First edition. Paperback. 2022. Cover illustration by Seweryn vvilczy Jasiński

@vvilczy

ISBN 979-8-9867176-0-9 (Paperback)

ISBN 979-8-9867176-1-6 (Ebook)

To the people whom have molded my imagination over my earlier years, these stories are a part of me that came from all of you.

<u>My Inspirations</u>

Clive Barker

Robert Bloch

John Carpenter

Wes Craven

Alfred Hitchcock

Tobe Hooper

Stephen King

Dean Koontz

Ozzy Osbourne

Mary Shelley

Kevin Smith

Dr. Theodor Suess

James Wan

Rob Zombie

FAR FROM PARADISE

A MONTH BY MONTH HORROR COLLECTION

WAYNE HOPKINS

Contents

Check the back for a preview of

"AT DEAD OF NIGHT"

Available July 27th 2023

November

Mother knows best

Prologue

Six-year-old Dalton Thompson was enjoying the fresh Nebraska air when an unfamiliar van came rolling into the mobile home cul-de-sac. The young blonde boy promised with he'd stay in the yard but due to a certain sound, he broke the promise.

The promise breaking sound came as the chugging of a loud car engine coming from the trailer next to his mom's lot. With the car engine getting louder and more defined, it was difficult for Dalton to keep his promise to his mother as he absolutely loved cars. Surprisingly, the car didn't roll past the front of his mom's trailer, but it seemed to stop at the lot before his house; the trailer on the left.

I didn't know we had another neighbor, Dalton thought. He knew of Mr. and Mrs. Fields to the right of his mom's but never had he seen anyone at the trailer to the left. *Maybe they have a hotrod!*

Dalton didn't know many different types of cars but before his father moved away, he used to point out all the "hotrods" on the road. They were always the loudest, meanest, and the fastest looking. Without hesitation, he ran outside of the yard and onto the gravel road of the trailer park to get a glimpse of the "hotrod".

Although, to Dalton's surprise, it wasn't a fast and mean looking hotrod at all.

The vehicle looked like something the people who come and fix your TV would drive except it wasn't as clean, the white had faded, and there was no logo. Just a long green stripe on the side.

With a screech, the van door swung open and one foot after the other brought out a towering, thick old man. A grey crown of hair surrounded his liver spotted head and connected with a beard of the same color. As well as, round, gold grandfather-like glasses that hung on the bridge of his long nose.

That made Dalton think of his grandpa in Lincoln and how they had to be close in age. From Dalton's distance—which had been about twenty feet—the elderly man seemed ordinary. Some would even say friendly. The bright colored clothes the man wore gave off a safe appeal to Dalton's eye. A bright white T-shirt, light blue jean shorts, and shin high socks, along with matching white sneakers.

Neither fear nor urgency struck the curious boy until the liver spotted man set eyes on him.

"Hi, little one!" the man said with a wide smile before he started to walk toward Dalton.

His face turned red as he remained in the same spot awaiting the man approaching. The tall, grinning geezer was now in front of the boy, casting a shadow on him like a tree. Up close, Dalton noticed the man had very few teeth, and the teeth he did have were yellow. His eyes were blue but the supposedly white around his eye color was actually a similar tint to his teeth and his cheeks were also covered with scars.

"Guess it's time for you to meet your neighbor, huh? My name is Mr. Hanson but my friends call me Joey and I would very much like to be your friend, bucko!"

At this point, he had no longer felt safe. He was never allowed to talk to strangers and now it was becoming clear why.

"What's your name, kid? It isn't really 'bucko,' is it?" Mr. Hanson chuckled.

A nervous smile formed on Dalton's face before he stuttered out his name. Mr. Hanson then cut his height in half by bending over to get more personal with Dalton at the boy's height.

"Well, Dalton, could you do something for your new friend?"

he asked.

Dalton stood still with his tiny legs shaking and his gaze down, focusing on his fidgeting hands instead of looking up at the man's wrinkled and scarred face.

"I go on a lot of business trips so it's hard for me to come back home as much as I'd want. Do you think you could keep your sharp eyes on it for me while I'm gone? Make sure nothing happens to my place? Huh, Dalton?"

Relief struck upon Dalton. Maybe nothing horrible was going to happen and Joey Hanson was a perfectly normal man. Although, before he had the chance to reply to his neighbor, he was interrupted by the scream of his mom swinging open the screen door.

"Dalton Michael Thompson! You get your ass inside now!"

With his heart thumping rapidly from hearing the wrath of his mother, he sprinted away from Mr. Hanson and through the door his mother held open. Trisha Thompson stayed on her porch, glaring at Joey Hanson while he held his right hand up in a neighborly fashion, wearing that wide grin displaying the few teeth he had left protruding out of purplish gray gums. After Mr. Hanson returned to his trailer, she followed her son inside.

When the front door slammed closed, she gave her son an intimidating and infuriated look. He was standing right on the line that separated the carpet and the white tiles in the kitchen with his head down, ready for a scolding.

"Dalton, what were you doing talking to Mr. Hanson?! I told you to stay in the yard! Did he tell you to come over there? Do you even know what could have happ—"

She was halted by soft sobbing emanating from her oldest son. It wasn't obnoxious but she could see tears trailing from his eyes, snot oozing out of his nose, and his chin was trembling as if he were freezing. From this, she knew he was scared. The rage she had once displayed in her voice had faded. Instead, she felt the urge to comfort her son. In an attempt to end her son's crying, she got down on one knee to Dalton's level. She then embraced him tightly and kissed his cheek while soothingly petting the back of his head.

"Shhhhh. It's okay, baby. Calm down," she whispered.

When he seemed more at ease, she released from the hug, then held him by his shoulders at arm's length. She wiped his tears away with her hand and then she decided she'd try a different tone.

"Dalton, honey, listen to me. You and your little brother are my whole entire world; all that I have, and I don't know what I would do if I lost one of you," she said, choking on her emotions. Now she was the one shedding tears just after Dalton stopped. "I don't trust that man outside. I haven't since I met him. I need you to watch out for him, Dalton. I believe he's a bad man. You can still go outside without me, if you please, just stay in the yard." Her hands gracefully shifted up from his shoulders to his face.

"But when Mr. Hanson is home, do not go outside! Do you hear me, Dalton Michael? Stay away!" she wept.

By the time Trisha Thompson dried her soaked eyes, the cries of her youngest son, Christopher, poured out from the back of the trailer. Followed by some not-so-motherly words, she walked down to the room in which the cries came from. Alone now in the living room, Dalton heard the loud chugging start back up. He glanced down the hall to check if his mom was out of sight. The wailing of his baby brother was still strong.

The curious boy ran through the kitchen to check behind the red curtains draped over the windows on the face of the trailer. The shunned geezer and his noisy vehicle were now nowhere in sight. While Dalton couldn't see the van with the long green stripe anymore, he could hear the chugging fading down the road and knew Mr. Hanson was leaving the mobile home park for who knew how long.

(2)

 It was a cold November day with forty-five mph winds whirling west, eight years after Dalton's encounter with Mr. Hanson. Blustery winds roaring outside forced Dalton to wake up in his bed. Instantly, he grabbed his phone to check the time and see if anyone had messaged him.   The phone read 10:30 AM and below the date was one message from Blake.

It was a Wednesday so his mother would be at work until eight at the least. However, it was the time of the year for Thanksgiving break and all public schools were closed. Therefore, Dalton and his brother Christopher were home during the day.

Usually at this time of the day, he would be sitting at a desk in a place where he felt he had to be stoned to attend. Three hours before that, you could find Dalton behind the high school and by the creek smoking pot with his closest friends, Austin Richardson and Blake Smithers. The once adventure-seeking boy who loved cars, and spent his time playing in the yard grew up to be a defiant teenager who would now spend most of his time with friends who influenced criminal behavior. Swearing, stealing, and smoking were always part of this particular motley crew's day.

Suddenly, before Dalton had a chance to open Blake's message, a loud snap came between the roar of the wind.

The snap made him instantly sit up straight in bed curious of the noise. Not very alarmed but intrigued, he started guessing what it could've been. Maybe a shitty car rolling past the trailer, or his brother getting into something he shouldn't. Either way, it seemed to come from outside.

Dalton chose not to investigate the sound but decided to get dressed and leave his bedroom to lounge in the living room.

He made his way to the couch in the next room. With desire to turn on the television, he started searching for the remote between the cushions. Just as he felt the remote with his fingers deep in the couch, the snap came again.

This time, it snapped twice about two seconds in-between each other. And they appeared to be coming not only from outside but to the left of his trailer, Mr. Hanson's property.

"What the hell is that?" he asked himself.

Abruptly, he stood from the couch and walked through the kitchen to peak out a window at the front of the trailer. In anticipation of pulling back the curtain, he was struck with a childhood memory. He remembered seeing that dirty old van stroll away all those years ago, through the very same window he was about to stare out.

Dalton shook off his thoughts of the old man and his van then took a look outside.

Hanson's driveway was empty like any other day. One could tell there was little to no attendance at the old man's trailer by the lack of maintenance on the property. His lawn had grown wild and now looked like an untamed meadow with grass taller than a child. Also patches of weeds started sprouting through the gravel of the driveway, right where Dalton once saw the van with the green stripe park. Although there was no van in his neighbor's lot today. Not a vehicle nor soul in sight.

Just when he started making his way back to the sofa, the puzzling snap blared yet again. Now frustrated and annoyed, Dalton grabbed his jacket then strode to the door. He swung the front door open, but the screen door did not open as easy. The wind had been forcing the screen door to remain shut. But with a little extra strength, he pushed the rusty door open then stepped out into the breeze.

(3)

Chilling and powerful; the violent wind slapped Dalton instantly, blowing his shaggy blond hair and all loose clothing on his body back. He stood waiting for the wind to break but it kept blasting. It was almost hard to see or even breathe in wind of this magnitude. The type of wind that trash cans, lawn furniture and children's toys could be seen tumbling in the streets.

Against the breeze, Dalton stepped off the porch, then creeped across the face of his own trailer, intending on getting a better view of Hanson's yard and hopefully find the source of the strange snapping. But in the midst of creeping, the snap came louder and more vivid than ever.

Discretely, Dalton peered over the corner of the Thompson trailer, and in the tall flowing grass of Mr. Hanson's yard stood his little brother with a handful of stones.

"Hey! Chris! What the hell are you doing over there?" Dalton shouted over the wind, before realizing he sounded like their mother.

The eight-year-old jumped with fright and immediately dropped the stones in hand. Christopher knew he had been caught red handed and took on an expression of guilt. Dalton gave Christopher an angry look in return, then shot his head at the trailer his brother stood guilty in front of. However, while examining the blue trailer, he noticed something that had nothing to do with his little brother, something he had never noticed before. The windows on Mr. Hanson's trailer had bars built in from the inside. That struck Dalton's curiosity, but he also saw golf ball size holes in the white skirting beneath the trailer.

"Did you make those holes? Dude, that's not cool! Why would you do that?"

"Calm down, Dalton. It's not like anybody lives here!" Christopher finally replied.

"Someone does live here, dipshit!" Dalton snapped.

The look of guilt on Christopher's face was now mixed

with fear.

"Who?"

"It doesn't matter who, just get inside and pack your bag for grandpa. Mom said he'd be here to pick you up around noon."

Chris ran past his older brother then went inside to pack his bag. Dalton on the other hand, stood gazing at the geezer's trailer. He wasn't surprised the bars on the windows went unnoticed all these years. This was actually the closest Dalton had ever been to Hanson's trailer. In his childhood, he wouldn't have dared standing where he stood now. Not after the way his mother screamed his full name when he was seen just talking to the old man. And if it wasn't his mother's screams that kept him away, it must have been the way the old man's eyes fixed on him. He wondered if his elderly neighbor was even alive today. If he was alive, where was he? And what business was he exactly involved with? Then all at once curiosity slithered into his head along with the strong urge to check if Mr. Hanson's door would open.

No. I shouldn't even try.

But curiosity knocked even harder.

I'm sure it's locked anyway, what harm is there in trying?

Despite his best resisting effort, Dalton quickly ran to Hanson's driveway to see if any cars were driving down the cul-de-sac. When the coast was clear, he ran up Hanson's two step porch and gave the door knob a twist. The door was locked tight. *Of course.*

Dalton's wondering thoughts had quickly turned into paranoid ones and now he was ready to get off Hanson's property and out of the wind. Although as Dalton turned away to step off the old porch, he made another observation. There was another window. Not quite as big as the other two but big enough to climb through and there were no bars on the inside. Dawdling, his paranoia grew stronger than his curiosity and then he hopped off Hanson's porch steps and into the tall grass, then fled the yard.

(4)

Afterwards, Dalton returned to the living room with his brother when he remembered he never opened Blake's text message. He pulled his cheap cell phone out then took a look.

From Blake:
Let one of us know when your lil bro leaves and we need to find a place to smoke cause of the fuckin wind.

He closed his phone and started brainstorming on places they could smoke inside.

"Hey Dalton," Chris said from the other couch, but Dalton just ignored him and kept thinking.

The boys usually just smoked outside, in the woods, under a bridge, or behind certain buildings in town. Not today though, not with the hellacious wind outside. Before Dalton could think of a place, a pillow was tossed at him by Chris.

"What, dude?" Dalton said, already annoyed.

"Why aren't you going to grandpas with me?"

"Because I'm going to see a movie with friends tonight. I'll still be there tomorrow for Thanksgiving. I'm riding with mom in the morning."

There was a pause, then Christopher spoke again.

"Is Blake going? What are you seeing? Who is driving? How do you have mon—"

"Why do you have so many damn questions? Just stay out of it. You sound like mom." Dalton interrupted.

An even longer paused came and Christopher spoke again but in a concerned tone.

"I don't like Blake; I think he does drugs and he's mean. I don't trust hi—"

"Well he's not your fuckin friend, now is he? You're so

annoying! Just shut up, cock sucker!"

Chris resisted crying, staring at his brother across the living room. Then a car horn honked in the driveway, and surely it was their grandpa.

Chris stood up and grabbed his bag, then went for the front door. Dalton just stared at his phone, ignoring his brother's existence. But that didn't stop Christopher from speaking yet again.

"Bye Dalton, I love you. See you tomorrow."

(5)

Truth is, the boys weren't going out to see a movie tonight. Really Blake, Austin, and Dalton had just bought three grams of marijuana and the plan was to smoke the entire bag on the first day of break, which was today. The whole movie story was just a cover up for Dalton's absence from home and his excuse to leave with his mother tomorrow.

Dalton and Blake have been best friends since the first grade when Blake moved in about a dozen trailers down from Daltons. His father was an abusive man who often claimed Blake as a bastard, as well as an inconvenience to him. Blake Smithers is the product of two substance abusers one-night stand, and as a result of living a substance abusing lifestyle, his mother had overdosed and died early on. That exact loss in Blake's life is what led him to live with his father and gain Dalton as his best friend.

They grew up doing everything together, always reflecting off each other. Over all the years they'd been friends, Dalton's mother had even taken a liking to Blake. But lately, Blake started walking in the footsteps of his drug fueled parents. And therefore, Blake's behavior reflected onto Dalton. Austin, on the other hand, had just moved into town for his freshmen year, and was desperately in need of friends. He's a soft-spoken boy who followed whoever was leading the charge. He met Blake in his third period and the rest was history.

 It only took ten minutes for Blake and Austin to arrive at Dalton's doorstep. That didn't surprise Dalton since Austin stayed the night at Blake's last night. Dalton met his friends at the door before they even had a chance to knock.

"Holy shit! That wind is a bitch!" Blake panted as he stormed inside with Austin trailing behind.

"I know, right? Earlier, I went out there because I heard some weird snapping and it was fuckin' Chris throwing rocks through the skirting of that trailer," Dalton said pointing before closing the door behind his friends.

"Damn dude, your mom will probably have to pay for the damages," Austin stated.

"Eh, I doubt it. The guy who lives there never comes home. I haven't seen him in like ten years." Dalton sat back on the couch. "I bet the old fucker who owns the trailer is dead by now anyway," he laughed.

"I've never seen anyone there either. You think someone owns it though? They just never come home?" Blake questioned in a strangely eager tone.

"I haven't seen anyone." He shrugged.

(6)

The gang sat in the living room brainstorming for a little less than an hour. The only one who actually had a suggestion so far was surprisingly Austin. He suggested they smoke in Daltons room with the window open, and they'd spray the room immensely afterwards. Dalton shut that idea down quick; he knew his mother would still be able to smell the stench and she would have his ass if he were caught smoking again. They all sat frustrated with the lack of ideas until Blake chimed in.

"What about that abandoned trailer?"

17

"What trailer?" Dalton questioned as he sat up, a confused look on his face.

"The one your little shit brother threw rocks at this morning obviously," Blake replied.

"Dude, that trailer isn't even abandoned though."

"Fuckin' might as well be! You said yourself he's probably dead anyway."

"That's true," Austin said. "You also admitted you haven't seen him in like ten years anyway, even if he's not dead."

"Eh, I don't know, man." Dalton shrugged.

"Come on, Dalton. Will you stop being such a chicken shit!"

"I'm not! But we could get caught, and what if he co—"

"By who?" Blake interrupted "Everyone keeps to themselves in this damn park; no one will even notice us, and we'll have a lookout on cars."

Dalton sat baffled and out of excuses. "Okay. Fine, we'll do it."

"Hell yeah! That's the spirit, but how do we get in?"

That's when Dalton thought back to the window without bars.

(7)

By the time Blake's hazardous idea was in full affect, the sky had grown grey, and the wind had yet to slow down and became more frigid.

"This wind is going to kill us before we even get inside this fuckin' trailer," Blake whined as they stepped into Hanson's yard. "Whoa, what? You didn't say there were bars on the windows! How do we even get in?"

Dalton threw up his hand then pointed to the smaller window. "That one doesn't. Do you think the window will slide up if we push up on it?"

"Yeah, it should I think, but how do we get up there? Do you even have a ladder?" Blake shouted over the wind.

"No but my neighbors on the right do!" he laughed and shouted back. "I'll go get it."

Earlier in the year, he saw his other neighbor, Mr. Fields carry a six-foot ladder to the back of his own trailer and store it by their propane tank. Dalton hoped it was still there. Moments later, he came back dragging the ladder through the tall grass of Hanson's.

The boys propped the ladder against the wooden trailer and just under the bar-less window. The three teens stared at each other standing in the chilling wind with realization. It had not been decided which one of them were going up the ladder and through the window of a home that wasn't theirs.

"Alright Dalton, get up there," Blake ordered.

"What? Hell no! It was your idea."

"What about you, Austin?" he suggested.

"I'm road lookout." Austin shrugged.

Blake rolled his eyes. "You both are pussies."

"Dude, just get up there, we're wasting time. I'll hold the ladder," Dalton said.

Blake stepped onto the ladder. "Fine"

Before he could take another step higher on the steel, Dalton gave him some advice about the window. "I think that window is above the sink like it is in my trailer. So, you'll have the counter to hop on. When you're in, unlock the front door and we'll run in."

Blake nodded and then scaled up the ladder quickly before going to work on the window. Dalton held the ladder steady at the bottom while Austin stood at the end of the driveway on lookout duty.

At first, the window was as stubborn as a spoiled child, and didn't budge a bit. The thought of the window being locked had crossed the boy's mind but neither of them mentioned it, seeing as how far they already were. Then, just as Blake was pushing the window up tirelessly, it went up about three inches.

"I got it!" He put his hand under the bottom of the window and pushed up as hard as he could. He managed to shoot the window all the way up and the three boys' adrenaline shot up with it.

"Crawl in! Crawl in!" the other two chanted.

Immediately, Blake crawled in the trailer, disappearing from Dalton and Austin's sight. He was in and a few moments later they would all be in Mr. Hanson's trailer. Dalton took the ladder down, laid it in the tall grass so it would be unseen from people driving by. With everybody's adrenaline at a high, suddenly, the old front door of Hanson's trailer creaked open with Blake inside and doorknob in hand. "Come on hurry!"

With all their hearts thumping tremendously, Dalton and Austin ran up the wood porch steps and into the trailer owned by Joseph Hanson.

The same man Dalton once promised his mother he would stay clear from.

(8)

Blake instantly closed the door once the other two made it inside. Now the only sound present was the muffled wind smashing into the outside walls but other than that, it was as quiet as an 'abandoned' house should be.

Similar to most mobile homes, the kitchen and living room were connected without a wall in-between. From the front door in the living room, the kitchen was on the left along with a narrow hallway holding a backdoor and leading to the master bedroom (Dalton inferred). On the right was another hall with three closed doors, two on the left of the hall and one at the end of it.

To Dalton's surprise, the inside of his elderly neighbor's trailer was comfier looking than he expected. There was a long purple couch next to a leather recliner with a wooden coffee table and a box TV in front. The stench of the house was dust, like in an antique market. Wooden antique signs, some photo portraits and a couple of taxidermy pieces took up most of the wall space in the front room.

"Let's get down to business then; we have already broken one law, might as well break another." Blake cracked as he pulled a bag full of pre-rolled joints out of his front hoodie pocket. Austin and Blake made for the couch, then sat while they lit the first, but Dalton remained standing and observant. He stepped closer to the decorated walls, ignoring the mounted deer head and the full-size wildcat on a branch.

The portraits grabbed his attention. They seemed to be school photos like the ones they would take on picture day. One was a black-haired boy with a bowl cut wearing a Spider-Man shirt and a contagious and genuine smile. The other two photos were twin blonde girls with matching dresses but different colors, yellow and blue. All about his brothers age, he guessed.

"Dalton," Austin called, handing the burning joint to him. Dalton never really feels anxious or frightened before smoking, but this time his hands were shaking.
"Bro, calm down. We've made it in, and no one knows, nothing bad is going to happen. And if shit goes sour, we'll just ditch out the back door."

"I know, I know, you're right." He took the burning marijuana cigarette and took a slow drag. "I didn't think this guy would have had kids though," Dalton coughed.

Blake then stood to his feet and joined Dalton by the portraits. "I didn't even notice these pictures with all the stuffed animals in this place, I fucking hate these things. They're gross."

"Taxidermy," Austin corrected.

"Whatever, asshole." Blake shot back. "Is this a bobcat?"

"I think that's a mountain lion," Dalton answered.

"Uh huh, you know what?" Blake said. "I think we deserve a tour of this old fart's place since we worked so hard getting in." He took off down the hall with the three doors. Austin and Dalton didn't take long to follow since they were just as curious.

(9)

When he got to the first door with the others, Blake twisted the knob, flipped a light switch on the inside and showed a windowless and near empty bedroom. Only a twin-size bed dressed in a retro Star Wars comforter. One after the other, they entered the small bedroom.

"This must be the guest room for the kids when they used to visit or something," Austin said taking a seat on the bed.

"Yeah, I guess so. I just never would have thought this guy would have kids or seen them around, even though they'd be older by now than they are in the pictures." Dalton sat down next to Austin. "When I talked to him, he was kind of a creeper."

"You actually met the geezer?" Blake asked.

"Yeah once, honestly he's pretty scary looking, he's really tall, probably about 6'6, but kind of fat and he's covered with these orange spots. Even then he seemed sick or like dying." Dalton took what was left of the joint from Austin before he spoke again. "He started talking to me when he saw me in my driveway. I was probably about five or six. But before he could say much, my mom screamed my name to get inside immediately; she sounded like I was talking to fuckin'

Hitler." The last part made the group laugh.

"Damn, she probably thought the old fucker was going to spread your cheeks," Blake joked, while standing above the two sitting on the bed.

"Shut up dick, you're the only one who spreads little boy's cheeks around here," Dalton laughed. "Take this fuckin' thing, it's burning my fingers."

"Just put it out. We got two more. Anyway, let's go to the next room," Blake said taking the roach to put in the baggie.

After they all made their way back into the hall, Dalton closed the door behind them. Austin checked the next one and found a bathroom behind it. Uninterested, he shut it then turned to Blake who was opening another one at the end of the hall. Behind that one was another small and windowless dark bedroom but with no bed, just piles of fat black trash bags.

None of them muttered a single word.

The three boys all had paranoid expressions as well as chilling thoughts on what those bags were full of, but decided against mentioning them. Blake bravely stepped into the room while the other two stood in the doorway, gazing with wide red eyes. He didn't bother turning on the light since the shine from the doorway was enough. Dalton's oldest friend grabbed one of the bags then tore the plastic open. Relief along with laughter struck the gang when children clothes poured out.

"Oh my god, dude, I'm so baked! I thought it was going to be something fucked up!" Blake said in a relieved tone, followed by more laughing from all.

"I think we all did," Dalton replied still giggling.

"Yeah dude, I thought it was going to be like, body parts or something," Austin mentioned. "Whew, let's get out of this room, unless you want some toddler T-shirts."

(10)

Another hour was spent digging and scavenging through the belongings of Joey Hanson. Blake and Austin had even started to pocket certain items they liked. For instance, Austin took a switch blade found in a kitchen cabinet. Blake took a tobacco pipe and vanilla incents found in a drawer of the coffee table. Meanwhile, as his friends snickered, smoked, and stole, Dalton felt more frightened by the minute being inside Hanson's trailer. The three hadn't made it to the master bedroom yet, but it seemed they were saving the best for last. At this particular moment, they all were hanging out in the kitchen, right next to the narrow hallway.

"Alright C-suckers! Let's check out this last room and smoke this last one before we bail," Blake suggested eagerly.

"You know, I think the wind might have slowed down, we could probably go back out and smoke that somewhere else."

"Why?" Austin turned to Dalton. "We've already gone this far; it would be dumb to not go in the other room."

"Right! Dalton just quit being such a pussy. No one will ever know we were here," Blake said walking away from Dalton and into the hall, but stopping at the entrance. "But if you want you can just run back home and hope your big scary neighbor never finds out."

As the other two started to walk toward the master bedroom, Dalton legitimately thought of abandoning them and going home. Though he would never hear the end of it from his friends, so against his better judgement, he followed them down the narrow hall, into Mr. Hanson's bedroom.

The self-proclaimed leader of the group twisted the golden doorknob and pushed it open. The room was immensely sheltered, they couldn't see a thing inside but a stream of sunlight from the window behind a thick curtain. Gradually, Blake felt for a light switch from the right of the door. When he found the switch, he flipped it then a loud *pop!* came from the light bulb but no light.

"Oh god damn it!" Blake cursed. "Let's just pull that

curtain back from the window, that'll give us some light."

Cautiously Blake and Austin stepped slowly into the dark room as if they were creeping into a part of a haunted house attraction. When the curtain opened, the sunlight filtered into a large room with a full-size bed, a night stand and a closed closet door.

"Man, this guy has a taste for plain ass bedrooms" Blake let out, circling the bed to the nightstand. He opened the thigh high night stand to only find nothing inside.
Dalton, whom had been planted at the door way still stayed silent but was curious as ever.

"Dude, will you stop being so nervous and get in here? You're freaking me out, Dalton," Blake stressed.

He took a deep breath and stepped into the room with the others, shaking off his fearful thoughts.

"Sorry," he let out with a little laugh. "I guess I'm still freaked out about being in this guy's house."

"Why though?" Austin took the baggie from Blake.

"Because I remember meeting him like it was yesterday, bro. I remember being so shook when he was just looking down at me." Dalton looked out the window with bars. "And now we're inside his place stealing his shit."

The trio sat in the near empty bedroom while they puffed on their final joint. Although Dalton couldn't wait to leave the trailer, he didn't want to mention anything else about it and earn flack. All he did was puff on the smoke until he was no longer paranoid about the horrifying Hanson and being inside his trailer. Blake on the other hand, felt disappointed with the break in, as if he were missing out on something.

"I guess the only thing left for us to do here is to search that closet, huh?" he said walking away with the burning reefer to the closed door.

"Why? So we can find more incents? Maybe some more children's clothes!" Dalton questioned sarcastically followed by a laugh from Austin.

Not surprising to Blake, the closet looked normal as

can be. All kinds of shirts hung up on the rack (mostly plain white T-shirts) and the floor below was covered with shoes.

"And nothing," Blake mumbled bitterly. The other two boys got up from the bed to see for themselves.

"He probably has bars on the window so no one steals his sweet collection of white t shirts." Austin joked followed by a huge outbreak of giggling from each of them. Although, in the course of laughter, Dalton Thompson noticed something very curious about the old man's closet.

There was another door behind the hung-up T-shirts.

"What the hell is that?" Dalton interrupted, then pushed all the shirts to the left side, revealing the mysterious door. Confusion spread like poison ivy once they all saw it; not one of them could find the courage to speak.

"It's the door to the breaker," Austin said, sounding unsure.

"No way, that's too big, this is a full-size door. It cou—" Right before Blake could get this sentence out, Dalton had already pushed open the door within the closet open.

There was a flight of stairs behind the door.

About fifteen gloomy steps going down to yet another door at the bottom. It looked like an entrance to a cave that held some sort of monster. But that didn't restrain them because curiosity had never been so tough. Especially for Dalton who was the first to step onto the stairs.

While stepping down on those fifteen shady steps that seemed to get darker the further down they got, the boys didn't make a peep. Their stoned imaginations were moving too fast for them to actually muster out a word. Tightly grouped together, as if they were kids crowding in front of an exhibit at the Omaha zoo, they arrived at the bottom of the steps.

Dalton swallowed the lump in his throat before he opened the hidden door only to be met with pitch black on the inside. With caution, he felt the walls on the inside for a switch but didn't have any luck.

"T-T-there's no switch?" Blake stuttered. "There's probably a string to pull in the middle of the room."

Maybe he was dazed and stoned from smoking, or maybe Dalton truly couldn't help himself from his curious nature. Either way, he wandered into the black space with his arms stretched out feeling for the string. About two steps into the dark abyss of the room, Dalton felt what seemed to be a piece of yarn dangling from the ceiling. Once he pulled the string not only would the hidden room be revealed but also the disturbing reason *why* it had been hidden in the first place. As the light bulb suddenly flashed on, the three teens knew they had uncovered something that was never meant to be found.

And Dalton Thompson was standing right in the center of it all.

(11)

In a room no bigger than the single bedroom upstairs, children stood stiff along the walls. On top of that, the walls were decorated with the heads of kids on mounts like trophies for game.

Everyone in the group reacted differently to Mr. Hanson's hidden hobby. Dalton became transfixed and did nothing but stare back at the departed eyes gazing at him. Austin, on the other hand, immediately turned around and ran back up the stairs, through Hanson's bed and living room then all the way home. Blake's jaw dropped, then he puked all over the carpeted floor. Though not long after Austin left, Blake was behind him and in panic, shut the bed door on the way out.

That left Dalton all alone in the room of children taxidermy. He also felt like puking then running but couldn't help starring at Hanson's displays.

Almost as if he was admiring the work. He recognized the full body stiff children from the pictures upstairs. The blonde little girls were facing each other, seeming to forever be in a game of patty cake. The bowl cut boy was staring at his hands while they were closed, just like how Dalton stood when Mr. Hanson stared down at him.

The heads on the wall all revealed different emotions on the children's face. Some looked surprised with their jaw dropped and eyes wide open, others seemed to be laughing, a few looked sad but most of them had a terrified expression. Probably the expression they had when Hanson turned on them. Dalton could tell the room hadn't been visited for a while by the spider webs all over the place. A number of spiders were even crawling on the children's hair and body, making homes on the faces and leaving their eggs hanging from the dead kid's ears.

With the heads on the wall and the three full size ones, there had to be near twelve kids in the room. He almost felt like counting to be sure, but eventually Dalton snapped out of his frozen stare and knew he had to leave. He turned around without switching the light off and raced back up the stairs.

(12)

Do I tell anyone?

Who? The police? But we broke in to smoke in his place!

This was a bigger dilemma than Dalton could have ever imagined. As he approached the closed bedroom door, another thought came to mind.

What if he finds out we were in here? We would be good as stuffed!

In that moment, he grabbed the doorknob and his heart dropped to his shoes when he found the knob wouldn't turn. It was locked from the outside.

"What! What the fuck!" Dalton screamed hostilely. "Blake! Austin!" The throbbing in his chest was so hard he could hear it, and with his trembling hands, he pulled his phone from his pocket.

 During Dalton's discovery of his entrapment, Blake was still shaking and feeling nauseas but safe on Dalton's porch steps. The images of those severed kids' heads were still fresh on his mind when his phone started to vibrate in his pocket. It was Dalton calling.
  "Dalton! Where are you?"
  "I'm in the fucking trailer still, dude! I can't get out! Did you lock the door? Where are you?" Dalton yelled over the phone, not giving Blake time to respond. "Come open the door now!"
  "Fuck, fuck, fuck! I'm coming!" Blake sprinted the short distance from the Thompson trailer to Hanson's. Dalton stayed on the line as Blake ran up the porch steps to front door. But to make things even more awful than before, the front door was locked too.
"Shit! Dalton, this door is locked too! I don't know what the fuck happened!"

  Dalton couldn't utter a word,

  "Could you break down that door?"

  "I tried kicking, but it seems really thick and heavy," Dalton replied sounding like he was about to shed tears. "Blake, you have to get me out of here, please don't leave me."

  "Dalton, I'm not going to leave you in there. Just stay calm while I think." He looked around him and saw the ladder laying in the tall grass. "Dalton I'm going to climb through the window and get you o—" Blake cut off his words and moved the phone from his ear. He heard someone coming down the road.

"Blake? Blake! What's wrong?"
"I think somebody's coming. I hear this loud car coming down.
I think it's a truck. Hold tight, I'm going to check it out."

Then Dalton could hear the loud chugging from the
engine himself and with that sound, Dalton could no longer
breathe. He stood in Hanson's room waiting on Blake's
response, more scared than he had ever been in his life. Even
more than when Mr. Hanson looked down on him, more than
when his mom screamed his name and even more when he
was face to face with a child's corpse moments ago.

Blake stood watching the road from Dalton's driveway.
"It's some dirty white van. I'm going to wait for it to
pass, " Blake comforted. "Wait, fuck! Dalton it's pulling in!"
Dalton didn't let out a breath or a word, not even a
croak. Not only did his heart drop again but so did the phone
from his sweaty hand. Dalton's friend since the third grade
stood in the Thompson driveway and watched an old,
towering, and thick old man step out of the van.
"There's an old man coming out! He's going to the front
door! Dalton! Dalton!" Blake just about screamed into the
phone walking away from the driveway. No response came
back. He felt there was no other choice than to just run home
like Austin, so he did.
Blake left his oldest and best friend, Dalton Thompson
trapped in Joseph Hanson's trailer. And soon, in seconds even,
Dalton would meet Mr. Hanson once again.

December

<u>WHATS IN THE WOODS?</u>

After her wife's accident, driving sixty-five mph now felt too fast for Bethany Savage. These days she was too skeptical to even go sixty on any sort of road. Fortunately for her though, the minimum of the I-435 interstate was fifty-five. Cars were constantly passing her, some even honked and felt obligated to give the finger as they passed. However, Beth didn't mind, and she understood, they all had places to be and so did she. Beth had just rented out her new home in the small town of Fairway. That was her destination and in less than twenty minutes, she would arrive; at least that's what Google maps read.

In her side mirrors, she could see her older brother, Nick, slowly trailing behind her in the U-Haul she ordered. It was full of all the furniture and other belongings Beth and Angela had collected in the last decade. She began to think of everything inside that U-Haul and how it was all hers now. That also included the blue heeler riding shotgun in Beth's Explorer.

Three years before the wreck, Angela adopted him as a puppy and gave him the name Bonzo. Named after one of Angie's favorite band's drummer, John "Bonzo" Bonham from *Led Zeppelin*. Beth looked over at the sleeping heeler curled up in the seat then scratched one of his pointy black ears. That was his favorite spot to be rubbed and scratched Angela used to mention.

At first, she didn't care much for the pooch. He pissed all over their house and always ran through the place at a crazy pace as if something were chasing him. It wasn't until Angela's passing when Beth started to warm up to Bonzo and it seemed like he warmed up to her as well. He started to sleep with her every night, listen to her commands, and he even stopped urinating in the house. She was starting to believe dogs had some strange sense for grief from the bond they had developed.

The car was quiet besides the heater's exhaust. It was almost as if she were scared to listen to music, another skeptical that had come after her first and only love's death. She loved music but Angela always had it on wherever she went. In the car, at get togethers or even at home when they were just simply lounging. Although, Beth knew she couldn't ignore music like she could ignore driving at a certain speed. She placed her right hand on the radio volume knob and turned up whatever was playing. To no surprise, she would have to make new presets in her car, doubting they had the same stations in Missouri as they did back two and a half hours where she came from. Which she was glad about, she felt even hearing the same stations Angie played would get to her.

Surfing through static and all kinds of genres, she settled on 98.5, a station that "plays it all." Behind the exhaust of the heater and the miscellaneous music playing, Google informed her she would be approaching her exit in less than a mile. Bonzo was now sitting up in the seat looking out the windows, seeming to be admiring the trees along the interstate. She scratched his spotted back, and he shot her a look.

"Are you ready, boy?" she asked her new best friend, but really, she was just asking herself.

Once she made it off the exit ramp, Beth was directed to a narrow road that eventually put her on fourth street, the main street of Fairway. The road was made of red brick, and tall town buildings stood on each side of the street. The paint chipped buildings looked older than her mother and besides the thrift away and hardware store she noticed, many appeared deserted. After approximately two blocks down the red brick road, it was a left turn on pine street then onto Woodend Road. The road she would start her new life on, and away with the old one.

(2)

Woodend Rd was a dead-end street that had more than six houses paralleled on both sides concluding with a wall of abundant trees that most likely went on to be a lengthy forest. In addition to Woodend, right next to the collection of stands was the two-bedroom house Beth had rented out online. Bonzo hadn't done any whining the whole ride, but as they approached their new home, he looked uneasy and let out a high-pitched cry.

"It's okay, Bonz. We are here now. Don't worry, we can finally get out of the warm car and into the cold, whiner." She scratched his ear and back again once she parked the Explorer in the tiny driveway.

Nick parked the U-Haul across the street then stepped out at the same time Beth was letting Bonzo out of the car.

"Come on, I know you have to pee, go explore the new yard and all the things to piss on." Bonzo hopped out of the vehicle and went on to the yard on the right side of the house, in front of the wall of trees.

"You know, you could have gone just a little faster on the way up here." Nick criticized while he walked across the street to his sister's new home.

"Hey, you could have passed me. You didn't have to follow."

"The only reason I was following is because this town is in the middle of butt fuck Missouri, sis," Nick laughed.

"Shut up, it's not that bad! It's better than Kansas was, *and* Texas for that matter!" She let out a breath into her hands for warmth. "I think it's exactly what I'm searching for right now."

"Uh huh, let's just get a move on with getting this stuff in the house because I'm freezing; Missouri is a bit nippier than Texas in December. And if we finish soon, we can just drop the U-Haul off tonight instead of tomorrow, so we don't have to worry about time for my flight."

"Okay, okay, let me just get Bonzo back in the car before we start then. I'll unlock the house." She moved her head around to seek the pooch. "Bonzo!" she called. Beth couldn't see him anywhere from the driveway and he didn't come running when she yelled.

"Do you see Bonzo anywhere?" she asked Nick when he was behind the U-Haul opening the trailer door.

Nick looked around and saw Bonzo sitting in the yard looking totally obedient, gazing into the woods. The heeler was focused, like he was listening intently.

"Yeah, he's right in the yard. Bonzo!" He cupped his hands around his mouth. "Bonzo!" Nick called again. The dog didn't move a muscle, still set on whatever he saw or heard in the trees.

"What the hell is he doing? Bonzo!" Beth shouted with aggression. Finally, the dog snapped out of its trance like state and glanced Beth's way before running to her. "What were you doing, pal? See something in the woods?" She bent down to stroke the top of his head.

"Do you have a tie out for him?" Nick asked when he returned from across the street. "You might want to tie him on a leash when he goes outside, he looked like he was about to take off into the woods there, Bethy."

Beth stared at him as if he had just insulted her and her eyes watered instantly. "Please do not call me that, Nick."

There was a moment of silence once he saw his sisters restraining anguish leak. He didn't feel like he needed to apologize but maybe that he should.

"I'm sorry," he said sincerely with a red face.

She ignored his apology and went on to open the car door for Bonzo and he hopped in willingly.

"Let's move this crap, getting done tonight sounds great." She flashed an ingenuine smile then walked across the truck.

(3)

Later, Beth, Nick, and Bonzo all sat in her new living room—a small room that now seemed even smaller with all of Beth's furniture inside. They really did get done moving in great time, which didn't come as a surprise. Nick had spent the last twelve years in the Marines so he was in phenomenal shape and his task doing skills were just as great. Beth wasn't in terrible shape either, she always went on runs with Angie every morning. The girls even medaled in track together in all four years of high school, although that was more than a decade ago. Now Beth had a feeling she would never run again, not without Angie.

"Can I say something? Just my opinion?" Nick asked sitting on the love seat across the couch Beth lay upon.

"Might as well, you're already talking."

Nick straightened his posture and scooted closer to the edge of his seat. "I know you're grieving, sis. Hell, it's only been a little over a month since the accident and I know everyone grieves differently but I don't think it's a good choice for you to run away from it all like this."

She was looking into his eyes at first then shifted sight onto her feet. Her socks were the fuzzy sort to keep your feet warm and they were baby blue. They were also Angela's and even in her favorite color.

"You're all alone out here with no one to talk too. You've cut all ties with everyone who even knew Angie. Honestly, I'm shocked you still kept in touch with mom and me." He scooted conspicuously closer to the edge of the love seat. "I just wish you would talk to someone about it or just stop run-"

"It's impossible for me to run, Nick! I'm constantly reminded of her everywhere I turn!" Beth got to her feet quickly, turned her back on him, then put her hands on her face. Once she turned to him again, her face was flushed, and a stray tear tried to slither out from her left eye. "Look around! All this shit is what we had together! I couldn't get away from her even if I tried!" She threw her arms up just to plant them back down at her sides. Nick just gazed up at his sister and listened to her, felt for her. Beth took a deep breath then plopped back down on the sofa.

"I just needed to get out of the home we made together and leave all the people that knew she meant everything to me," she said in a much calmer tone than before. "I didn't want everyone I ever had a conversation with to know I've lost what means the most to me."

Nick walked over to the couch and put his arm around her as he sat down. "I miss her too. She really was great. And she would have wanted you to move on with your life without her." His muscular arm wrapped around her tight. "I'll be with mom until she gets better so anytime you need me, you just call, and I'll answer, Beth. Texas isn't so far from Missouri, not far enough to keep me from my little sister anyway."

"Thank you, Nick." She wiped her eyes with her long sleeve and then Bonzo jumped onto the couch joining them. She scratched his favorite spot with a pinch and pulled him closer while Nick held her.

(4)

The next day, after Nick boarded a 3:00 PM. flight back to Houston, Beth spent the rest of the day unpacking. When she was going through boxes, a tie out for Bonzo was found. Angela had bought it when he was a puppy; it came with a silver chain and a metal stake to put into the ground. She figured her finding was a sign to take her brothers advice about putting him on a leash when he went outside by himself. When Angela and Beth lived in Kansas, he was able to roam free since he was good at staying in their area. However, now they were in a new area, and she felt he would run off to explore then not be able to find his way home.

The ground wasn't completely frozen, so the stake went into the ground without much force. No snow has fallen in Missouri or Kansas so far this December, but it was still quite chilly to be caught outside. While Beth stomped the stake deeper into the dead grass of her yard, she saw a grey Oldsmobile pull in the neighbor's driveway. Relieved she even had a neighbor, Beth waited for the mystery person to come out of the car so she could introduce herself.

A tiny elderly woman with a hunch in her stance stepped out of the vehicle, then went around back to the trunk. The grey-haired woman had a puffy black winter coat that covered half her legs. Still standing by the stake, Beth watched her take seven plastic bags out of the trunk and saw the lady had noticed her standing and staring. Her neighbor made eye contact for a moment only to ignore her presence while proceeding to her bags. Despite that, Beth decided to approach the woman anyway.

"Hello ma'am, do you need a hand?" Beth asked in a light, warm, and helpful tone as she walked into the woman's yard.

"No." She grumbled and limped away carrying the bags ahead of Beth.

"Oh, well, I just moved in next door, my name is Beth Savage," she introduced herself picking up her pace.

"That's nice," the woman muttered, pulling the bags up higher to hopefully move faster from Beth but she was clearly struggling.

"I can really help you with those, miss, you seem to b— "

As soon as the grey wrinkled woman made it up her doorstep, she finally turned to her new neighbor and interrupted her. "Listen lady, I don't care who you are, where you came from, or how you are settling in!" Her eyes were sunken and bloodshot as she looked down on Beth holding a confused expression.

"Just stay away from me, out of my yard, and out of those damn woods!" She turned away from Beth, managed to get the door open with all the bags hanging off of her arms, then slammed the door after she limped her way in. Beth started to make her way back home and while she was leaving the old hag's yard, she saw a mailbox in front. It read "Percy."

"Nice to meet you too, Ms. Percy," she said to herself sarcastically.

Before stepping inside the house, she inspected the leafless trees to the right of her home. It was a safe bet to say the woods probably went on for miles. Even from Beth's doorstep, she could see an army of stands behind the first row of trees. She studied and thought back to what Ms. Percy had said to her then wondered, *What's in the woods?*

A week of unpacking went by along with her settling in and getting back to work as a web designer. It looked to Beth that most of the boxes had been emptied besides some kitchen equipment. Those boxes were next on the agenda, and she would get to them later today. Settling in for her has been half decent, but Bonzo eased in swimmingly and seemed to be loving all of it. He was sleeping well, not having any accidents in the house, and was always scratching the front door to go out on his chain.

At the moment, Beth was lying on her couch while surfing the web on her phone, Facebook to be exact. She hadn't been logged in since the first week after Angela's death. The grief felt messages and posts from friends were difficult to read and she became annoyed by all the sympathy. Although, now, the messages quit coming so she felt safe to skim through the feed.

Everything seemed fine until Facebook sent her a memory post that featured Angie from three years ago today. It was the day they picked up Bonzo from the shelter or at least the day they posted about it. Facebook's memory showed her three pictures that were posted, one of just the spotted tiny pup, Bonzo, and the other two were of all three of them snuggled up in bed with big smiles on both of their faces. She felt tears flood to the brim of her eyes and closed her phone as she tossed it away.

Swinging her feet off the couch and onto the floor, she sat up and found Bonzo sleeping at the bottom of the sofa. She placed her hand on his head and scratched the grey stripe between his eyes then went to his ear with the pinch itch that he couldn't get enough of. His multicolored head popped up and looked up at her with big eyes. The rubbing and scratching from Beth went on until he stood up on all fours and went to the door, clawing at it.

"Fine, fine, I'm coming, big baby." she whined looking for her winter coat.

Nearing dusk, Beth clipped Bonzo on his chain and left him outside while she would start putting away the boxed kitchen items. Walking back inside, she knew it wouldn't be long until she'd have to be back outside to rescue her fury best friend from the frosty air. In a matter of minutes, he'll start crying and howling to come back inside and that would be her signal to bring him in.

(6)

Like the rest of the house, the kitchen was compact, and it wouldn't take long to finish putting everything away. Possibly finishing before Bonzo's fussing outside started. All the kitchen equipment was packed into three boxes, one being a lot bigger than the others. Beth decided to start with the larger box and when she lifted it from the floor, the box was heavier than she inferred. Pots and pans, perhaps even the microwave, was expected to be inside, though she wasn't too sure. Her memory of packing was faint, since at that time leaving the house was all she wanted to do; she had even left some stuff behind. Plus, Nick had helped her pack too so maybe he packed this one.

Inside the heavy box were the pots, pans, and microwave she had expected but also, a tiny black radio. Not surprising, Angela had done most of the cooking back in Kansas and when she did, music was blaring like usual. Beth stared at the radio in her hands as if it were staring back at her. Hesitant at first, she proceeded to plug it in and tune to 98.5. A pop song was playing, she wasn't sure who it was or if she had heard it before. Most pop genre songs sounded the same to her anyhow.

Three songs later, everything inside of the big box was put away and Beth was now stacking glass plates into the cabinet from the second box.

As she reached to the counter for one of the final plates, a loud smack of a drum snare played from the radio had nearly startled her. *Led Zeppelin's* John Bonham had just pounded the intro to their song *D'yer M'yker.* One of Angie's favorite songs from one of her favorite bands. A very happy sounding song with its reggae rhythm but also had lyrics full of heart ache. Memories of Angela dancing and singing to this exact song came rushing back at Beth. Her eyes started to wince as she fought back upcoming tears.

Body shaking and stomach cramping, her legs went weak before she sank down to the ground sobbing on the white tiles of the kitchen floor. She felt this precise moment was her rock bottom, the moment where the shield she put against her suppressed grief burst like a dam creating a flood. Beth was trapped and she was drowning as she stayed on the kitchen floor bawling until the song was over.

(7)

Right as Beth finished with the big box and before D'yer M'ker played on the radio, Bonzo had just finished his business outside and waited for her to bring him back in. He hadn't started whining yet, but it wouldn't be much longer until he did. The weather wasn't exactly freezing, but cold nonetheless, especially with the sun dropping at a winters pace.

Frustrated after a few more minutes went by, he let his fussing begin and started to run around the area his tie out would allow him to go. Regardless, he quit his fussing and running when he heard a whistle come from the woods. Bonzo faced the trees, much like he did the week before and his attention was set.

The whistling was calling.

Tree branches creaked in the rushing air and the heeler tilted his head to hear better as the whistling continued. "Bonzo," the woods called in a voice familiar to him. Whistling continued and got louder, and closer. Despite his leash choking him, he pulled toward the woods. The stake in the ground began to wiggle with the first pull.

"*Bonzoooo*," the voice called with a dragged finish and continued with more whistling from in-between the tall trees. Harder than ever, he pulled forward and the stake came farther out of the dirt.

"Come here, Bonz," the woods whispered in that familiar voice.

All of that pulling succeeded and the stake was yanked out. He sprinted into the wall of trees with the chain and stake dragging behind him.

The calling and the whistling hadn't stopped when he went in but became more distant, like it was running away from Bonzo, making him chase the caller. Panting heavily, he ran farther into the forest with his collar tight around his neck from the weight of the chain.

About half of a mile into the woods, Bonzo was immediately stopped when his metal stake caught on a fallen branch. Realizing he was stuck, he pulled forward yet again but even more aggressively than before. Then the whistling came closer.

From behind a wide tree, surrounded by shadows, a single glowing eye the size of a cantaloupe appeared. It was about four feet off the ground seeming to hover in the darkness. The eye was stalking Bonzo and began to creep near him. He growled viciously as well as letting out some deep barks. The thing didn't back off or hesitate, it breathed like a horse and just kept marching near the helpless and isolated dog.

(8)

By the time Beth realized Bonzo was still outside, she was sitting up straight with her back against kitchen cabinets under the sink. Her face was red and still moist with tears.

"Shit! Bonzo!" she cursed and then slapped her thigh prior to getting up and running to the door, not bothering with her coat.

The moment Beth made her way outside, she felt how icy the air had become since night had come. This was the coldest she had felt Missouri or Kansas this year and that worried her even more.

"Bonzo? You frozen, boy?" she inquired while passing the front of her truck where she clipped Bonzo earlier. Her gut twisted when she saw he wasn't there anymore. Gone without a trace, besides the hole in the dirt where the stake had been. She checked all around her anxiously before calling for him.

"Bonzo!"

Nothing came. Not a sound nor movement approached. Feeling nearly ill, she went to the middle of Woodend rd. and called once more.

"Bonzo! Come here, boy!"

Nothing again.

He could be anywhere, Beth thought.

Searching for him with the truck had crossed her worried mind, driving around on every nearby street, checking yards and bushes he could have got caught up in. That was best case scenario. She would find Bonzo in a yard down the street, only to be tied up in someone's yard unintentionally and in such case, all she would have to do is apologize to whomever had rescue him.

Then a sudden gust of cool wind that forced the branches to sway, made her acknowledge the worst-case scenario.

He went into the woods

Driving the truck in search would be a major waste of time if Bonzo were actually lost as well as freezing in the depth of the forest. Beth thought back to when Bonzo gazed into the woods and what Nick said about him looking like he was about to take off into them. That's what pushed her to check within the trees first. Not wasting any more time, she went inside to retrieve her coat and when she came back outside, off into the woods Beth went.

(9)

With the moon and stars hiding above the cluster of branches, it was practically pitch-black underneath the canopy pf branches and leaves. Not very far into her search, Beth pulled out her smartphone for its flashlight in order to see where she was going. Looking for Bonzo, if she couldn't see, wouldn't do her much good.

All of the trees stood about four feet from each other, and the ground had a blanket of dead leaves that crunched under her feet with every step. She felt frightened searching through the moonless forest but the idea of leaving Bonzo to freeze to death, lost and forgotten, seemed to upset her more. Therefore, Beth kept strolling cautiously through the quiet blackness. Behind her, she had gone so far that Beth could no longer see the moonlight from where she had come from, it seemed like the forest had closed the door on her. Despite that, she didn't even think about turning around until she saw the gruesome sight at her feet.

There were the remains of a raccoon, the bottom half ripped from its body poorly buried under a pile of dead leaves. She gasped as her face turned pale. The raccoon's remains had made her more nerve racked and more frighten than ever before. For Bonzo that is. After Letting out a gasp, she stopped for a moment to check out the topless rodent. During her pause of searching, Beth strangely felt too warm for her winter coat now. She could feel her shirt underneath her coat was damp at the armpits. At first, she brushed it off as a nervous sweat but as a cool drop slid down her face, it was clear it was humid in the air. Weather-wise, a frosty December night appeared to bizarrely transform into a post rainy summer day, excluding the sunshine.

The change in the air made her frantic and confused her beyond belief. Nevertheless, and even more now, she had to find Bonzo and get the hell out of the woods. She kept walking and calling, swinging the phones flashlight all around her for any sign of the heeler. The humidity under the trees drenched her face more than the tears she cried earlier and randomly her throat started to hurt as if she had been chain smoking. Not only did the pain make yelling difficult, it also caused her to have shortage of breath, almost as if she were running out of air. Nearly to the point of giving up, she found something to lift her spirts and give her hope. Bonzo's metal stake was caught under a fallen thick branch, but the chain was broken off. Relieved she chose the right place to look for him, she kept walking forward, faster than ever.

"Bonzo! Here boy! Bonzo!" she called.
Committed, her walk became a light jog as she kept yelling for her lost best friend—practically her only friend. The

flashlight had to be pointed toward the ground if she wanted to see where she was stepping. The last thing she needed was to step in some decayed rodent's corpse. Sweat started to slide its way down to her eyes, making the search even more miserable. With the preposterous humidity, the absolute black atmosphere and mangled racoon she saw, Beth stood at the edge of hysteria. Taking a second to wipe the pouring sweat from her eyes, she heard the most satisfying sound. Nearby, a chain was rustling, a chain like Bonzo's.

Now filled with excitement, she wasn't far from smiling when she called in a tone delivered with great enthusiasm.

"Oh, Bonzo! Come here!"

Switching the phone light from the ground to the right and then to the left of her, she was disappointed when nothing appeared or approached her. "Bonz!" Beth called as loud as she could. For another few moments it was silent until the chains started to rustle again. She could now identify the noise was coming from straight ahead, and readily, she moved forward with the light. Still not seeing anything ahead but a tree that looked to be thicker and taller than the others, she kept on calling Bonzo with every breath she took.

Following the rustling that only seemed to be teasing her now, she ended up right in front of the mighty tree because that's where she could hear the rustling the best. Desperately, she put her back to the body of the tree and shined the light all around and saw nothing. Much like earlier in the kitchen, tears came to the brim of her eyes and all she wanted to do now was give up. Bonzo was gone, Angela was long gone and not only did the emotional dam bust, there was no rescue team coming for her. In that sense, she was being left to drown in the flood of depression and eventually it would kill her. And for Beth, that seemed better than anything right now.

All her weight was leaned on the wide bark of the tree. She was just beginning to bawl right there in the depth of the forest when from the humongous tree, something dropped in front of her. The impact from the fall sounded like it was an acorn, not too big but before Beth could push off the tree and look down, cool drops dripped on her neck and back. Instantly, she took her weight off the bark and turned around to face the tree and what had fell.

It looked like a patch of carpet or fur in a triangular shape. Curious, she bent down to take a better look at the patch. There was a pinkish color on the edge and red inside the pink, like a jelly filled pastry. Beth picked it up with a pinch and once she did, what she was holding became more than clear to her. And that's when the chain started to rustle again then it fell from the tree, dangling from the top.

She dropped her dogs severed ear and shinned the light on the silver chain. A shaken and overwhelmed Beth followed the shinning silver up with her phones light. Splatters, streams, and drops of blood were on the tree's bark farther up behind the swinging chain. Bravely, she stepped closer to the tree. Beth stood directly underneath the branches and tilted her chin up, then pointed the light toward where she was looking. Her jaw lost all control as it dropped wide at what was sitting between the branches.

Its body shape was similar to a praying mantis but it was the size of a grizzly bear and looked to be a scaly shade of violet. The thing had one eye and was already looking down at Beth by the time she shined the light on it. Holding itself on three different branches about nine feet away from her, it held Bonzo's bottomless corpse in its thorn covered arms. Beth had not let out a single breath since she laid eyes on the beast in the trees. Yet she didn't run, was she accepting death?

What else do I need to live for?

While the thing looked down on her, it dropped Bonzo's top half, hitting several branches on the way down and landed next to Beth, chain and all. In Seconds, the one-eyed, dog ripper crawled down to Beth. Now only three feet away, she saw this thing had a mouth like a spider's and its eye was snake like but so big she could hear it blink. Below its fangs, a long yellowish horn stuck out of its chin, she looked at the horn not moving a muscle. Pondering death, she gazed into its eye and out of its spider like mouth. It spoke in a voice that was more than familiar to Beth.

"*Bethy*," it said in Angie's voice.

She ran like hell. Faster than she did in high school track and those morning runs with Angela. Dodging trees and trying to watch where she was stepping with the flashlight in her hectic swinging hands, not looking back and not slowing down. She was stopped abruptly by the same fallen branch Bonzo got himself caught in. After she face planted, Beth was up in no time and continued to run for her life that was now worth living. Getting closer, she felt the rushing winter air on the outside of the forest.

The frigid Breeze felt godly while she dashed through the wall of trees, soaked with sweat and tears. Running to the passenger side of her explorer, she checked her inner coat pocket for her keys. Luckily that's where she usually kept them and she retrieved them, also moist with her sweat. Not once did she look back at the trees. She crawled into her truck and hopped onto the driver side then started the engine and pulled out of her new home. Beth drove forty-five mph on Woodend Rd and fifty on Pine, disregarding the stop signs. Her car shook violently going fifty-five on the red brick road of fourth street, but she made it through to go seventy on the narrow road out of Fairway. And with her foot firmly pressed against the gas, she got up to eighty-five mph driving away from it.

<u>Giving back</u>

"We'll hit the road on Sunday, after mass." That was Steven Kramer's response the previous week when his eldest daughter asked when they would be leaving town. Abbigail Kramer was only eleven years old, but she knew driving from their home in west Nebraska all the way to central Indiana would be a dreadfully long car ride. With her little sister, Alyssa, only being two years old, she wasn't surprised her parents decided not to fly. Plus, Abby heard her dad mention driving would be saving them some money.

Though, it wasn't a vacation the Kramer family were headed to Indiana for. More of a family event or an obligation. Steven's wife and mother of their beautiful brunette daughters, Amber, grew up in Indiana and still has a younger sister there. Her name was Jackie, and she was nearing the end of her first pregnancy. Just like Jackie once did for her, Amber insisted on being present at the hospital when she went into labor. Despite living about two states apart, the two sisters retained a close relationship. They both had always made the effort to be there for milestones and celebrations in each other's life. Weddings, graduations, the birth of both the girls, and both of their baptisms.

No doubt their family was the strong-willed catholic type, both parents grew up in religious households and therefore, they built their own family with the same structure. Everything from baptisms to church camp, confirmation to confession, and also attending mass every Sunday. The word of God was strong in their everyday life.

This Sunday in early January, their car had been packed full for a week stay and Abby sat with the rest of her family in church but felt incredibly eager. Head down, trying to listen to the prayers Father McClellan cited, all she could think about was her new cousin she was going to meet and seeing her beloved aunt. Abby thought the world of her mother and aunt Jackie, she would always follow by example when it came to the most important and coolest women of her life. Seeing the baby was just icing on the cake. She naturally adored babies, as did most little girls. She reflected on when Alyssa was even smaller than she is now, back when she used to be held in church but now, she would sit on the church tile and play with her toys.

"Lord, hear our prayer," Father McClennan preached.

"Lord, hear our prayer," the audience repeated. Well, everyone except Alyssa and the other toddlers playing on the floor or screaming in the hall. Surprising to Abby, her mother was tuned in to the service. Lately, Amber had hardly been able to focus on anything else with her sister's due date coming up. She was most likely even more eager to hit the road than her daughter. Although, that didn't seem to stunt her in church, but Steven and his daughter could tell she was overflowing with excitement for her sister and lately looked about ready to get on a plane to Indiana herself.

After communion, Amber had her purse clenched to her chest and all of Alyssa's toys picked up. Her foot was tapping at a swift pace as she waited for the last lines of mass. She knew she had to wait for Father McClennan to leave first, like every Sunday. Amber also told Abby to grab Alyssa and follow her quickly to the car to beat the church rush prior to the last lines.

"Now let us go in peace," he lastly said

"Thanks be to God," they all replied in unison.

The Kramer family stood up in the fourth row, waited for Father McClennan to walk down between the crowd, then hit the road for Indiana.

Inside the Pacifica was a tight fit for the girls in the back with all their clothes, toys, and snacks, but the new stroller Amber bought for her upcoming nephew or niece took up a good chunk of space. Jackie and her husband didn't want to know the sex of their baby. They wanted it to be surprise, but Jackie had her heart set on a little baby girl to match her sister's two gorgeous girls. Abbigail had a feeling it would be a girl, too.

Steven took the first driving shift and wanted to cover all of Nebraska by himself, more than likely some of Iowa as well but the eager mother said she would take over once they got to Iowa. The whole entire trip was roughly about fourteen hours by car. The parents, especially Amber, wanted to do the whole entire trip in one take. However, they both agreed if they were completely drained and had trouble staying up, they would check into a hotel wherever they were at and call it a night then continue tomorrow. Additionally, Steven mentioned the lengthy car ride might be too much for the girls, exclusively Alyssa.

The last time the family took a trip to Indiana, Abby was only five years old, so at eleven she had trouble remembering what the ride was like. She couldn't recall if it was fast with beautiful sights or if it was long and dull. For the first few hours of the car ride Abby was gazing out the window, though there wasn't much sight to see. Nebraska, like most of the Midwest consisted of farmland and in January, as well as the dead of winter, farmland was even less interesting. Plain fields with a light sheet of snow on top, dead trees with ice frozen on them, and a city every now and then would be the only sights to see.

Eventually, Abby got bored of what was outside of the car and started to play with her sister. That always made their mother happy since Amber and her sister always had a great relationship. It was nice to see it reflected on her own daughters as well. Nonetheless, within the hour Alyssa was passed out in her car seat and Abby turned her attention to her parents.

"How much longer do we have to go?"

"Hm, I'd say only about eleven hours," Steven lightly laughed. Amber giggled with her husband then smiled and reached her hand back to touch Abby's leg. "You don't remember the car ride last time we went, honey?"

"Not really, I just remember being there."

"Yeah, I guess you were about five years old then and how old are you now? Twenty-three?" Steven asked sarcastically, looking at his daughter through the rearview mirror.

"I'm eleven, dad!" Abby grinned and shouted back.

"Shh, Abby don't wake up Alyssa or she'll be a nightmare for all of us," Amber stated with a pleasantly smooth tone.

"Are we going to stop at any hotels, dad?"

Steven shot a look at his wife then replied, "Maybe if we get too tired. But the plan is to keep going and get to Aunt Jackie's real late at night. We'll see what happens though." He switched his stare from his wife, to the road, then to his daughter through the mirror. "Think you can make it, Abbs?"

"We'll see, I don't know."

(3)

After four hours on the road, they made it to the state line of Nebraska and were about to cross into Iowa. Once they made it through Iowa, it would be Illinois, then finally Indiana.

Neither of the parents seemed fatigued but it was clear they were bored of driving. Alyssa was again fast asleep for more than an hour now, but Abby was still so excited she felt she couldn't even try to sleep. Her goal was to stay awake with her parents the whole entire car ride.

"Mom?" Abby called from the back seat.

"Yes?" Amber answered, catching Steven's attention while driving.

"Do you think Aunt Jackie will have a boy or a girl?" she leaned as far forward as the seat belt would allow. "I think it's a girl."

Amber smiled and slightly giggled before replying. "Well, that is what your aunt wants too, but myself, I think she's having a boy. A smelly little boy." She then gave her husband a light rub on his shoulder.

"You guys hungry?" Steven chimed in.

"Yeah, I guess we did skip out on lunch, huh?" Amber turned around to face her daughter. "Where would you like to eat, Abbs? You pick."

Abby thought about it for a moment but came up short in ideas. She wasn't exactly a picky eater, but her appetite wasn't huge.

"Um, I don't know. Dad, you pick!"

"I saw a sign for a Flat Patties on one of the upcoming exits. Does that sound good enough for the queen and princess?" Steven said and laughing at his own joke. Amber gave a light slap to his arm this time while she laughed quietly with her family.

"Yeah, that sounds fine. You good with that, Abbigail?"

She was, and at the next exit they would stop, then go inside to eat their late lunch.

(4)

Flat Patties was practically empty. Behind the counter and in the kitchen were a group of teens from a nearby town. They were all laughing and chatting when the Kramer family came in for their four in the afternoon lunch. It was Amber's duty to get Alyssa up and out of the car and whenever she did, the two-year-old was aggressively cranky. Once they got inside the fast-food spot, Steven noted the crankiness was from being in the car all this time.

Abby stayed by her father's side and helped him carry the food and drinks to their table. Now that they were out of the car and away from the road, she thought her father actually did look a little beat. Which wasn't terribly surprising, the car ride drained both her and her mother and by the looks of it, obviously Alyssa too.

While they ate, Steven informed his family they still had about ten to eight hours left and they wouldn't be getting to Jackie's until after midnight. When Steven let his family know this, even Amber had her doubts about driving all night. All she did was sigh and say, "We'll see."

Then, something happened that would change the Kramer family forever. All of a sudden, the doorbell chimed as the entrance door was pushed open. Abby looked up from her food to the entrance and saw a man.

He was short but wide, wearing a cheap looking and off brand Carhart with dirty jeans. A bandana was tied around his head bandit style to cover most of his face from the cold air, and when he removed it, his nose and mouth were drenched in snot. He had a thick black untamed beard and his skin looked red from the outside's chill but also filthy from not bathing. After his entrance, he went to a booth and sat down, cupping his hands together and rubbing for warmth.

Despite the cold, the man was awfully sweaty and panting as if he were having a heat stroke. It was clear this man was homeless, drifting and probably ill. Abby couldn't take her eyes off the unsanitary and less fortunate derelict. As soon as the man entered, Abby felt scared from the man's presence. She glanced back at her food and suddenly lost her appetite. She then peeked to her family and realized her mother was staring at the man too.

Deciding on what she should say or whether she should say anything, Abby stared at her mother who appeared just as intrigued with the homeless man as she was. A few moments later, the stares stopped, and they finished their food while the man now rested his head in his arms at his table, minding his own, and trying to keep warm.

When it was time to get back on the road, Steven threw away their trash and asked if anybody needed to use the restroom before they left. Amber suggested he take Alyssa and clean her up. He did so, and Amber took another look at the man at the table, still with head in arms. She grabbed her purse and got out of her chair; Abby followed but instead of her mother going to the exit, she went to the counter.

Pulling a twenty dollar bill out of her wallet, she ordered a number six on the menu. Which was just a burger, fries, and a medium drink and told the cashier to take it to that man at the table and give him the change. About a minute after, Steven and Alyssa returned from the restroom then they all left the Flat Patties in a matter of seconds. Surprised but very confused, she stayed quiet about it and wouldn't mention anything to her mother until later on.

(5)

As they drove through Iowa, the sun was falling, and the night was born. Still flummoxed in the back, Abby stared at her mother while she drove but hadn't said anything about what had happened at lunch. Alyssa was talking and playing with her stuffed rabbit and their father sat in the passenger side, clicking through the local radio stations. Neither of the two knew about the deed Amber had done at Flat Patties but Abby couldn't get it out of her head. She wasn't sure why but she felt extremely nervous to address what her mom had done but her nerves didn't stop her. Eventually, she found the courage to ask.

"Mom?" she finally called.

Amber put her gaze on Abby through the rear-view mirror then back on the road.

"Why did you pay for that man's meal?"

Steven quit his clicking with the radio and looked at his wife who had a certain smile on her face while she looked at her daughter.

"What man?" Steven interrupted.

She replied but still had her eyes on the road. "Did you see that drifter come in at Flat Patties? He looked awfully dirty and cold, he had that big jacket and beard? I think he was the only other person there besides us."

Steven lifted his cap off his head then gave a scratch as he thought back. "Yeah, I guess I do remember seeing him. You bought him some food?"

"Yeah, when you guys went to the bathroom, and I also gave him the change."

"That's nice of you, Hon! Did he seem happy when you gave it to him?"

"We left before the food was made and brought to his table," Abby noted to her father.

"That's right," Amber nodded.

"But why did you do that, Mom?"

She didn't speak at first as one could tell she was trying to find the right words. "Well, when I saw that man, I totally forgot about what we were doing and where we were going. The excitement I felt for Aunt Jackie stopped for a minute and all I could think about was how cold and hungry that poor drifter probably was," she confessed to Abby, with her eyes switching from the road and back to the mirror.

Abby nodded as her mother spoke.

"You see, Abbigail, it's important to be grateful for the life you have, and also to be excited for the things yet to come, like Jackie's baby. But at the same time, you should be considerate and thoughtful of the people around you, even the ones you don't know." Amber held eye contact with her daughter through the mirror before she continued. "Whenever God blesses your life and makes it that much better, it's important to give back."

She understood loud and clear. Her mother was practically always right, and she was such a role model to her daughters, especially Abby. Her mother always went above and beyond for anyone and always knew what to say and when to say it. She wanted to be just like her mom; she listened to the words she spoke, repeated the things she said, and tried to do the things she did. To Abby, her mother was a living angel and to have her as a mother was a blessing on its own.

Down the road, she thought back to that man at the table and wondered just how he felt when his food arrived. She predicted he was grateful and happy; the thought made her smile.

Yet again, Alyssa fell fast asleep and after the cheeseburger and fries Abby ate, she felt tired too. With little resistance, she fell asleep looking at her mother who was a constant inspiration to her.

(6)

The earth beneath her feet was sand and the violet moonlight was able to show her that. It worked more as a spotlight rather than the moon, only lighting a circle that Abby was the center of. But she knew it was the moon, it had craters. The center of the circle—Abby—was about eight feet from the outside and everything that was beyond that eight feet span was an abyss.

Nothing but black surrounding her purple spotlight and sand. And no matter how far she ventured, the scene remained the same. The moonlight was following her.

I'm dreaming, she gathered.

Although, it felt all too life like. The sand between her toes was pilling, she could feel an itch coming on, and the back of her neck was damp with sweat. All her senses were there but the scene was mute besides a continuous, mechanical-like purr and if there were wind, she was sure she could have felt that too.

There was no wind, though; the air was still and without a chill.

Suddenly, something was under the uncanny moonlight with her and the first breeze blew it in the moment she saw it. Or maybe what she was seeing was the breeze. It looked like the thick smoke that came from burning a vast number of leaves. White but also grey, it had a strong opacity, so strong it was questionable if you could even put your hand through it, as if it was a solid with no particular shape. The dream figure flowed around the edges of the circle and with every lap it drew closer. She watched it go around and around, it wasn't fast, and Abby had the impression it was watching her watch it.

Eventually, it was right next to her, almost touching her. Twirling around Abby, she could feel its breeze again, and also, she felt it inhaling, like it was smelling her. In total astonishment of her dream company, she stayed still and let it do what it wanted.

Then it stopped. Didn't move or shift at all, seemingly standing right in front of Abby at her short height. Was it her turn to do something now? Did they want her to feel them?

Cautiously, she put her hand out like she was approaching a dog that may or may not bite, and when she was inches away from placing a finger on it, it backed off. And it got bigger, taller, and darker. It looked angry to Abby, and when it got to be taller than any man she'd ever seen, it struck down through her. The impact of the smoke on Abby was unlike anything she had ever felt. It wasn't painful but it was cold, colder than any breeze she had ever embraced, and she had felt it inside her. And her insides remained cold even after it left her body.

Her breath was gone, and her face felt like ice. She turned around in search of her dream mate but it was gone, out of the violet circle and into the abyss. She could still see it but not the way it was before. Now it was merely a pair of leering blank eyes floating tall in the shadows. Eyes the color of a gravestone.

(7)

Awakened by the Pacifica's interior lights due to the passenger door being opened, Abby's eyes spread with surprise. In the first few seconds of consciousnesses, the memory of her once vivid and unusual dream already began to dry and once Alyssa's door flung open and the cold air rushed in, it was nearly all the way gone. Rubbing her tired eyes, she saw her father unstrap the still asleep toddler from her car seat. At first, she assumed they had already made it to Aunt Jackie's and it was way past the midnight hour. But when she looked at the radio clock and then outside her window, she assumed wrong.

The clock read 10:42 PM and they were at a hotel that was just off of the highway they had been traveling on. To the right, she could see the exit ramp they had used and the quiet highway it was connected to. A little after Steven grabbed Alyssa, her mother opened the driver side door, then went around to the back of their vehicle where the bags were packed.

"You awake, Abbs?" Amber called after she opened the Pacifica's rear door. "Come and get your bag, we're done for the night."

"Mom, where are we?" She yawned while unfastening her seat belt and stepping out of the car.

Amber handed Abbigail's bag to her then answered, "A hotel, sweetie, your father and I got too tired to drive and thought it would be a better idea to stay here tonight."

"Are we in Indiana?" Abby asked.

Steven shut down the back while still holding Alyssa asleep in his arms and Amber picked up the bags she set on the ground. "Not yet, pretty close to Illinois though. We are at the edge of Iowa right now."

Abby let out another long yawn before saying, "Oh, okay." She picked up her bag. "Dad, are we going to get something to eat? I'm kind of hungry."

Walking to the hotel's front doors, she saw a sign with the hotel's name on it, in black bold letters reading "The

Sterling Inn." Perhaps a little above mediocre, not a resort by any means, but not a total dump either. It had two levels of a decent size rooms, with a brick build. And just as they were about to escape the late-night January air, the big sister looked to the sky in desire to see the pale moon but it wasn't there. It was buried behind abundant clouds. Abundant clouds that resembled smoke.

(8)

Whenever they made it inside the lobby to check in, there was a middle-aged man reading a paperback book at the front desk. He looked exhausted, and by his face, someone could guess he wanted to be anywhere than where he was now. Everyone but Steven went to the couches and chairs the lobby offered, then took a seat. Steven dragged to the front desk and started to discuss with the exhausted man, though one could say both were exhausted.

The lobby was poorly lit and immensely silent. On the way in, Amber pointed out how they had very few cars in the lot. To no one's surprise though, not many people took trips in the middle of winter. Regardless, this January the Kramers were traveling, and tonight they could travel no more. And when Steven returned with a room key to room 35, that's where they would call it a night and rest. The family exited the lobby but not in the same door they had entered.

The door they did go through was on the opposite side of where they entered. Behind this entry was an outdoor patio and pool area that the rooms surrounded. There were two levels of rooms and two stair cases on different sides, room 35 was on the second level.

Taking in her surroundings, Abby studied the outdoor area once they made it to the second level. She saw the pool had beach chairs all around and had a huge black cover on top along with a dead garden to the side. Right across from their area, she saw a dark passage with two soda machines casting a faint light on what appeared to be an ash tray of some sort, and the passage, as far as she could see, led to the parking lot.

As soon as Steven found room 35, it wasn't long until they were all inside and putting their bags down. However, in that short window of time between unlocking the door and entering, Abby took a better look at the vending machine passage.

In the vending machines shy light, it wasn't a large ash tray after all, it was a tall body resting. Assuming it was a man, she saw he was sitting with his back against the wall but with his head upon his arms as they rested on his knees. He looked awfully skinny and even from a distance she could now tell he was wearing a flannel shirt along with a large hat on his head. The man wasn't right in front of the vending machines but toward the right near the exit to the parking lot.

Now sitting on one of the hotel's beds, she considered the scrawny and poor man and couldn't help but feel bad for him. It was pretty cold outside and that flannel he had been wearing couldn't be doing any good for warmth. She hadn't seen much of his body before, but she saw his arms were incredibly thin, nearly as wide as the neck of a guitar and his legs weren't far off from that either. She looked at her mother who was now watching the box television beside Steven with the local dinning guide in his hands. Alyssa was up again, and she was watching the television with her mother but still looked exhausted from the road.

Abbigail wondered if any of them saw what she had seen. She thought of asking if they had and then telling them what was out there but, in the end, she decided to keep it to herself.

It was slightly past eleven when Steven abruptly stood up and announced he would be picking up a pizza for their late dinner.

"Where at, hon?" Amber questioned while still watching T.V.

"There's this place that about fifteen minutes away, they're open 24/7 and advertise to always have pick up ready," he explained putting on his coat by the door.

Intrigued by the mention of food, Abby involved herself in the conversation. "What if they don't have any pizza ready, Dad?"

He looked down at his daughter laying on the bed. "Well, I guess if that's the case," Steven stepped toward her, "we'll have to eat each other!" He then proceeded to tickle her ribs, making her laugh so hard it could be mistaken with crying.

He returned to the door and swung it open. "I'll be right back. Try to stay up."

Steven rushed out the door and with food practically on its way. His oldest daughter was hungrier than ever. Although, despite the upcoming food making her hunger boost, she knew the man outside had to be hungrier than she had ever been in her life. Suddenly, Abby had a righteous idea.

"Mom?" She sat up and called from the bed beside her own.

"What's up?" she answered in a sleepy voice.

"Can I go out and get us some sodas for dinner? There are a couple vending machines not too far from our room."

"Sure, you payin?" Amber smiled. Abby returned a smile then her mother grabbed her purse off the floor.

She pulled out a five-dollar bill from her purse and handed it to Abby after she put her coat on. "That should be enough, babe."

Abbigail's thoughtful idea was to go down to the vending machine, grab four sodas and give one of them to the poor man and mention that she would bring him a slice of pizza soon. She chose not to tell her mother just because Abby figured it would be better to tell her after she returned with the sodas, then she could ask about the pizza. Her mother would be touched and proud, she thought.

Leaving the room, she looked back at her mother who appeared totally relaxed and ready to pass out any minute. Never in her life had she met anybody who she wanted to imitate more than her mother. As stated before, Abby always followed her mother's lead, mimicked her actions, followed her greatness, so to speak. And that's what encouraged her to go up to the man at the vending machines.

(10)

As soon as Abby closed the room's door, she went to the rail and tried to see if the man was still in the dim passage. He was still there and in the same position, basking in the vending machines blue light. But it wasn't appearing blue anymore. Once she stepped closer, she recognized the machines light as a shade of purple. Or *violet*. Now second thoughts made their way in her head as she got a whiff of the dream Abby thought she had completely forgotten. The steps down to the pool area now seemed like it was ten stories.

Consider others, she reflected, and urged herself to keep going. She also proceeded with asking herself why that violet light seemed so significant. Abby made it to the patio area and then crossed the width of the covered pool. She was getting closer to where he was. Now she could not only see the man, but she could see what he was wearing entirely. The flannel she saw was correct, but he also had a dirty blanket around his shoulders and the large hat he had been wearing had been a straw hat. He had sweatpants on that were dark grey and covered in little tears. Below that, were what looked like snow boots. She had never seen anyone actually ever wear a straw hat, but Abby insisted a poor man probably took whatever he got.

Next to the dark and dead garden, she stopped walking. The resting man was so close to her at this point she thought that she'd be able to see him breathing, but he wasn't moving at all. While she stood at the entry, the eleven-year-old felt like turning around and telling her mother the machine was jammed. At this moment she felt too scared to even go near the machines, let alone approach the man on the ground.

In addition to her second thoughts, another one came. She thought back to that sweaty and sick man at the Flat Patties and how her mother unexpectedly bought his meal. Her mother didn't do it for herself, she did it because she was giving back.

Maybe it's time for me to give back a little.

The doubtful child continued into the dark passageway. The man remained still as Abby approached the R.C. cola machine. Sliding the bill into the dollar slot, she looked back over her shoulder to see if the derelict had noticed her. No movement whatsoever, the machines hum or purr must have been soothing him, but she knew once the sodas were selected, the drop into the receiving bin would make a rambunctious fuss that could wake anyone up.

Post making her last selection, she prepared for the drop of the four sodas by keeping her eyes locked on her sleeping company.

CLUNK...CLUNK...CLUNK...CLUNK.

He stayed still as a statue. Perfectly motionless as if the cold air had frozen his scrawny bones. Abby recovered the bottles and turned around to face the man who even sitting on the ground, was at her chest. Everything around her seemed inaudible as she mustered up the voice to speak.

"Excuse me? Sir?" she nearly whispered.

No adjustment or acknowledgment; he stayed with his arms across his thin knees and head resting on top. She couldn't see his face as the massive hat tipped toward the front, hiding his face and hands.

"Mister?" she called in a louder voice than before.

Nothing changed. The preteen stood with her arms full of bottles, still with those second thoughts lingering.

"Hey, excuse me, sir?" louder than ever.

Frustrated and cold but set on doing what she felt was right, Abby unwrapped one of her arms from the sodas. She reached out her left arm to touch the man and hopefully wake him up.

But right before she even got the chance to touch the cloth of his worn-out flannel, the man clinched onto her extending arm and the man turned out to be perhaps anything but a man.

Its hand had long, green and crooked fingers but no thumbs. The grip on her arm was firm as the head of whatever it was popped up, losing its hat, and revealing a deformed and disturbed appearance in the process. Its skin was tight and green like the fingers, and the skull was comparable to a human's but had a softball size crater on the right side.

Although, it was the thing's facial features that made Abbigail scream but before she could let out a sound, the ghoul jammed its lengthy fingers into her mouth, holding down her tongue.

The teeth were sharp, yellow, and long enough that they went above and below its mouth like some bizarre fish. There were two holes for a nose that looked like they had been poorly done with a dull pencil. Eyes like a person's but no detail or presence, just foggy and grey as if smoke were trapped within them.

The Kramer's eldest daughter dropped the sodas in attempt to escape and cry for help. Only quiet muffles made it through as the terrible thing now covered her mouth with its long hands. It swept her off her feet and ran like how a predator does after it steals a cub in the wild. The fiend took Abby under the same ramp that led her family to the hotel to do, unfortunately, God knows what.

February

Used

Prologue

The bedroom of her studio apartment hasn't seen sunlight or city light in almost a week, and currently, Holly doesn't care if she sees either one of them ever again. The only light that has graced the room recently is from her phone screen. All her app's signature colors illuminating her chubby, flushed, and damp face as she scrolls down her newsfeed. Appropriately, the color that appears the most is blue. *Facebook's* blue, to be exact.

It was a constant painful reminder for her to be on the social platform though, considering that's where she had met Sage when it had all started. But of course, he had blocked her the minute after she read his departing messages, and before that, likely only an hour before, they were having sex. Which made her feel even more disgusted and used.

She knew a shower would be essential tonight, especially with finally returning to work tomorrow morning after being off for five days. More heartache was surely to be received there as well. The subject could not easily be avoided, not with how she handled it at the beginning. If she could go back, maybe she would still hook up with him but not get attached or led on. However, her biggest regret, as she dwelt on the impending workday, was what she had told her co-workers before the falling out. Previously, she was telling everyone what she *thought* was going on between the two.

Holly, as naïve and trusting as she was, never shut up about Sage to her coworkers despite only seeing each other for a little under a month. Always commenting on his strong facial features, his caramel toned skin, and his fit body. Sometimes she went on about his voice and his jokes or things he simply said to her. The sex she didn't bring up as much. Not that she hated talking about it, she liked sex just fine, but it wasn't her favorite aspect of him. But too bad for her, from Sage's perspective, sex was the only thing he cared for from Holly. She knew that now. No matter how painful it was to accept it as the truth, it clearly was.

All week she lay in bed and half of the time Holly was reflecting on her previous outlook. What she considered to be wishful thinking was nothing but empty and unrealistic dreams she had with a man who never even liked her enough from the start to finish. Four years ago, way before Sage Torres, before she moved to Chicago and away from the more suburb area of Illinois, when she was going to high school at Champaign Central, she had run into this problem a handful of times. She was disappointed she fell for it again, but this time was way harder.

When will I learn? When will I learn that all these Illinois boys are good for nothing but leading on and fucking over women like me?

Her phone charge was at a dying six percent and despite laying near the charger this entire time, it wasn't plugged in. Her charger was in between the bed and the frame. She plugged it in and flipped over to her back. The urge to cry was still lingering over her after all this recovery time she had. Holly avoided crying this time and instead let out a massive quivering sigh then continued on to the shower.

The bathroom mirror was spotless, but she loathed the view. Parts of her strawberry blonde hair were loose from her bun and stuck to the side of her face, making it look like she had some gnarly and greasy sideburns. Rather than dark bags under her eyes, Holly had red sacks that held more luggage. The T-shirt she had been wearing the last five days smelt sour when it dragged up her face as she took it off. Looking at her bare body in the mirror, the urge came hauling back and harder than ever.

I bet if I was smaller, I would have actually had a shot at being his girlfriend.

Now, Holly wasn't obese or covered with rolls, and some most likely wouldn't even say she was fat but what ate at her was that she believed Sage would say so.

The water was cool at the start, then it slowly went lukewarm and then, a second later, it was scalding. Making sure to pick up her feet to resist slipping, she stepped out of the shower range and went around to turn down the hot water in an effort to let it cool.

Quickly, she began to think of work again and how she was going to respond to them when everyone asked if she was feeling better. Or an even more dreadful question, "How's everything with Latino-heat lover, Holly??" The first question she could bullshit through, but the second question, her answer might expose her.

Not too long after Holly was blocked, she ultimately decided work wasn't manageable the next day and some of the days that followed. Without much dispute—being such a reliable and hardworking employee allowed such privilege—Holly was able to squeeze the five days she spent "recovering" from a bogus stomach flu excuse. Her paycheck would suffer but she didn't care at the moment. Before, she knew she wasn't going to be strong enough not to cry at work in front of everyone. People always made it worse when she was sad or heartbroken. Putting her hand in the water to feel if it was still too hot, she hoped she would finally be strong enough tomorrow, but like she should have when she met Sage, Holly doubted it.

Once the water cooled and became reasonable for bathing, she washed up and returned to her bed. While her phone charged, she skimmed her Facebook feed and saw a relatable post in the process. Posted by "Vintage Love," was a photo with a caption in the middle. It was a gloomy looking woman gazing out of her rainy window. The caption said, "One of my biggest fears is that I'll meet someone and believe they're *the* one, only to find out I'm just one of *theirs*." Within finishing the caption, her eyes wilted with tears. Holly felt she couldn't have seen a more relatable topic unless she made it herself. She shared the post, wiped her eyes before a tear could fall, and put her phone on rest.

The bed she had been sobbing into all week no longer comforted her. Every time she had fallen asleep recently has been enforced by self-pity and the crying that tagged along. Tonight, would be no different. She could feel it around her, already feeling so damn sorry for herself while he isn't sorry whatsoever. The shove of sobbing finally got her down, but it wasn't all night.

Around 3:00 AM, her phone screen lit up with a notification from Facebook. Immediately she thought it was Sage unblocking her and asking for a booty call, or maybe to apologize. He didn't though, it wasn't him at all. It was a notification from someone liking her shared post. The thumbs up was from a friend from high school, though they hadn't talked since freshman year. Briefly Holly wondered if this girl was feeling the way she felt. Again, doubt became apparent in her head. This particular girl was beyond gorgeous and strong, very unlike herself. Sleep still had a firm grip on her since she only opened her eyes to see the like. As she put her phone to rest again, she did the same to her eyes but as if sleep weren't an option, her phone lit up again and her eyes opened with it. Someone had sent her a message on Facebook.

(2)

He hadn't snapped the picture, not yet anyway. Sage just wanted to see what a picture would look like in his formal date clothes. But if he liked how he looked in the picture—which he usually did—he would send it to all the girls he had daily streaks with. *Actually,* Sage decided he shouldn't do that. Instead, he would just send it to the one girl. *Maybe it would be for the best to just get use to that*, he thought. To be fair, that one girl was the reason he was dressed so nicely tonight.

The picture was snapped in the mirror, and he liked how he looked in his violet sweater shirt and light jeans. It was simple but he hardly ever dressed nice to see a girl, but then again, he hardly ever went on actual dates. On his *Snapchat* via *iPhone*, he went to his contacts to find the receiver for his selfie. At the top of the list with a two-week streak across from the contact's name, was Marcie Welsh.

He had already sent her a few snaps today, but Sage really believed he looked good, and also, he had already resisted sending her other photos throughout the day. Nothing that could get him blocked. Especially not with this girl. The entire experience with Marcie so far had been surreal and enlightening for Sage.

At age twenty-three, the young man had seen and been with many different types of women. He liked them all to a point, he guessed, but none of them made him crazy or love struck. In the past, he was never one to become clingy. Though, now he had a hard time trying to stop his dwelling over a future with a woman that wasn't even close to solidified. What was straight hypocritical about the whole thing was he hated when girls did that to him. A huge turn off to say the least but it regularly happened. Some women just couldn't catch a vibe even if it were thrown directly at their chest.

Nevertheless, here he was, fantasizing and hoping for a girl he hasn't even personally met yet. Tonight, that was set to change. Sage had been asking Marcie out on a date ever since she and him became friends out of nowhere about two weeks ago. When Sage had first seen her, he didn't believe her to be real. Thought maybe she was just a scammer or virus the way she debuted into his life.

Shockingly, she added him, but the surprises didn't cease there. If looks really could kill like the saying goes, this girl would be a walking massacre. Her hair was thick, wavy, and hung to the middle of her back and was as jet black as Sage's own hair but unlike him, her skin was pale and flawless. The only thing her skin did bare were these tiny freckles around her nose and tattoos that decorated her whole right arm and half of her left.

On the surface, she looked like a girl who would be hard to make smile, but he had seen it in some of the photos she was tagged in on Facebook. Her teeth were perfect as far as Sage could see and the way the corners of her lips curled up next to two deep dimples on both cheeks pressured Sage to quit looking at other women completely. Excluding her aesthetic, Marcie had traits of an angel but looked like a cemetery had puked on her. To complement her black hair, there was a straight forward goth aura around her but the natural features of a human barbie. Dark clothes, dark nails, and the darkest and sharpest eye make-up to strengthen her emerald eyes. Early on, he found himself infatuated with her. Certain that he had never seen a woman even a shred like her before, he knew he would never see one again.

Staring at himself in the body mirror for the last fifteen minutes gave him the assurance he needed. He looked good, damn good in fact. She'll look great though. Something told him that. Sage turned away from his reflection and retreated to his made bed. Before getting ready, he prepped his bedroom as well. Although, there was no guarantee Marcie would see his bedroom or his apartment tonight, he did it just to be safe.

He would have hated if Marc—funny, he was already giving her nicknames in his head—came up and saw his room dirty. He didn't like to appear unprepared under any circumstance and as if it were some kind of ritual, Sage also took time to jack off before showering. Unnecessary as it seems, he usually did so every time he was set to hang out with a girl. Relieving stress was nice, but that wasn't the main purpose of him doing it. To him, it was merely the same thing as cleaning his room or making his bed. Just to make him look better later on if he did get some action, which, to be fair, he usually did.

With Marcie, on the other hand, Sage felt a different approach was beneficial. He wasn't after sex tonight. All the bedroom preparation and masturbation was merely insurance. In some sort of way that made him feel gentle (a rare feeling in his tactics). Sage was hoping they wouldn't have sex tonight or anything. Sitting on his bed looking at Marcie's vague profile he told himself he didn't deserve to know her like that yet.

The time in the corner of his phone was twenty minutes away from being done with seven o'clock hour. Marcie told Sage she would get him around eight, but she might be a little late. Fine by him, he knew driving in the city was a bitch, and it was hard to predict anything. While considering the time, he caught yet another thing he liked about her. She was independent and knew what she wanted and what she didn't. The whole date tonight had to be on her terms, or it wasn't happening and Sage, well, kind of got turned on by that. Sage had his own car in the parking garage, but she still insisted on her picking him up and going to a restaurant she wanted him to try. He liked that. Probably because independent women never gravitated to Sage. Assumingly because they could always see through his bullshit in a second.

"There wouldn't be bullshit with Marcie though," Sage committed.

Eight was coming in closer by the literal second and he was determined to make this girl his. Not by tonight, but after eight, it'll all be a part of the process.

He felt so lucky to have this chance but nervous just the same. To prepare for the night, he began to think of questions that would move the night along smoothly by striking up conversation. Their texting over the last couple of weeks had been brief—sometimes she would be irresponsive for hours, another new experience for Sage, but he knew the basics about her, just not a fair amount. Once she had told him she was twenty-two and that she didn't grow up in Chicago but she did spend a good deal of her life in Illinois. He could work off that. It was pretty similar to himself anyhow.

In a joking manner, but with a touch of sincerity, he asked himself where she had been his whole life? Chi town was a big city, anybody could tell you that, but Sage swore if he ever saw Marcie before all of this, he would have known. She stuck out that much to him. Still sitting on his bed, he was curious what school she had went to during her teenager years. He was certain she didn't go to Urbana High like he did. He would have sniffed her out there but additionally Sage didn't believe she went to any local school in the Champaign cou—

A message found its way to Sage's phone. It was from Marcie and with a smiley face (a simple but new touch that made Sage expose his cocky, shit eating grin). She said she would be there way sooner than expected. In fact, she was pulling up to his building within five minutes.

(3)

A storm-colored PT Cruiser took a rushed right turn onto Hubbard Street. Sage could see it from the entrance of his building, standing and shivering. Why hadn't he grabbed a jacket? The excitement, he assumed.

The cube shaped vehicle was screaming a very distorted and garage-like sounding band that could be heard through its tinted windows. "That's her," he already decided. Though he really had no way of knowing but he still got rid of the idea of grabbing his jacket. Behind light traffic, the car halted its speed but not its tunes. Sage and the PT were a lane and about five cars away from each other but he didn't take his eye off it as the cars pushed forward.

Closer, the Cruiser filled with the sounds of a drummer who perhaps loved his double bass pedal too much came. The anticipation had slayed the feel of the winter for Sage by this point and appearing to add to the suspense, when the car made it directly across from him, the passenger window started to drag down. The music escaped. Now playing louder than anything else on the street in an acclaimed noisy city, and from the same place the heavy music came, was Marcie driving. Exactly like he imagined, but no matter how much he dwelled of her looks before, when he saw her, Sage saw he had still been deceived.

This girl was stupendously stunning.

She waved her dark painted fingers swiftly, signaling Sage to hop in and fast. The cupid's bow-struck young man didn't need more than a millisecond to respond. He was off. Dodging and maneuvering around cars and putting a hand up to ease the honking driver behind Marcie. Usually, it would have been the finger but there was no way the dildo honking could spoil his mood tonight. Not when he's about to get in a car with a girl whom he wanted to change his life for.

As soon as he got into the PT, she yelled something over the music but it was too loud. He was pretty sure she said, "What's up!" So he just smiled and nodded up to her, returning the favor.

Sage was not very involved or in-tune with heavy music or the rock genre at all. His music preference evidently didn't matter in Marcie's wheels as a band he had never heard of—most haven't heard of truthfully—was blasting in his ears at about full rage. He didn't care for it, hell no, they were just a bunch of freaks screaming about death or about how life was so terrible. She cared for it though, and he could tell by looking at her. Hell, he couldn't stop looking at her.

Along with her violent music taste, Marcie also drove like a lunatic escapee driving with a stolen ride. At first, Sage considered that the loud music might be encouraging his perspective that she might be driving recklessly. Then the moment passed where she curb checked a stop light island and only thinly smiled without looking his way. But damn, did she look good doing it.

He restrained gazing at her as much as he could. And she didn't look his way much at all. They had only been in the car for about ten minutes, a long time or a short amount in a different pair of shoes. Besides "singing" with her music, she had not said much to him. The thought of her being shy suddenly jumped to his head. With that fresh idea, he waited for the band to cease so he could get a word in before the next song played. Hopefully something funny but Sage was aware he would only have a few seconds to speak.

Awaiting his moment, it came earlier than expected when Marcie got a text on her phone—that the aux cord was plugged into—and the music came to an early halt. *Here it goes.*

"So, what kind of music do you listen to?" Sage asked, with a smile that displayed how funny he thought he was.

The music returned but not for longer than a flash as Marcie manually shot down the music with twisting the stereo knob left. "Huh?" she answered.

Swing and a miss.

"Oh, nothing. I was just kidding around and asked you what your favorite kind of music was. Ha-ha." His red face spoke. "You know, I thought it would be funny since we're head banging as a unit right now!"

Marcie replied with a smile, a thin one like she had when the Cruiser's passenger side wheel (his side) smacked the curb but now, she was looking right at him. Her eyes on him felt like heat from a blazing bon fire, inviting but viscous. It made him feel that gentle way again that was never relevant before. Once she put her eyes back strictly on her driving, Sage believed a proper introduction would be smooth.

"I'm Sage by the way. I'm the stalker who has been howling at you for a date for about two weeks."

Sticking with her light smile, and her sight on the road, she made her quick response.

"Marcie." Then acting as if the music was her punctuation, she went back to the stereo knob and twisted toward the right this time. The music blasted higher and louder than Woodstock '99.

He didn't have a single idea where they were going out to eat. It didn't matter so much to him. He wasn't hungry but sure, he could eat, though he had other things on his mind. Like her and what she was thinking.

Did she like what she saw when she (barely) looked at him? Did she think he was funny? Is she really shy or just not interested and only said yes to the date to shut him the hell up? He really didn't know. Sage was sure he would eventually find out though.

Thirty-five minutes past the last time they "talked," and twenty-five minutes away from the city, the Cruiser was finally put in park. Sage rode in the passenger seat confused the majority of the ride, and with a pinch of being annoyed and handful of getting ignored. They were in a blink-you'll-miss it kind of town named Dawson. Some who lived there or live-in smaller towns would correct that statement saying it was a city. That didn't really add up to Sage. Especially with how close they were to the windy city and all its noise, history, and lights. Easily took in more of a town vibe when Sage scoped out the few sights on the way in.

He had never been to Dawson before tonight, never even cared to drive through it to get somewhere else. The whole town just came off as so *useless.* Like why not just be a part of Chicago? He hated that the little shithole place, thought it was independent enough to take business land from the big city. On the way in, he only saw two gas stations and one *Dollar General* with one other local super market. The only sit-down restaurant he saw was the one they parked in front of.

She parallel parked on a street that was the home of a joint called, *Glenda's pie and wine, A café'*. He liked the café add on. Just so people knew she didn't just sell pie and wine, but probably expensive burgers and coffee too. The building had a brick build and looked to be a size as a common *McDonalds*, perhaps a little bigger.

Once her car was turned off and the key was removed, the band, who had been playing as loud as they could, finally quit and the doors unlocked. "Finally, some *wanted* silence," he bitterly praised quietly to himself, a jiffy before his brief bitter mood changed for the night when she got out of the car.

Perfectly put together, she stood looking around her and up at Glenda's neon bar lights above. She had these tight black jeans on that made Sage wonder how she got them over her hips or butt, and below that, she had leather boots that gave her more height. She was almost as tall as he was in them. Rather than the boots making him feel insecure, they made him feel powerful and badass to be standing next to her.

Her coat was also a jean material and black with some buttons of what he assumed to be horror characters pinned to the vest of it. Under the jacket was just a causal black T-shirt with a surprisingly bright design on the front. He had out dressed her formally without contest. Nevertheless, Sage could not be happier with how she looked. Anybody else would have looked like a wannabe vampire with the amount of black she was covered with. Not her though. She almost looked *too* good in black to wear any other color. The fucking *night* even looked good on her.

Sage looked toward the building with Marcie and tried to find something to say that might make her give him another smile.

"Aw! This looks fuckin dope! This one of your favs?"

No smile, no look, she just spoke. "It's okay."

Sage, discouraged but still with a smile, rolled his eyes and chuckled. "Wow, you really sell it."

Involuntarily, she smiled and then chuckled some. Sage's smile only grew bigger off of hers. Gotcha. He was still in this, and she did think he was funny despite her strong guard. After she covered her little laugh, she went forward and led the way to the double doors at the restaurant ahead of them.

(5)

She had beat Sage inside by a full-size beds length and met the host first. By the time Sage met up with the two at the podium in front of the place, Marcie had already told them everything they needed to know. All he heard when he came up was, "Booth? Alright follow me this way."

The place was pretty packed on both sides and that surprised Sage. Not that it looked shacky or ugly, but it was just in such an isolated and quiet area. He figured they all must be regulars to some point, kind of like Marcie. Looking at the crowd before going to sit down, Sage noticed how divided the crowd had been. On the right side—the bigger side of Glenda's—were full tables with multiple seats and families filling them. The other side—the smaller side but perhaps with more people—was full of booths lined up on the walls and a bar that was doing pretty well tonight. Couples and single drinkers took up most of the left and thankfully for him, the host had led them left.

First, they uncomfortably sat without any conversation for over two minutes. All of a sudden, and at the worst time, he felt silently nervous. He didn't know what to say or what to do. What did he do with his hands? Put them on the table? Wasn't that rude? So much was crossing his mind, but nothing at all coming out of his mouth. Sage also had a hard time trying to find where to look. He didn't want to look right at her; well, he did, but he thought that wasn't the best idea.

To distract him from her wicked beauty, he looked at the atmosphere of Glenda's. Everything was fall decorated and even smelt like October with scents of pumpkins and cinnamon. Pictures of cheesy witches like from the wizard of oz were framed on the wall. He knew they weren't all from the same movie, but they all looked similar. Big and sharp noses that could make a bird jealous, ghostly pale or with green skin and giant moles with no discretion and blac—. Marcie slipped off her jacket and unmasked all her tattoos on her arms. Sage had fought to not stare since they had sat down but now nothing was going to stop him.

"Ha-ha. Damn, those look so badass. You easily look ten times tougher than me just with those. Not to mention your music." Sage let go.

Marcie looked down at her arms like she wasn't aware she had tattoos, "Oh yeah? Thanks." She gave no smile and that defeated Sage along with her simple response. This was the first time Sage had ever been the one wanting more than the girl had. He went back to the walls to look at more witches and fall themed decorations but was interrupted when she better-late-than-never added to the tattoo talk. "Why don't you get some?"

Sage laughed and gave a half smirk. "Well, there's an idea but I don't know what I would get really. I'm not that creative." He looked down at her arms and could identify some of the images she was painted with. Most of them, if not all had to do with nature in some way. Sage was about to ask her to go through her tatts but was cut off by their waitress who had arrived with a drink menu along with three other menus.

The girl had red hair that was boy length and curly in the front. She was very thin but not very tall and looked middle aged. He wasn't sure how she worked here, there was no way she could move huge orders to tables. He also inferred she was gay, not that he had a problem with that by any means. Just an observation.

"Hey there, guys, how is it going? My name is Amanda and I'll be taking care of you tonight. Do you know what you guys will be having to drink?"

"You can get whatever, it's on me," Sage said to Marcie before returning his attention back to the waitress. "I think I'll just have a water to sip on for now."

"Yeah, me too," she added.

The waitress delivered that customer service smile and said she would be right back with those.

Marcie chuckled at her own expense, stealing Sage's eyes. "I hardly even like drinking water but she took me by surprise when she came up here."

"Yeah, I know what you mean. I haven't even been thinking about food or drinks since you picked me up ha-aha, I'm really not that hungry."

"Then why did we come here?" she said with real curiosity, but her eyes looked to burn a hole in him again.

Sage felt his face go warm for a moment but soon realized that they were there because of her. He would have been fine hanging out anywhere, but Glenda's was her plot.

He bellowed with laughter shortly then sharply said, "It was your idea, jerk!"

"Oh shit. That's right," she said with a laugh. A stoner laugh at that. Adorable, he marveled with also the thought of how they actually were slowly, but surely settling into the night well.

In a hurry, Amanda the server dropped off their waters and continued on to her next table. Sage hoped it wasn't a huge order for her sake.

"So, are you thinking either the pie or the wine?" Sage asked, reaching for the menus their server had placed at the front of the table. He separated them in his hands like they were a giant hand of playing cards. "Ope, they accidently gave us three menus. Guess I'm stealing one," he joked, grabbing his deceiving coke labeled glass that held the water.

"That's weird, and I'll probably just order the blackberry pie. The crust is soooo good. Legit makes me want to change my panties thinking of it."

Sage, who had a throat full of water, choked on her comment. While resisting spitting up his drink, he smiled hugely to let her know he was okay during his coughing/laughing fit and Marcie looked amused and pleased with his reaction. She even laughed with him, but not choked.

"Ha-ha That good, huh?" his throat cleared.

"It is! You should try it. We can even share a slice."

Sweating and feeling hot in the face from his struggle of swallowing his water, he agreed and finished off with a small single cough.

"What about the wine though?" Sage retrieved the smaller menu from the stack he had placed in front of him.

"They actually call drinks 'brews' here. To go with the whole witch theme," Marcie said.

"Ahh, that's cool. Do you have a favorite one? Do you drink?"

"Wine is my favorite, in general. I have countless bottles I save at my place."

"That's cool. Do you have an apartment in the city or something?"

Marcie had no problem making eye contact with Sage while he spoke or while she did. She wasn't shy nor was she scared after all, and Sage could read that from her as soon as they sat down across from each other. He wasn't sure what to make from it, but Sage believed he liked it.

"Something like that." She looked away for the first time since the conversation had started rolling.

"Alright, guys! Did you find anything else out? There is a brew and stew special tonight if you two are interested." The server came back right in time to rescue the two from any further silences.

"Um I thin—

"Just a slice of blackberry pie and two forks, please," Marcie butted in and ordered but somehow still in a charming and polite way.

"Coming right up, beautiful." The waitress walked off, probably feeling some kind of way after having Marcie's powerful gaze on her. He wondered if she felt as vulnerable in its warmth as he did. As Marcie returned her eyes to Sage, he strongly considered it was probably just him.

(6)

The date swept by with casual conversations due to basic questions. There were a few more silences but none that Sage was too upset about. Most of them were from pauses between answers and different questions and therefore he felt they were natural and weren't worth over criticizing. Though, his fear of running out of topics from before came back to haunt him and was only inevitable at this point. Had he never gone this far with a girl without sex? It was silly to think but he began to. He needed to brainstorm to keep her interested.

Marcie practically made the plate the pie came out on spotless. He had a good amount of it and the crust along with its blackberries were enough to get excited about. At one point while eating it, he had thought about referencing back to her underwear joke from earlier, but he thought better of it since he didn't want her to think that was where his head was, even though it was her joke. Couldn't be too sure with some women.

He let Marcie have the last few bites as she continued to scrape any other residue with a fork. When he had watched her drag her fork in the left-over guts and crust, he had told her she could get one of the pies to go and she could take it home if she wanted. She accepted his offer carelessly with a shrug. That's when the lack of conversation really started and where the uncomfortable silences were born.

Up until this point in the night, their date had only been decent—filled with green lights that influenced him into thinking she liked him, and red lights that would switch from the green unexpectedly and give him the impression she didn't give two shits about him. It was the erratic reactions that left him encouraged at times and discouraged for what seemed like most of the time. But what Sage didn't catch in the midst of their first uncomfortable silence since they sat, was that everything was set to not only go downhill from here but to roll at the speed of the interstate with no brake nor foreseeable conclusion.

"Can I get that outta your way, sweetie?" Amanda, the server snuck up on them.

Marcie helped out and picked up the plate then met her hand halfway with it. Sage remembered the pie to go, and he also started to think about what the "to go" part entailed; the date was probably ending. And who knew if he was going to get a second one. He admitted at this rate, it wasn't looking too promising but he wasn't willing to accept that. He needed more time.

"Excuse me, can I place another order? I want to get a slice of the same pie."

"Can we get it in a box?" Marcie spoke up.

"Absolutely! I'll get that for you in a sec."

In a box, she mentioned. God damn it. He bit his bottom lip like a punishment for sealing his own fate.

"Oh, can we add to that actually?" Marcie chimed again.

"No problem! What else?" the short haired potentially gay woman eagerly asked.

She pointed at Sage, "Can you get him a glass of Amityville apple?" Amanda nodded and quickly stepped into her next tables direction.

"I thought about the wine again," she said, almost like she wanted to reveal a secret. "If you like your glass I'll drink one with you," she ended with a smile bigger than he had seen on her all night. Sage was flushed with the reoccurring gentle feeling once more, and little did he know it would never leave him again. *I'll buy the wine, but you just bought me the extra time,* chimed only in his head, for it was way too cheesy to speak.

"I'm sure I'll love it." He grinned back.

The wine arrived more than punctual. In a long neck glass, it bubbled as Sage looked at its transparent green color from the side. He put the glass to his lips and took a drink. Just like a real green apple, it shared the sweet and sour appeal. He winced at the sour flavor but was genuinely pleased with the taste. He looked to Marcie at the other side of the table. She was staring at her lap, obviously into her phone.

Marcie switched her attention to him like she knew he was looking and awaited his review. She let go of a yawn that seemed suppressed from how long it lasted. She even lifted her tatted arms to the ceiling from how strong it was. Above her head, her right hand caressed the belly of her left arm that held a black circle logo. Like she was stroking it. He never did get to the bottom of her tattoos, he reflected.

"It's good! I wonder how many apples they had to squeeze to get this glass." Sage cracked, expecting a laugh, giggle or at the least a smile to show her model-like teeth but she wasn't even looking at him. Her head had returned back to her lap already.

"Good." She lifted her head up.

"So, your tattoos, point 'em out. Which ones are your favorites?"

Curiously, she looked upon her arms again. "How about you tell me instead… Which ones do you like?"

"Hmm." He searched her designed arms from across the table. Her entire right arm had been covered with numerous themed patches. The outdoors was heavily illustrated throughout with leaves, roots and birds with their wings spread, all around her bicep, elbow, and wrist.

"Show me your birds," he shrugged.

Marcie extended her arm and began to point them out with her shiny gel painted nails. "This owl was actually my first. Always said that owls were my favorite animal." She touched the big-eyed brown owl above her elbow. Sage thought the owl looked cartoonish and more cutely drawn than the others. He looked to the next bird, a dark and skinny feathered creature who didn't have its wings spread. It was resting on her bicep.

"Cute. What about that one? Is that a crow?" Sage picked up his glass in order to take another taste of his wine.

"Yeah, it is. Then I have a vulture on the back of my arm and my raven on my wrist." She showed him her wrist, reaching over the table next to his glass. Sage was pleased to see there were no scars. Some girls—especially of Marcie's style—had a habit of cutting themselves. *Who are you to profile anybody?* Flew across his mind. And that was true.

"Super cool!" Sage admitted. He continued to search her tattoos to find one to spark more conversation. Some others were potential band logos and more animals like a snake spread out on her forearm and a racoon with his little hand up.

On the other arm, the partly inked arm, were leaves and what he imagined to be stars surrounding a round emblem. Sage was positive he didn't recognize the symbol from anywhere. It looked more like a religious or club piece with how much space it had around it. Like it was important and loved. The tat was on the belly of her forearm and the ink in it was darker than any of the rest. Looking at it, someone would think it was fresher than the others, but Sage strangely believed it merely looked deeper.

"What about that one?"

Marcie seemed to know exactly which one he was referring to without looking and let out her curb-smacking smile before turning her head toward it. "This one? Well, why don't you tell me what you think it is?"

He looked at it more closely. To him, it looked like a mushroom, or a tree. But on second thought, he believed there was a deer standing in front of the tree. Or was that just the skull of an animal? He wasn't certain, but he knew he wasn't going to guess right anyway.

"Is it a tree? Or some kind of plant?"

She laughed. The hardest she had all night so far Without a joke to have even sparked it. Sage smiled at her and shared in the laughter though he had a feeling the joke was way over his head.

"Ha-ha, am I right though?"

Marcie slowed her laughing down and then cleared her throat. "Something like that," she said, with just a dose of seduction. "I think I want my wine now. Can you go find our boyish server and get it?"

"Hell yeah. I think I'll get another too. She can't run from me!" he joked and laughed before he went. She decided to give in and laugh too. He saw her wince when she did, it made her winged eye liner look even sharper.

He found the server without much looking. She was at the post talking to the man who had led Marcie and him left. He placed their order and she also mentioned the to-go pie was on the way! When he returned to their booth, Marcie had her arms stacked horizontally on the table. Her head was resting on them, she was grinning, and waiting.

Sage plopped back into his leather seat. "Should be coming soon!" he claimed prior to taking another drink of his wine. About finishing it this time.

"Cool," Marcie said. She looked more and more pleased with him with every passing minute it seemed. Her attitude seemed to grow more preppy, and she was laughing at anything that had a scent of humor. Her eyes looked eager and though her smile had been luscious as usual, it hinted that she waiting for something. Other than the pie and wine, he feared. Sage found it incredibly difficult to brainstorm on conversation when she had her eyes on him with that patient smile.

Saved by the brew, two more tall neck glasses came out to snatch their attention. He quickly finished his first glass so it could be taken away in exchange for his new one. The last of it wasn't as sour as the rest. It had finished sweetly with a vague and bitter aftertaste. For a moment, he wondered what the alcohol percentage was on a bottle of Amityville apple. Already, his stomach felt warm, and he could feel himself gradually becoming looser in his shoulders and jaw. Sage considered the fast-working wine and assumed it was just that.

Heavy wine. Who knows what they really put in this stuff? Still, he almost looked at the new glass as downright daunting.

Marcie took her glass from the table and looked to, if not through Sage. Subtly, she scoffed internally like she had just thought of something funny. With no intention to share her piece, she tilted her glass back, taking half of her wine away with one drink.

"What?" Sage asked. "What is so funny?"

"Nothing really," Marc replied, still with her inside joke scratching a grin. "So do you have any more questions for me?" She leaned in. Sage could see her tits press up against the table as she came in closer. It made his mouth water like a dog watching its food being poured. Yet, he didn't feel aroused.

This had never happened before, so why now?

Sage foolishly pawned it off as the side effects of love at first sight. But he had no questions. Not on the spot. He felt like as soon as he got something in his head to talk about, it would drift away land he couldn't hang on to it.

"Actually, I was going to ask you if you had many for me?" He slurred and pulled out of nowhere. *Heavy wine,* he thought as he knew he had just misspoken his words.

"Hmm." Her dazzling eyes rolled.

"Do you believe in God?"

Sage did. Raised in a traditional Mexican household, the catholic version of the church was always shoved down his throat whether he cared for it or not. Therefore, yeah, he did. He hadn't been to church weekly since he was thirteen, but he did. He guessed.

But was that the answer she was looking for? The idea halted him from speaking his answer.

"Well. I do—

"How about the devil?" she changed up.

For some enigmatic reason, the word devil coming from her delicious lips gave him chills at the back of his neck. He was puzzled for a choice of words and came up speechless. Unbeknownst to Sage, he was physically incapable of talking anyway.

"You know what? I'm going to hit up the rest room and you can dwell on your answer until I get back? Cool? Cool." Marcie winked, took another drink of her wine, and then went off to the bathroom.

(7)

Well, of course I believe in both. How does someone put faith in one but not the counter part? Sage decided. Though the question seemed out of the *blue.*

Quickly, he declared this was the time to gather some ideas for conversation. He reflected back on what he had asked her and what he knew. The basic questioning at the beginning of the date hadn't done him so good in an information sense. It was time to get more personal and make an impression to seal the deal on a second date.

Her Facebook!

He had stalked it dozens of times in preparation for their date, but he was hoping if he looked again for inspiration, he would luckily score it there. Sage sloppily dug in his pants pocket. *He-he heavy wine,* he loopily thought.

Her profile was active; Sage could tell by the green circle on her main photo. Humorously, he pictured Marcie on the toilet, scrolling through her feed. He smiled at the image though he was losing feeling in his face rapidly. *Heavy wine and those heavy nerves.*

Or was it the pie?

Am I allegoric to blackberry? I don't know but I'll be fine.

He skimmed her profiles info and came up thin. Marcie hardly posted on her account but she occasionally shared or was tagged in others post.

Desperate, he slid the page down on his phone in order to update the feed on her profile. He really believed he had struck some white luck when the page actually pulled more down to offer. Far from luck, instead he saw what he should have seen or realized weeks ago.

There was a photo an older woman posted and tagged Marcie and about five other girls in. The picture consisted of the girls, around middle school or early high school age, all circled around a dining room table with a lit birthday cake on it. The lights were low in the photo but the candles on the birthday cake revealed the girls easily. Marcie stood next to the birthday girl wearing black and a smile.

Even without the tag showing and her teenage years ahead of her in the photo, Sage knew exactly who she was.

Her name was Holly Davis. And she was, without reason, obsessed with him.

Worried, Sage tilted his head back up from starring at his phone then put his suddenly clammy hands over his eyes. He tried to achieve a deep breath to compose himself better before Marcie came out. His hands went to the table, but he kept his eyes rested as he breathed in and when he let his air out, he opened his eyes. He stared straight but lacked a purpose of looking. There was nothing to see but couples in other booths. Casually but still freaked out from his new discovery, he turned his head right for something to see. Anything to see. And what he saw only swiftly confirmed what he feared when he saw the photo on Facebook.

For, the girl he had been staring at in the photo just a minute before was staring back at him.

What little feeling Sage had in his body left, he felt it all. A lump developed in his throat like he was trying to swallow a marble; his stomach felt as if it were boiling on the inside and the pain was so great it made his balls ache. He suddenly was under a massive pressure and became rightfully paranoid and sick.

She was about four booths down on the opposite end of the young side of Glenda's. They mistakenly shared eye contact and Holly, in little time, put a menu up to hide her face once it happened.

Sage's jaw was at the table, but his eyes were jerked back to Marcie when she returned to her seat across from him. She was glowing. She was the most alive and ready he had seen her since she picked him up.

It then dawned on him without a doubt that this was a trap. Nothing but a ploy that was set up to get him to this point and time. Her adding him, the cat and mouse lead on, the circumstances, the win—

The wine, the heavy fucking wine.

He had been played, and drugged. Or from an older standpoint, *poisoned.*

Sage, shaking, looked at Marcie with a look that whispered painfully, "Please, don't." The outstandingly pretty woman across the table was relishing the whole scene, Sage could see it in her face. Under the table, his foot wouldn't stop bouncing, his eyes were as wide as a full moon, and he was shiny with a fresh coat of sweat.

"So, Sage, have you thought of your answer?"

He said nothing nor thought much. Actually, he wasn't looking at her when she spoke anyhow. He was looking at Holly, standing up and walking over to them with the same type of eager grin Marcie had.

Sage's mouth was a pond of saliva. It became wetter and more flooded the second after he would swallow. By the time Holly came up to their table, he could have puked right there from the horror that had been unmasked tonight. But likely, the nausea had been from whatever Marcie slipped in his wine.

"Oh my god! There you guys are!" Holly shouted. "I have been sitting by myself because I thought you guys were late!"

Marcie laughed with Holly as Sage looked at the two girls with vulnerability and fear in his eyes.

"What's wrong, baby?" Holly said to Sage with what seemed like true empathy in her voice.

Sage wanted to curse and scream at the women in front of him but literally couldn't. When he tried to speak, it was as if the wind had been knocked out of him for good. Though, he could breathe fine, but just not say a single word or mutter a moan.

"Here, scoot over. Sagey." Holly scooted herself in with her thick hips. She put her hand on his leg, but it wasn't long until he brushed it off with a messy slap to her arm. He was moving like he really was hammered. "Ohh, take it easy. I think it may be time for us to go home. Looks like you guys got started without me." She spoke with her chest up and with more volume.

Where the hell are they going to take me? he thought.

There was no need to try fighting, he could feel in his muscles that they weren't for the cause. Sage was pretty sure he also couldn't stand up on his own as well. They had pinned him and got him exactly where Holly wanted. He assumed it was Holly.

Why would Marcie even agree to this? I never did anything to her. He asked himself this as he watched the two women get up. Marcie took the full glass that he never touched and downed it with two drinks. Holly looked at Sage still in the seat like he was a toddler with his arms spread out.

"Come here and be easy, you fucking dick," she said quietly just to him.

Holly took a hold of his arm and attempted to get him on his feet. It worked temporarily until Sage felt a rush up his throat when he stood. Holly had been wearing an open button up shirt that showed a generous amount of cleavage. He had never seen it before because they never went on dates. As if he meant to, when he stood up, he turned his drooling head to her chest and vomited all over her shirt and breast.

Holly dropped him like a bag of ice. For the first time, Glenda's fell a little quieter and most of everyone looked to Sage on the floor with Marcie and Holly above.

They all laughed. No one was concerned with the man on the floor, if anyone, it was the young lady who had puke on her tits.

The fall didn't hurt him in the slightest. He couldn't feel a brand from a hot iron right now or ponder over the simplest things for long. Now for the time being, he was just a dummy with skin, bones, guts, blood, and vague thinking but probably still no soul. Holly mentioned that to Marcie many times over the last month. That Sage was soulless. She never really cared though. Marcie knew what men did but she did know for a fact that he had a soul.

They all had something to offer.

The male host from the front of the restaurant came over and helped a distressed and disgusted Holly get her "boyfriend" in Marcie's car. The host put him in the back, sitting right up behind the passenger side but once the car door shut, Sage's top half fell to the left. Holly came in not too long after with her shirt soaked from cleaning it off in the restroom.

"That wasn't funny," Holly lectured to the somewhat coherent man.

His eyes were open, and he could see her looking forward, waiting for Marcie. Holly dashed her eyes to the corner of her sockets a few times to see what Sage was doing. Not that it was going to change anytime soon. Eventually, she turned all the way around to look at the mess the slip had made him.

"You did this to yourself, you know that, right?" Holly said.

Sage of course didn't respond but he looked at her.

"You can't just treat women like that or be a total pig and get away with it. You fucking led me on and hurt me so bad. They made fun of me at work because of you! You stupid fuck!" she screamed.

She looked over her shoulder. "Where is this bitch? Jesus Christ…" Holly returned her attention to him with one more thing to say. "I don't know what Marcie is going to do with you. She could kill you," Holly said sincerely but with no pity.

"I'm kind of hoping for that but she won't tell me what her plans are. Truth be told, I don't give a fuck what she does. I just want you gone, and she did promise me that."

The car door opened, and Marcie hopped in without glancing at Sage. "What took you so long?" Holly asked as Marc started the PT. "Oh, we ordered a slice to go." She held up a to-go box, then they both shared a mad cackle. The slip was coursing through his blood stream swimmingly now and he felt exhausted in a matter of blinks while watching them drive and laugh in the front. Sage, in his awkward and uncomfortable resting position fell asleep in the back.

(8)

Epilogue

Sage hasn't seen any light or anything in an undecided amount of time. He couldn't count his first day because the sun and moon could not be found where he was kept. There was freezing stone beneath his feet and different types of wood surrounding him; *confining him*. When he felt the walls of what he assumed to be his prison, splinters would slide into his palms and fingers with hardly any force.

He would eat and drink but not when he called for it. At times when he would start to feel hungry and thirsty, it would stretch until it was agony. Then he would go blacker than the black in which he already lived. A heavy sleep would take him against his will as if it were routine. When he would wake up, he would be full of food but not knowing what he ate. Any desire for the bathroom would be gone and the splinters would also be removed from his hands when he felt them later.

Marcie didn't want him to know where he was, and she was immaculate at keeping it all from him. He was clueless to where he was trapped and that allowed him all the time in the world to think, about what he had done to get here, how he had treated women and especially Holly. It was ironic to Sage, how after he blocked her, he never thought of Holly again until he saw her at Glenda's, and now he felt that he would never stop thinking of her for the rest of his life. If someone could call it a life.

Around his ankle was a chain that was attached to the ceiling. He never bothered trying to break it or mess with it as the energy in his body was at an all-time low constantly. She took care of him in a strange less-than-a-pct way, that kept him alive but not well. He felt drained all the time like he was working for her without even knowing it.

Sage felt he was being *used*.

<u>Underneath the Sheets.</u>

Spring is the season of resurrection. Not only speaking of Easter, biblically said to be the day Jesus arose from the grave, but also the rebirth of nature itself. Figuratively and nearly literally, mother nature seems to wake up or come *alive* when the winter's cold conditions cease. Nude trees regain their vibrant leaves, the once frozen soil sprouts flowers and weeds with personality, the birds return with more songs to sing and the weather, well, becomes more tolerable.

Of course, not everyone shares the same enthusiasm over the spring. Some may not like the warm and prefer the cold, others may get sick with allergies, but certain individuals have a more legitimate reason than the rest. A reason that doesn't seem to make any sense to anyone else but them. For them their greatest fear roams once more and they can never truly escape it until the winter arrives. And even then, it's never actually gone.

Brendan had already unbuckled and placed a hand on the passenger door handle before Eddie pulled his Silverado in the usual drop off spot. As soon as the truck would come to a complete stop, he would nod, routinely say thanks for the ride, then head upstairs to his apartment. There he would start his highly anticipated two days off.

Though, to Brendan's surprise, as soon as the truck was stopped, Eddie put it in park then killed the engine. That meant he wanted to chat for a moment, and probably smoke a cigarette, too. Wanting to sigh but not wanting to come off as ungrateful for all the rides, he removed his hand from the handle and looked up at the star smothered sky through the truck's window.

"You wanna smoke a cig with me before you head up?" Ed asked, pulling his pack of menthols from his center console.

Brendan redirected his gaze from the sky to his apartment complex in front of the truck. "Sure," he replied, feeling like he had to, not because he wanted to. "Do you have one I can bum though? I ran out at work."

"Yeah, no problem. They're menthol though." Ed pulled another smoke from his pack for Brendan. "If you'd like, I can swing you by *Quick-Trip* and you can snag you a pack."

"Nah man. I'll just take one of your toothpaste flavored ones." Brendan cracked, retrieving his lighter from his pocket and the cigarette from Ed's hand. "I'm really thinking about quitting anyway."

That wasn't entirely the whole picture though. There was more to Brendan's decision on getting a new pack that wasn't quite as obvious. For starters, Brendan's night had just ended and that's how he planned to keep it. No more destinations to arrive to, no more task to be done, and nothing else he *had* to do, except relax. He was done for the night. He wouldn't go straight to bed when he got up to his apartment, Brendan would stay up for a couple more hours, but by his own will and by himself. That time seemed well deserved in his eyes, and spending more quality time with Eddie was the last thing he had in mind.

Eddie Green was a friend and a good one at that. Anybody who gives someone a ride to and from work every shift has at least earned that title. Still, friend, best friend, good friend or not a friend at all, they had just spent an entire eleven-hour shift together at Flat Patties and a departure between the two sounded glorious to Brendan. The midwestern food chain kicked their asses all day and he wasn't sure how Ed was holding up but as for himself, Brendan felt physically tired just as well as socially drained. Also, regarding his decline on getting a new pack, there were actually about two left in his Marlboro light pack. Quitting was a real idea in his head, just after this pack was empty. *Probably tonight*, he guessed.

They lit their smokes, then went on to bitch and moan about their hard day at work for about five minutes. Ed brought up the burn he had received from the fryer and how he put mustard on it to ease the pain and it worked. Brendan still thought it was stupid to walk around with mustard on your arm. Their departing time was coming closer and closer; Brendan could hardly keep his foot still from how eager he was to leave. Soon, he would be trotting up the steps to his single bedroom apartment with his burning desire for solitude about to be fulfilled.

Both of their cigarettes were puffs away from being thrown when Eddie asked a genuine question. "So, why do you want to quit smoking? Not feeling cool enough?" He smiled.

"It gives you cancer, duh?" Brendan answered, blowing smoke from a drag of his cigarette before he laughed at his own wit.

"Hey, cancer has to be better than Flat Patties, right? Count me in."

"Has to be…maybe I should keep smoking…maybe I should smoke more." That last bit threw both of the burger joint employees into a chortle. Eddie then flicked his smoke out his window and onto the sidewalk.

"But seriously, why?" he asked again.

Brendan found himself hesitating on speaking the truth. He thought about giving another joke answer or just flat out lying but he figured a vague answer would do it justice.

"I just don't like smoking in the spring or summer is all," he said, rolling what was left of his cigarette between his index finger and thumb.

"Cause of the heat?" Ed guessed.

Damn it, just let it be, dude, Brendan thought, but didn't speak it. He took one last drag of his menthol and then tossed it where Ed flicked his. When it was in the air, surrounded by the night, it looked just like a firefly.

"Yeah, it's the heat," he lied.

Despite that Eddie didn't pick up that Brendan had been lying, there was a moment of silence in their conversation like he did know. "Well, alright man. I'll see you on Wednesday around noonish," Eddie said, starting his truck back up.

"I'll see ya then." He shut the door and started toward the steps leading up to his place.

(2)

While walking up the three levels of stairs to his affordable abode, Brendan first reflected on why he didn't tell Ed the whole truth.

Am I ashamed of my own fear?

He shouldn't be, as he Believed it was more common and not quite as *irrational* as the majority makes it out to be.

At the second case, those self-critique thoughts were shoved away. There was no point in badgering himself, especially with the next two days looking so bright. Granted he was worn and smelt like French fries, he still felt so liberated and energetic from being off work. Overthinking would just spoil that mood and the rest of the night.

But isn't fear just overthinking?

That thought swept away just as fast as it came, buried with the rest when he approached the final staircase.

In seconds, the worn-out fry cook would be back at his front door. A moment he has been anticipating and desiring since Eddie's truck pulled into the parking lot at noon. Perhaps he would turn on his *Xbox* as soon as he got in or maybe he would do that later and first he would put on a movie with a bowl loaded in his pipe. Both sounded appealing enough, and his excitement was at the brim as he climbed the last few steps.

However, right when Brendan made it to his level, and with his door in sight, that near overflowing excitement morphed into a belly rolling anxiety. Already nauseous, he felt his mouth begin to water like he was going to spew the burger he ate hours ago.

They were here, and seemingly right on time. Swarming and fluttering around his front light like mad. The same light he insisted on keeping off for this exact reason.

Brendan Shoemaker deeply suffers from entomophobia. More commonly known as insectophobia, and more bluntly known as an individual who is deathly afraid of bugs.

He loathed them all. Every single one and not excluding even the smallest or least harmful but also not exclusively insects either. The hatred and fear were driven from any creature remotely close. Spiders, slugs, crabs or just anything that could potentially be confused with an insect. They were all the same to him anyhow. The beady black eyes, no legs or several legs, the abhorrent and vicious looking mouths. Traits of many different types of insects as well as traits of fictional monsters. Yet, to Brendan, bugs really were monsters, but people typically were deceived by their small size. People like him just don't underestimate them like the others.

But here they were anyway. The legitimate reason for his halt on cigarettes in living form. Those ugly, tiny, and brainless but stealthy pest that could be found at his door, it was them that made him dread going outside at all. He couldn't stand being anywhere they were lingering, therefore, he decided it would be wise to quit smoking. *Can't get me if I don't go out for a smoke,* right?

It wasn't until this moment, as he was keeping a safe distance from his own front door, he realized just how absurd that idea was. He would always have to go outside. Even if the nicotine wasn't pulling by his pockets, every time he would go out, they would still be there.

Every day they would fly or crawl around him whether he knew it or not. He was positive that someday, during the bright spring season or maybe in the humid summer, he would be minding his own business when a horse fly or worse, a *wasp* would buzz near his ear. Immediately he would panic, swing his arms around and scream then run as if he were engulfed in flames. Oh, and how everyone would love it. That was probably the worst of it all. Anybody around would laugh at him, actually they would crack up as if it was the funniest occurrence they had ever seen. Then they would tell him to come back, "It's gone!" and when he would, someone would act like or really throw a bug at him. That was the routine every year when someone discovered his greatest fear.

"Oh, calm down it's just a bug." *Yeah, and you're just an asshole.*

With his keys in his pocket, Brendan still felt locked out. An excessive number of Moths, crickets, and June bugs surrounded his door. *June bugs? But its only March!* He also hated that joke but couldn't resist thinking it. He likely did so to gather the courage he needed to unlock his door, open it, then burst in. All while in the swarm, of course.

The biggest concern here wasn't that they were going to get on him—although, that was an issue—it was making sure none of them came inside with him. There were more June bugs than the rest, then it was about a dozen moths, and a few crickets at the lower part of the door. The population of insects appeared excessive to him. Was this the only active light on this side of Ohio? It sure as hell seemed like it!

Why is the fuckin light on anyway? his mind quickly came up with. In the winter, he kept it on almost every night but since the weather has been getting warmer, he careful about having it on. At one point he considered unscrewing the bulb, but he concluded that would be unnecessary. Now he wished he would have.

Preparing to set forth into the swarm, he retrieved his keys and plugged his nose, looking like a child about to do a cannon ball.

One of the most fearful ideas of his phobia was inhaling or swallowing a bug. Whenever Brendan pictured that, he was certain he would seize up and his heart would literally explode into a million pieces and the explosion would be so massive his eyes would pop out of his skull and his brain would flood out of his ears. Okay, maybe all of that wouldn't happen but he felt that wasn't far from the real result. Brendan really despised these little monsters.

He took some deep breathes through his mouth—with his back against the swarm—and after which, he proceeded to the door with his key pointed straight ahead.

Before he could put his key into the slot, a June bug zoomed to his shirt. "Shit!" He screamed and plucked it off then tossed it down the steps.

Once he recovered from his "attack," he tried it again but this time he wasn't letting anything stop him. Brendan did it as fast as he possibly could, and the key found its way into the lock then he twisted it and barged in. He slammed the door the second he got himself in, then locked the top lock. Next, he switched off the light outside and hoped they would all leave by the morning.

Like his usual paranoid self, Brendan couldn't help but feel like one of them got in. He turned on his living room light and searched around but luckily saw nothing. Then a thought arose that made him shudder, *what if they're in my hair!* Likely a June bug, crawling through his scalp, making itself comfortable, getting warm, and burrowing in deep, waiting to be found all night. Without waiting a beat, he took both his hands and ran it through his messy black hair. Nothing.

Finally, back on track with his night. The excitement was reimbursed, and he felt somewhat at peace again.

(3)

For a man in his early twenties, his apartment was kept pretty tidy. His cleanliness could probably be rooted back to his phobia. *No messes or dirty dishes equals no bugs*, he hoped.

Being the age that he was and not having the upfront money to buy furniture, there wasn't a lot of stuff in his place.

A tv stand—if a crate was considered one—his twenty-inch box television, a ragged purple love seat, a DVD player and his beloved *Xbox* were the only objects in his whole living room.

His bedroom was even less than that. Merely a twin sized mattress without the frame along with one clothes basket. When Brendan wanted to watch a movie or play *Xbox* in the comfort of his bed, he would simply move the T.V. and the stand from the living room, then place it in front of his mattress.

Currently, right as the microwave clock in his modest kitchen blinked to 1:10 AM, the duo of Brendan's T.V. and video game held his attention firmly. War was appearing on the screen but in the soldier's point of view. It wasn't a familiar war that someone could tie into a piece of history, it was set in the future, assumingly on a different planet. A Glowing sword and Laser rifle were part of his soldier's cache, and at the moment, the character was yielding the sword while Brendan held the green controller in reality. He was sunk into the couch, his eyes attached to the screen, at last enjoying his time off.

Moments prior to the gaming system being turned on, a movie was considered. The idea was more vital whenever he was walking up the steps, before he encountered his unwanted guest.

The initial plan for the movie was making a big bowl of popcorn and pouring a cool glass of soda then topped off with a tight bowl of reefer. Though, eventually, Brendan decided against *the fellowship of the ring*, the snacks, and the weed. Told himself that a game would be better and more intriguing choice, but it was really that he couldn't stop thinking about his worst enemies on the other side of the door.

Were they still there?
Did any of them get in?
Did he miss the ones that came in?

The grass would just thicken his out-to-get-me thoughts and a movie wouldn't diminish them either, but a game could, and it did.

Proceeding with that logic, the game was started, and his attention was forced on his solider. The thrill of the hunt and the essential interacting with the game made his paranoia slip away. He was only focused on killing the aliens on the opposing team and Brendan had just found a rocket launcher to help him achieve that. Things were looking up tonight.

To hell with those bugs and to hell with these alien fucks, too.

He humored himself, right as he pushed in the back-right trigger and firing a massive missile to where two of his opponents were. Once it hit its mark and killed them in a vast explosion, it gave Brendan's team the lead.

It was dire they keep this lead until the time expired. He desperately hoped time would fly by because Brendan wanted to win this match, but also, and suddenly, he had the strong urge to use the bathroom.

For those remaining five minutes of the game, his solider had been placed in a dark spot of the map. There he could pick off the enemy if they were around.

Now more comfortable with his characters positioning, his bladder became more uncomfortable—actually quite painful, as if his bladder was shrinking by the minute. Feeling like his penis was swelling and dripping out pee onto his boxers. Pissing was now a necessity and his foot tapped at a rapid pace from the urge, much like he did when he was stuck talking to Ed earlier in the truck.

There was three minutes left on the clock, but now Brendan really had to go. Though, if he were to leave, someone could easily kill his solider.

The pull of the bathroom was undeniable and now he felt regret toward not asking Ed to come up earlier. If he would have, they would have smoked together, taken turns on the game, and laughed, but most importantly, Ed could have taken the controller while Brendan ran to the toilet.

With two minutes left, he wanted nothing more than to drain the main vein. Could he wait? His hands were tightly gripped on the controller and his legs were crossed to fight the urge.

Fuck it, there is only a minute left.

Brendan sprinted off down to the restroom and the second he started to urinate a great sigh of relief followed.

The stream was powerful and clear, identical to how water would shoot out of the super soakers he would play with as a kid. The memory drew a smile on his face. Summer wasn't so paranoid back then. He guessed his fear of bugs wasn't on his mind all the time like how it was these days, but Brendan didn't know why his fear grew fatter over the years. It just did.

His stream kept going longer than usual—probably an unhealthy length from holding it in. He looked down at it and also at a dead leaf behind the toilet. Must have been from the days of fall, he presumed.

But then the leaf twitched.

And after that twitch, it crawled forward. The peeing man threw himself back into the wall and pissed on himself and the floor when he did. The false leaf stopped moving but that's when he really got a good look at it. A bug of some kind, and a rather intimidating and undefinable one was behind his toilet.

The little beast was diamond shaped and a murky red that could be confused with brown. A row of spikes was on the center of its back like that of a triceratops and its whole body was a little bigger than a half dollar coin. Brendan shuddered, feeling so foolish that he didn't see what it really was from the start.

It was so close to me. He counted six legs while his back was pushed up against the wall.

Confounded and furious, he bellowed, "How the hell did you get in here!" The mysterious bug only stood looking thoughtless toward the toilet.

Just as soon as he realized there was an insect—if it was an insect—in his apartment, he knew it had to be squashed. Brendan was not one to be merciful when it came to a bug being in his area. Usually on the outside, he would try his best to stay away from them but when they were in his home, it was *seek and destroy* and kill or be killed. At least that's how Brendan's "irrational" mind perceived it.

But what was he going to use to get rid of it? Not his bare feet that was for certain. *Jesus, that rocket launcher would sure be helpful right now.* Brendan kept his gaze on the diamond shaped critter while he attempted to slide to the door and escape. The bug only kept his stance looking at the toilet, not knowing someone was plotting to kill it at any cost. He also saw the *freak* had four antennas, two upfront and two at the rear, but maybe the back ones were wings.

The frightened man kept sliding his back on the wall, the door was close, hardly a foot away and when the little bug on the floor twitched again, he flung it open and slid out of his bathroom. Right after he slammed the door, he ran into his living room to find his shoes, in the same sort of panic used to retrieve a gun during a home invasion.

His shoes were in front of the couch and the tv and on its screen was the final kill of the game. It was his character. Someone had found him and killed him without a chance of him defending himself. However, this was not the time to dwell on his loss in the game, he put his shoes on tightly and returned to the bathroom door.

Sweat was pouring from his forehead and arm pits as he stood by the door. Trying to get himself to make the first move before the red sucker went into hiding. His moist palm squeezed the doorknob, he was about to twist it when a noisy fuss blared from inside. It was a buzz and an aggressive one. It sounded like an active electric toothbrush left on a countertop and it did nothing but discourage Shoemaker from entering his bathroom.

Oh, what am I going to do? Shit outside from here on out?

The buzzing ceased. Without thinking or *overthinking* at least, he flung the door open and saw it right in front of the toilet. At first, it was looking at the bathtub but when Brendan marched in, it took its beady eyed gaze to him. Its stare was nerve pinching and froze him. And he couldn't even begin to fathom what occurred next.

The critter stood up on its back legs and as if it were roaring like a lion, it buzzed, consciously looking into his eyes. As if it knew Brendan was sickened by his presence.

The two antennas in the rear spread out and it started to rise off the floor.

Luckily for him, he didn't let it get any higher.

His right foot was brought up higher than it was rising, and he brought it back down with a stomp. A loud *pop!* cued when he made contact and a cool sweat relieving feeling washed over him with the sound.

His heart rate was steady when he removed his foot from the kill shot. The bug was smashed, looking like a pressed skittle, if a skittle had brown and green guts. With toilet paper, he scooped it up and then flushed it down the toilet. *Just like the piece of shit it was*, he thought.

The game no longer sounded fun or inviting in the least. He had lost the game for his team due to his bladder and the menace in the bathroom.

"Fuck tonight," he whispered to himself, downhearted and angry with his night after work.

(4)

Two hours and just twenty minutes shy of three hours went by before Brendan decided it was time to hit the hay. He spent those former hours spraying his apartment with an anti-bug fume. What he really absolutely revolted about bugs, maybe the most, was how if you found one, an army or herd of them was close by. The bathroom was where he stressed spraying the most, but the kitchen and closets were also done. He would spray his living room and his bedroom tomorrow. Refraining from doing it tonight since the fumes were so chemically powerful that sleeping would be awful.

Certain he wouldn't be able to get the altercation in the bathroom out of his head, but knowing he should try anyway, the TV was brought into his bedroom. He chose to put on a movie Ed had once brought over during a winter day they never got the chance to watch. Brendan wasn't positive, but he assumed they got stoned and played Xbox that day instead. *The Hills Have Eyes* was the title and Ed had stated it was "totally fucked up." Sounded like the perfect distraction he needed tonight.

Brendan had to admit it was funny how horror movie slashers or Boogeymen didn't scare him near as much as say, a pile of ants. If he had to guess why, he would probably say movies are fake and bugs are as real as can be and also that he felt he could *try* to reason with a killer, but there was no reasoning with a bug. They weren't conscious or articulate enough to do so. Either that or they just didn't give two shits about what you have to say.

Taking off his T-shirt but keeping his athletic shorts on, Brendan felt the most euphoric he had all night when he was getting ready for bed. Work was rough and long, the bugs who were at his door upset him, and the peculiar bug beside the toilet broke his high spirit for the night. Try again tomorrow is what they usually said, and that's exactly what he would have to do.

The movie was playing at this point, but it didn't steal his eyes like he wanted. The bug still had them and though it was gone, flushed down the toilet, he could still see it in his head as if it were still right in front of him. That creep gave him the impression it knew what it was doing. It looked right at him, right at his face. And that awful buzz it produced, never in his life had he heard such a powerful noise from a bug. No cicada or wasp or bumble bee could have ever paralleled it. It wasn't just outlandish; it was otherworldly.

(5)

A mutant or an incest character, or an incest mutant had just stolen the main character's baby in the movie. At least that's what Brendan thought was going on, he wasn't certain. It was in and out for him with this film. He had lost a good amount of energy since he lay in bed. The weight of his workday had finally put him down and he didn't feel like getting up.

Falling and fading pretty swiftly now, Brendan was glad sleep was coming over him so easily. Considering all the shit that had happened tonight, he felt he would just lay and stare at the celling all night. A long-lasting yawn came to him and his eyes watered. He turned away from the TV and tripped into a light sleep.

No more than five minutes later, he was jolted awake from the screaming of the teenage girl in the flick. Needless to say, achieving sleep with those grotesque and traumatizing events on the screen would be tricky. Not a lullaby by any means. Yet, he lacked the energy to get up out of bed. Motivation needed to be found and he was still looking for it.

Seconds away from falling back asleep, a scream from a different character woke him up. It was a wail from the killer shockingly. One more yawn was forced out of him and this one made his eyes water even more than the last. When his vision cleared, Brendan ultimately found the motive to get up that he had been looking for, and it was right on the TV screen.

A white moth had flown onto the screen. Captivated by the film's bright scene of the desert. Offensively he threw the blanket off his half naked body then swung his feet onto the floor. "This better be the last time or I swear," he said harshly.

Something made him stop.

Another moth flew to the screen, and it was followed by a mosquito and then a house fly.

He wasn't able to react, though, because as soon as he witnessed the extra bugs, his sheets started moving. They felt like they were vibrating.

No, not vibrating, they were *buzzing*. Straight away he bolted off his mattress and stood in his television lit bedroom, inspecting the sheets. They really were moving, shifting around, looking like it was bubbling under the surface. He tore off the sheets and simultaneously let out an incredulous yelp at the sight of what was underneath the sheets.

Ants, flies, grasshoppers, and cicadas partnered with mosquitos were lathered on his mattress. Sheet still in hand, he threw himself back with a palpating heart and a mouth full of a pre-vomit spit. That was before he even realized the bugs weren't just on his mattress, they were also still on the sheet, and scaling up his arms. Aghast and at a lost for action, he slapped all the ants he could manage off his arm and when they hit the floor, the ants went for his bare legs. The flies swarmed around his eyes while the grasshoppers and cicadas went for his hair, rattling and springing off his scalp only to get back on. The mosquitos landed on his neck and no matter how many he swatted and smashed, more just kept coming.

From the start, Brendan had his hand over his mouth with his thumb and pointer finger plugging his nose. He ran into walls, knocked his TV on to his DVD player, and stripped naked once the ants completely coated his boxers.

As disorientated and horror struck as he was, it took him a moment to find his bedroom door. Shoemaker brushed off as many crawlers and flyers as he could right before he left his bedroom, but the instant the door was closed, they swarmed after him from under the crack.

Still with a substantial amount on him, he sprinted through his apartment to the front door. On his way out, he saw his walls were an active bee hive. Bumble bees, queen bees, and regular worker bees covered his walls and began to attach themselves to him, but not stinging.

Dizzy is too modest of a word to describe his clumsiness at that moment. He could hardly stay on his feet and half of the way to the door, he was crawling.

The doorknob was in his free hand; he swung it open, and when he did, a blast of June bugs sent him back like a defensive lineman. The door left open, brought in wasp, walking sticks, crawdads, and spiders along with a plethora of insects. The snails, who came lastly, closed the door on their way in.

He lay in a pool of his most monumental and truest fear, wearing the pest in layers like winter clothing. Vomit had begun to spew out of the sides of his hand as he still held his nose and mouth closed, hardly breathing at all. The bugs were now moving him around, but he couldn't feel it.

He was numb when on his chest, he saw the murky red bug from the bathroom.

But bigger.

Now it was nearly the size of a tennis ball and it looked down on at his face while standing on a pile of maggots. All he could spare at this point was one eye to look out of. The spiked bug looked pissed off as they met each other's gaze. Then all of a sudden, his body began to rotate, the ants below him were putting him on his stomach.

Like thumb tacks, sharper than any other bugs legs he had felt, the red one was now on his back, crawling down to his bare bottom.

Brendan could feel it digging between his cheeks, clawing to his anus then it forced itself inside and continued through his rectum. He wanted to scream, of course he did, but he couldn't, they would get in hi —.

An inevitable urge to puke came to him. No stifling this one and it felt thick rising in his throat. The impact of his vomit was so powerful his hand was blown away from his mouth but as it turns out it wasn't even puke at all. It was *them*. He had projectile vomited June bugs, crickets, and also, smaller versions of the red bug that crawled into his rear.

They joined the puddle of their kind on the floor then went back to irritating Brendan. Every time he would stand up, he would slip on a slug, and whenever he would start to army crawl away, the ground beetles and worms would carry him back. He could feel his body giving up, his breaths becoming shorter, and his consciousness disappearing. Like sleeping but with a rapid heart rate.

(6)

Wednesday came as it usually does and that's precisely the day Brendan Shoemaker's body was found by no other than Eddie Green himself. He arrived at the complex around noon, smoking his menthol and honking obnoxiously after a twenty-minute wait. Concerned Brendan was going to make them both late for their shift, he stepped out of his truck and headed up the apartment stairs.

Ed knocked on the door just as obnoxiously as he honked before. He tried the door's handle. It was unlocked and he pushed it open without hesitation. A pungent smell flew at him as soon as one foot was inside the apartment. The stench was vomitous but strangely sweet, like a piece of rotting hamburger in Flat Patty's dumpster.

Eddie called for his friend in the stale and amiss abode but there wasn't a sound returned. Not a single peep so far. Empty like the last time he was here, Ed looked around anyway. The TV wasn't present in the living room but the *Xbox* was and near the *Xbox* was a can of anti-bug spray. Thinking nothing of it, he walked on down the hallway to Brendan's bedroom.

His bedroom door was closed, and the sickening sweet smell not only remained but became unbearable. Then finally, since his arrival, there was another sound besides his own noise. A small buzzing on the other side of the door. It was hardly there, but in the midst of the quiet zone, the smallest sounds are loud. It sounded exactly like a fly stuck on a window.

This time Ed nervously knocked three times. The suspense was making him sweat, and his face was as red as a ladybug. He just wanted to go to work already. Killing the suspense, he opened the door and within the first minute of viewing what was behind it, he turned his back and tried not to puke.

Brendan lay face first on his bed, naked, and pale with eyes slightly open and his jaw uncontrollably hanging down. His right arm must have been hanging off the bed for some time now because it was purple and covered with veins. Ed turned back around to have another look. The TV was on the floor next to a smashed DVD player and a single white sheet was in the corner of the room. Before he ran back out to tell the office to call the police, he had another look at the corpse.

There were flies and gnats circling above him.

April

<u>Shut the Door and Lock it</u>

Coupled with a yellow fade in certain areas on the walls that were originally painted tan, the apartment already stunk of cigarettes. The obvious former presence of a heavy smoker didn't upset Jessica Carver like it would have others, though. On the contrary, it was part of the reason—unbeknownst to Melissa—she had settled on Stoneleigh and not the other affordable three bedroom in Lawrence they had looked at. Now she could skip out on the fee and still smoke in the apartment. Or with the window still open at least.

  The other complexes were a little better looking than this one, but the location was closer to the university and work. The rent was also fifty bucks cheaper. And as college students and with Jessica additionally being a single mother, twenty-five bucks each was going to go a long way.

  Still standing at the doorway of her little family's new home when she said she was just going up to unlock the door, Jessica took in the place privately for an extra moment. The living room was cut in half for a small kitchen with a bar, a space for dining, and a tight hallway that led to their rooms. The bedrooms in the back were the best-looking rooms and she felt that was fortunate for her son. Sean was at a commonly stubborn age of five but the kid he was shaping up to be told Jessi he wouldn't care what his room looked like anyway. Though, it still mattered to her.

  Twenty miles north of Lawrence was the only other home her and her son had ever known. An old-fashioned town by the—most times—inaccurate name of Pleasant is where Jessica's own mother moved her when Jessi was five. When her mother was freshly divorced, and hungry for a good environment for her and her daughter. A mere reflection of what Jessi was doing now but with her son. Without a man and with her own hands.

Looking toward her new kitchen, she began to think of Sean's father, Sean Sr. She thought of the time when he had first moved into her mother's house when Jessica had found out they were pregnant at the age of nineteen. It was a house full of hope back then, despite the natural and truth-based discouragement around their relationship.

Jessica grabbed the doorknob and made sure it rotated, even though she was just going leave it ajar and kick it open while their hands were full. Still with a headful of her past, she continued looking back on what had brought her here.

She met Sean when she went through her "party" stage. He was younger but that didn't matter to her. All their peers always thought he was so charming and funny with his careless antics and delinquent attitude. His whole family had contributed to putting a rotten reputation around the Carver name, including Sean, but she was still foolish enough to take the name and birth another.

Nevertheless, Sean Jr. was the best thing that ever could have happened to her, and she truly did think that every day. *So, by association*, Jessi thought as she turned away out the door and closed it over, *Sean Sr. was the best thing to happen to me too.*

She was just about to start making her way down the outdoor steps when Meli shouted. "Damn, bitch, what are you doing up there! Your son is about to get out of the car and find friends if you don't come down here and get him."

She laughed leaning over the guard rail watching Melissa walk up. The staircase of complex D had three levels and they were at the top with D5. Meli appeared at the second level holding three large bags on her broad shoulders and a box in front of her chest. Jessi quickly met her at the third staircase.

She shivered and touched her own arms. "Why is it so cold out? The suns out and it's April!"

"I don't know? Why did you approach me like I'm some kind of meteorologist?" She laughed with her arms full. "What do you want me to tell you? Kansas fucking sucks and knowing that, I'm sure it'll be nice out tomorrow."

"D5 is ours! Just kick it, the door should be open," Jess shouted over her shoulder, going back down to the car.

Right when she stepped off the stairs and into Sean's view from the back seat, he smiled at her. No teeth showing, just his big cheek bones pulling up his puffy cheeks, encouraging his eyes to squint behind his glasses. She wasn't exactly sure where he had got that smile from, but she smiled back just the same and gave him a wave.

The car was still running and blowing hot air on medium, and while she appreciated Melissa making sure Sean was warm, it still half-way pissed Jessica off. What if someone just hopped in the front seat and stole her son and car? Meli got on Jessica's nerves that way. Sometimes she was inconsiderate with how she wanted to raise Sean. She was nice to him, and they got along well, but sometimes Meli didn't think twice about shit and you needed to with a small kid around.

She shut the car off and attempted to cool herself down by taking a thoughtful breath. On the way out, Sean spoke to her in his *wanting* voice. "Mommm," he called, humming the m.

"Yes, babyyyy," she mocked.

"Does this new house place have a playground like Dad's?" he asked. Jessica took some silly offense from the comparison between the two homes already.

"I don't think so, but your daycare does! It's so big, Sean! Only two days left, and you'll see it!"

"Does it have a rock wall, Momma?" he enthusiastically asked, but the excitement wasn't in his voice. His brown eyes and the way they seemed to glare told her he was excited about a dumb rock wall. And Jessica was smiling without realizing it because she was excited too, just to be able to see him that way.

"I think it might. Now, get out of this car and help carry some things inside the apartment. Follow me up there!"

"Okay!" He unbuckled himself, grabbed a small bag and a small box, then took off to the stairs.

"Sean, wait!" Jessi called. He quit at the fourth step up and sharply turned around to her. She giggled at him and his little legs about to race up the steps. *Oh, fuck it, he will be fine,* she decided, but before the words left her mouth, her eyes were yanked away by a distraction in a near window in someone else's apartment. Their blinds were shaking.

"Never mind, son. Go up there. Our door has the letter D and a five on it, honey. You remember what a five looks like, right?"

"Yes! I'm five, Mom!" Then he ran up the steps, leaping really but conquering them, nonetheless.

The day was skipping out on them soon and Jessica could feel it through her light jacket without even looking toward the sky. There wasn't much left in the car for them, most of the other stuff like the beds, furniture, and decorations were coming in a truck the next day with help from her mom. All that was left in their pathfinder was her giant bag with most of her clothes, her and Sean's bathroom stuff, and a wimpy box that held last semesters textbooks. Meli must've had all her stuff she needed for tonight when she passed her on the steps.

Jessi scoffed to herself, knowing she was about to attempt to grab everything at once. Melissa was bigger than Jessi, but not by much really, or that's what she believed anyway, so why couldn't she? She put the strap of her bag on her shoulder, then put the other bag on the opposite side. Jessi instantly felt unbalanced, but she was still confident. The box of textbooks was wider than her torso when she hugged it and picked it up.

Within the first minute, the bottom of the box started to give. She could feel one of the books about to fall out. It was heavy enough as it was, but with her clothes throwing her to the left and the box falling apart in her arms, it was a near impossible to walk up the steps.

But she tried anyway, and all the books spilled out like water down a drain.

"Shit!" Jessi shouted but in a library tone.

Suddenly a loud dead bolt unlocked and a chain started to rattle near her. Jessica quickly peered around to see where it was coming from. It wasn't until *D1*'s door flung open that she gathered it was right in front of her.

A very thin, pale, and snooty but good-looking older woman came out with a slight hunch and peppered hair that was once healthy. The woman and Jessica made eye contact instantly and she froze and was sure that this old bitch was going to yell. She had light eyes and Jessi only saw them briefly before the woman spoke. "Let me help you, hon! I heard what happened inside."

She was genuinely surprised. She was certain that the light eyed woman was about to holler at her for being on the steps or something else stupid, but there she was, helping Jessica pick up the text books and place them in the box.

"Thank you! You don't have to, but I really appreciate it, ma'am."

"Oh, no, hush. It's not any trouble and I'm always willing to help. I just sit inside all day and wait for something to happen, I suppose," the woman said, handing Jess a thick textbook with a shaking hand and arm.

Jessica saw it, then thought back to the shaking blinds. She clearly didn't want to bring it up, there was no reason to, so she just thanked her more and introduced herself.

"We just moved in today, my name is Jessica Carver and my roommate's name is Melissa."

"The brown girl with the big shoulders?"

Jessi smiled at her old-minded but American remark, she was used to it since Pleasant was full of it. "Yes, she's Mexican."

"Ahh. I see. What about the little boy with the bowl cut you were talking to?"

"My son. His name is Sean jr."

"He's a cutie! But awfully ornery looking, isn't he?"

Jessica laughed but felt finished talking to her newly found neighbor already, plus the straps on her shoulders had begun to hurt. "He's never that much trouble really. He is very sweet, and he won't stop talking ever since he's learned."

The mid-seventies woman looked at Jessica while she spoke like she was dying to know every detail. And when she finished, the woman had looked like she was waiting for more. Had she really been this lonely?

"Where is Sean's father, if you don't mind my asking?"

"We are divorced. He lives somewhere in Kansas City. We don't get along too well outside of our son."

The wrinkled lady smiled at her with empathy spewing from it. "I've been there, hon."

For a moment, she wasn't shaking and then Jessi thought of how good looking she actually was for her age. Better yet, Jessi wondered how beautiful she must have been when she was twenty-three. She was probably stomping on hearts like cigarette butts in her day. When her hair was surely long and jet black, and when her breast didn't sag and she was perky as well as threatening. Back when she was the full package, she must have been everyone's favorite eye candy.

"Well, it was nice to meet you…" Jessi realized she never got her name.

"My name is Linda Ortega, but please call me Linn."

"Okay, Linn." She smiled and shook her again vibrating hand.

Linn must have known she was thinking of her condition as she spoke on it, "It's called essential tremors, dear. I'm okay, trust me," she laughed.

Afraid her looks might have come off as rude, but relieved to hear Linn laugh, she laughed too.

She finally was able to turn away from Linn, grab the box from the bottom this time, and start back up the steps, but Linn was still out, watching her go up.

"Oh, Jessica!" Linn shouted in what turned into a raspy voice midway.

Jessi turned around to see her. Awaiting what was so important that she had to be stopped and could drop the books all over again. "Yeah?"

"I know you girls are in school and you guys probably both have jobs too. So, if you need someone to watch little Sean sometime, I would be more than happy to do it!"

She considered this but not for long. They already had everything covered. "Thanks! But we have a day care arranged here in town. The one-off Kentucky. It's called Little Angels."

"Oh, I know it! Nice little building they have there. Well, offer still stands, ma'am." She mocked Jessi with the "ma'am" part then winked and went inside.

She made it inside without spilling the books again. Later, they ordered pizza and slept on the floor all together in the living room. Jessica didn't tell Melissa about the elderly woman living below that she had met until they were just about to go to sleep.

(2)

Sunday was broad but went by as fast as a holiday. The day was packed full of moving stuff in, and afterwards, buying stuff to move in. They were in and out of their apartment all morning and afternoon, scaling the stairs from multiple trips up and down. Jess had anticipated her some-would-say, nosey neighbor to come out and say hello to Meli but she didn't.

Sean had a fantastic and hopefully memorable day with his grandmother, and Jessi gathered that her mother had missed him already. Not having to watch her grandson all the time was definitely creating a void she would have to fill someday, (though she regularly griped about having to watch him), and Jessi wondered what it would be. Maybe a vacation? She certainly deserved it. Around dinner time they finished moving in, and they went out to eat at Melissa's work since the discount was significant.

For about two months they planned this move, and it was coming closer to paying off tomorrow. Work was only ten miles from their apartments and school was even less than that. It was going to save them in gas, sleep, and time. Even if Jessica had to pay for Sean's daycare now, it was worth it, and she would be picking more hours up at UPS anyhow.

The daycare would be holding onto her son until five, then Meli would come and get him because Jessica's shift started at two. She did trust her watching Sean when overlooking things that Jessi overthought on, and it really was a blessing she had such a good friend to volunteer to babysit when she was scheduled late.

Unlike the first night, they had their beds the second. She set an alarm for 7:30. A good amount of time to get herself and Sean ready before her first business class started. Sean was tucked in and asleep by nine thankfully, and he was excited for his daycare and rock wall before passing out. Before she fell victim to sleep, Jessica thought more about how easygoing tomorrow was going to be.

(3)

The sirens, she couldn't hear until she was right next to their door and when they made it to the parking lot—the sirens being way more defined now—Jessica saw the smoke in the sky. She didn't think much of it. Meli had already left for her eight AM class and her own didn't start until nine. Same with Sean's 'class.'

Her anxiety for being tardy didn't spike with the traffic leading up to Kentucky or when she unintentionally was driving closer to the smoke, but it sky-rocketed when she saw the Little Angels center puking orange flames and black smoke.

The fire raging inside had clearly been burning for longer than the firemen cared to admit, and by the time she saw it, the once appealing white building was scorched a charred black. Jessica was baffled by its condition with all the emergency cars and trucks around the sight. They were attempting to take it down, but their hose seemed to be nothing but a tease to the fire burning.

Police cars stood around and closed the right lane the accident was closest to. Along with some civilians and some of the people she recognized to be teachers, some kids were looking on, curious and/or terrified of the fire. Jessica was wanting to see if anyone was hurt and what had happened, but selfishly, she knew she couldn't find out right now. No matter how furious or worried she may had been, Jessi couldn't miss her class. Not even a mile away from the fire behind, she knew she needed a sitter close by and promptly.

Following the detour, the police had arranged due to the fire, the answer came to her, and she told Sean what the change of plans were, but she had a feeling he wasn't listening and was only wondering what was on fire outside.

She was reluctant to give the door a knock, but nine AM was running toward her at a finishing speed. Sean stood next to her holding her hand confused to why they came back home with his backpack on. Jessica knocked rapidly three times and the door was opened without being unlocked first. Linn was standing at the door smiling with a surprised look with her eyebrows. She was wearing a flower printed button up shirt and jeans that she didn't really fill out.

"Yes, dear? Is something the matter?"

Jessica sighed and pushed her mostly blonde hair past her ear and glasses. "Well, do you remember when I told you about Sean's daycare the other day? Well, it burnt down this morning."

She gasped and put her hands over her mouth. They were practically slapping her lips from how bad they were shaking, but they were painted with a fresh black coat. "Oh my, how!"

"I have no clue. I didn't have time to ask because I have class in less than a half an hour. So, that brings me to this," she hesitated but knew she didn't have another choice. "Can you watch him? Just until five, ma'am, then Mel—"

"Of course, I will! Come on inside, guys!" she exclaimed. "Oh, I guess you better get going." Linn laughed and pawed her hands toward the Carvers. "Go on, everything will be fine and fun here. I've spent more than half my life babysitting. And he doesn't look like too much trouble now that I'm closer." Linn grinned and winked at a still nervous Sean. Though, he blushed and showcased a shy smile when addressed.

Jessica hugged her son tight and told him she loved him, reminded him that Meli would get him soon, and that Linn was going to take great care of him. She prayed that was true when her son walked into a near stranger's house.

(4)

She had pulled some money out for Linn right after work then did close to fifteen over the speed limit to get to Stoneleigh. She was already so paranoid about Sean's situation when Meli made it much worse by her reaction when Jessica told her what had happened with the daycare and what she had to do with Sean. Her eyes went wide, and she gasped, "*You what?*"

She thought of borrowing someone's phone at work if someone had one or using the offices to call Stoneleigh's manager to check on them but that seemed to be untrusting. *He's fine,* she said, *she's been baby-sitting all her life.* She left the idea of ever calling. *Why didn't we get a fucking home phone yesterday!*

Complex D was quiet. She raced up the stairs to hopefully see her son sleeping, but if he wasn't, she wouldn't get upset. Jessica just wanted to be sure her son was safe. She went to their door and barged in hoping it was unlocked and it was.

Melissa was sitting on their new couch with none other than Linn. "Where is Sean?" she asked, first thing. Noticing she probably sounded controlling asking that sharply.

"He's sleeping, Jessi, damn," she laughed, and Linn shared in the laughter.

Relief cooled her body. "Ugh, I'm so sorry. How was he?"

"That boy," Linn started, and shook while she paused. "Is so talkative." She giggled. "I could not get him to stop talking about this show he likes on TV. The Ninja turtles, I think?"

Jessica better late than never, joined in with a laugh. "Yeah, Don is his favorite because he has glasses like us."

Linn nodded and Meli scoffed.

"Well, I better get back to my own place. I just wanted to let you know with my own words that everything was perfect today and any time you need me to do it again, I'm downstairs."

"Oh, here I pulled out some ca— "Jessica started.

"Please, don't worry about it. I'm just happy to help." Then Linn exited out the door and when the door closed and latched, Jessica ran to Sean's room to see him tucked in his bed like he was last night. His lips looked puffy when he slept, his cheeks colored red.

"She's a pretty chill lady, Jess." Meli snuck up on her and startled Jessica. "I think you have a sweet setup with Linn watching him even if the daycare didn't burn down. By the way, did you ever find out if anyone was caught in the fire?"

(5)

Toward the end of April, the weather heated up and finally got to its expected spring feel that most Kansans were only tickled with since mid-march. With School coming to an end within the next month, finals were only giving Melissa and Jessica very little air to breathe at a time and that was with work included. Jessica—more so than Meli—would go to school tired, then go to work right after exhausted, get off, go home and be able to see her son sleeping already, and then repeat it all over again.

Her motherly duties, she felt, were unachievable with how hectic things have been lately but she was becoming more confident that her son was in good hands over the last month. They hadn't had a day to their selves since they moved in, but Jessi was sure that once summer hit, she would be able to spend a great amount of time with him and Linn wouldn't have to watch him. She had done good living up to her offer to watch Sean as much as needed though. In time, the four of them had developed a routine every weekday that consisted of Jessica dropping off Sean before class and Meli picking up him from Linn's around five if she didn't have to work.

Every morning Sean would wake up excited to go to Linn's as if she had her own rock wall in the living room. Sean and Linn had become an adoring duo. Whenever Jessi did get to speak to her son—not often—he would mostly talk about Linn. Never about starting school soon, about his dad, or even the ninja turtles. He would just go on and on about Linn, and what she made him for lunch, her apartment, or things they crafted together. Every once in a while, Jessi would actually feel quite jealous of their relationship. Not long after the feeling, she would laugh at it but that didn't mean it wasn't legitimate.

Things became regular by a late point in the month, and with school tightening around their throats, it was making things as comfortable as possible. But, around the same time, on a non-particular ordinary night, things got a little more uncomfortable.

She came home around 11:20ish; Jessica knew that because she glanced at her Pathfinders clock right before she turned the engine off. Stoneleigh was pretty dark, and nobody's lights seemed to be on, which was fair for a Tuesday night.

Meli didn't have work tonight so she told Jessi that she would get Sean right after class. Being use to the routine, she thought she would come home and they'd both be fast asleep with the apartment would be utterly silent.

But as she finished the second level of steps, Jessica saw a troubling sight.

Her front door was wide open.

Numerous explanations ran through her head, most of them mistake oriented but it still didn't calm her. She creeped carefully up the third rack of stairs and peeked into her apartment.

The lamp in the living room was on like usual—Jessi had told Meli to leave it on so she could see when getting home so late. She peered around the corner, behind the door, in the kitchen and all around. She closed it soon after, not completely sure what she was looking for. *Sean!* she internally screamed. In a short sprint, she ran down the hall and pushed open his bedroom door. Asleep like every other night with red cheeks and fat lips, he lay there glowing in the moonlight. She smiled, closed the door, and thought about how she was going to ask Meli about incident in the morning.

(6)

The following morning, Melissa apparently left earlier than usual. Jessica got out of bed about the time Meli would leave the house to catch her before she left. Although, with a night's sleep behind her, she had cooled down from the open-door incident but still felt the need to address it.

After dropping Sean off at Linn's, she had already planned to talk to Meli the next morning. Most Wednesdays, Meli worked later than Jessica and those were the days Linn had Sean the longest. Trying to find her on campus during the day wouldn't be a promising effort with Easter leave coming in and delayed classes before the actual finals.

While she drove and sought out why Melissa might have left the door open, Jessi wasn't surprised. Her best friend and roommate had become interested and invested in a classmate lately. A liberal arts major, who was obviously liberal in more ways than just the arts. The two seemed to be spending a lot of time together over the last week or so. Jessica was excited for her, thrilled actually, but sometimes when Meli found another girl that actually liked her back, everything else in her life became of less value, making life outside of the liberal art student white noise. So, it made sense if she did mistakenly leave the door open.

If?

What else? Or who else would it have been?

Ms. Carver shook off that thought right before getting out of her car to get to class.

(7)

Her alarm clock still beeped and buzzed annoyingly at 7:30 with no class to attend. Jessica felt relief of not having to get up, so she hit the off button on the clock and let her eyes stay shut for a little longer. Meli was off class today as well, but Jessica had expected her to leave at any moment, if she hadn't already. They both had work tonight, therefore Sean had to go with Linn at two and Meli was probably set to leave and hang out with her girl before then.

Throwing off her comforter, she swung herself out of bed and got to her feet. The room had a golden, sweet, and warm tone of lighting in it from the rising sun peeking through her blinds. Picking up a pull over jacket out of the dirty hamper, she left her room with a cool and level head about the other night.

That was until she took two more steps around the corner of her utility closet and saw sunlight blasting through the living room door frame. Inside smelt like outside, there were a few moths above kitchen bar, and the front room felt dewy and cold.

All fucking night, she marveled.

Livid, she clenched her fist then looked at anything quick to hit. Only finding the wall, she resisted throwing a punch and put her fist to her forehead. Jessica took a moment to collect herself. She opened her eyes and saw that Meli's door was closed. She imagined charging in with a mighty boom, scaring Melissa awake.

For some reason, likely to spare Sean the trauma or experience of them fighting—God knows he saw enough with

Sean sr. — she didn't act on her vision. Attempting to cool down, she unclenched her fist and continue to the living room, shut the door tight, and make breakfast.

Melissa came out fully dressed and ready to go by the time the last pancake was ready to take off the skillet. She was walking at swift pace and turned to wave Jessi goodbye when Jessi stopped her at the door.

"Hey!"

Jessica instantly snagged her attention. Meli looked obedient, but happy and prepped. Her outfit was a clean white zip up jacket with dark jeans and white *adidas*. She stood there waiting, genuinely curious to what her best friend had to say right before she went out the door. And suddenly, Jessica didn't feel so paranoid or as angry. Most importantly, she wasn't so sure it was Meli who left the door open now.

Then what? Or wh —

The thought was short lived as Meli looked at her.

"I made some breakfast."

Meli scoffed, and then let it roll into a full-on laugh.

"Bro, you straight scared the shit out of me. Ha-ha you used that voice you use when Sean gets into something."

"Yeah, I guess I did sound kind of bitchy," she said. "I'm sorry I'm just a little on edge." Then she just decided to ask. "Hey, um, did you maybe leave the door open two nights ago? I know you wouldn't have on purpose, but it just worried me."

"The door was open at night? When you got off?"

"Yes. Wide open."

Meli thought back, Jessica could see it on her face. "Hm."

"That's fucked. I even remember shutting and locking the door after Linn stopped by."

Jessica lifted her brow slightly in small confusion. "Linn stopped by?"

"Yep. She knocked on the door and asked if Sean was awake. She had baked some peanut butter cookies. He was asleep. They were fucking great, though."

Jessica's confusion was stroked but not scratched. Although her mind went back to the door. "Well, I, um." She stepped on her own words trying to find something to say that would put her worries of the door to rest. "Just make sure you close the door tight, I guess. Lock it too, both of them."

"Will do," Meli finished, made her eyes big and went outside.

Meli closed the door behind her and left Jessica in their subtly smokey kitchen. Jessica thought more smoke wouldn't hurt, she then lit one of her cigarettes, and wondered if she had offended Melissa somehow.

(8)

A crash that was not only loud, but powerful sounding, made Jessica open her eyes. At first, she assured herself it was merely part of the dream that came with her sleep that night. However, she couldn't recall a whiff of a dream if there was one. The more and more she delt with the crash in her head, Jessica became certain there was no dream at all, and that crash was real. She then felt fresh fear from the noise in the night. She looked at her alarm clock. The time was a quarter after three A.M.

Puzzled, and hardly awake, she still was aware that Meli sometimes came home this late in the past. It calmed her down just a notch.

She never woke me up coming in before, though, Jessi critically thought.

With a blanket hanging over her shoulders, she got off her bed and ventured to her bedroom door. She stood still and tried to listen for any movement on the other side, good or bad.

Quiet as a moment of prayer.

A sudden dose of courage struck her, and swiftly, she opened her door, then walked out in the living room.

139

It was just as black as her room; all the lights were off. She could only see what she *knew* was there, like her furniture. On the wall by the utility closest there was a backup switch for the top light in the living room, she found it with her hand and flipped it.

She woke up quickly when the lights exposed the front door as open as it could be.

She was at a loss for words. Though, she didn't care much for words anymore, now it had to be delt with swift action.

Jessica, without taking a breath, stomped to Meli's room and uselessly twisted the knob then shoved the door open with a painful shove of her palms. She simultaneously turned on the light as the back of the door slammed into the wall it was attached to.

Meli jolted and shot up in defense mode and panic. Her eyes grew large but not in a annoyed or playful way. Her eyes now told Jessica she was shocked and scared, but also that Meli had been in a heavy sleep before she came in.

Jessica felt like the biggest bitch in the mid-west at that second, but then she stomped out the thought and returned to the door issue.

"What the fuck, dude?" Meli said, aggrivated and not at all in a kidding manner.

"Why is the front door wide open, Melissa? What the fuck is with that? This is the third time I've seen it like that and it's fucking three A.M!" Jessica shouted, not as loud as she could since Sean was still asleep.

"Yeah, it is three A.M! So, why are you in my room screaming at me about the fucking door, Jessi?"

"Because you keep leaving it open for some dumbass reason."

"I didn't leave it open, bitch!" she snapped.

Strangely, in the heat of the argument she believed Meli when she said that but felt she couldn't back down. She was in too deep, and Meli really was the likely reason it was open.

She fought back. "If not you then who, Meli? The fucking wind? Just shut and lock the fucking door when you come in and out!"

(9)

The only thing that Melissa said to Jessica the next day was that she wasn't going to be home all weekend. She also felt she needed to add, "So, don't worry about the fucking door," before she left in the morning. Jessica wasn't upset for her leaving, or the comment about the door, she was quite the opposite really.

She had the whole day off work, school, or anything that would take her away from time with her son. Which is exactly what she intended to do with her time; spend it with the boy of her dreams. They had plans to go rent two movies from Blockbuster, get something to cook together—whatever he wanted, of course—and she was going to surprise him later on in the night with a brand-new Game Cube. Jessica couldn't wait to see her son's reaction when he saw his game and be contagiously happy all night.

The best part about it was that it didn't just end with the first night. With Easter on Sunday, she had the whole weekend off as well. Her mom was hosting a dinner that day and Sean was already beyond ready to see his grandmother again. Lucky for Jessi, her mom was currently on vacation prior to the holiday and was coming back late on Saturday. Therefore, that meant she had Sean all to herself. It's what she needed. No schoolbooks, no work, no Meli, no Linn and no grandmother to steal her son away.

(10)

Sean's reaction to the whole night had flown by her expectations. He cuddled his momma all day, told her he loved her more than once—especially when he got his new game—and also ate all of his hamburger helper she cooked up.

141

She was beat tired now. Sean had crashed out around ten and she put him in his bed right when his controller fell out of his hand. Jessica was on the couch now, smoking a cigarette and watching one of the movies they rented again. As she lay her head down on one of the sofa pillows, she tried to think of what they could do tomorrow. She did have plenty of money right now with all the work she had been doing. *Work but hardly any sleep,* she thought, and yawned.

Her cigarette had only been burning for a couple of minutes but Jessi felt she couldn't finish it. She grabbed her glass ash tray off the coffee table and smashed it out, then put the tray at the edge of the table.

Jessica told herself she should turn all the living room lights off and go to her own bed, but she couldn't. Well, she could, but she didn't want to. The couch had been keeping her warm and felt good on her back. She closed her eyes with her head toward the celling. In her last thoughts of being conscious, Jessica had her ex-husband in mind. She wondered how things would have turned out if they just stopped fighting over their son, and then, she was out like the moon was.

She woke up but not as tired as she would have felt waking up in her bed. Jessi had to recall how she ended up on the couch from just being asleep for about an hour or two. With some groans that were fitting for a woman much older, she stepped to her feet and went to the kitchen. The oven had a clock and it read 3:33. *Longer than I thought,* she saw.

From the living room, she heard a *klink*. It didn't startle her nor frighten her, but it did get her attention. She exited the kitchen and saw her ash tray had fallen off the table somehow.

"Fuck me!" she exclaimed, as she saw the ashes in the carpet. After grabbing a rag that she had dampened, Jessica went to the mess, knelt down, and tried to clean it.

The title screen of the movie was on loop and playing it's score at a modest volume. Still, Jessica found it obnoxious and dropped the rag to turn it off with the remote. It was now eerily silent. Though, only lasting a few moments, the quiet was disturbed by the clashing of small metal and a dragged-out screech that followed.

The front door was opening slowly.

She felt frozen with horror and Jessi's sinuses cleared up while she didn't even know they were blocked. Her heart was pounding in her head as she watched the door open.

"Melissa?" she guessed, hoping it was her with any spirituality she had.

She stood to her feet from the floor. Against her will, her brain started to think of the horrible things that could be on the other side waiting. A lunatic with a cheap, thin mask but thick blade, a robber or rapist who had been stalking her apartment, or a starving, murderous beast that had more eyes than fangs.

Grinding her teeth together, from a teeming of suspense pacing in her head, she began to rapidly plot her next move. Was she supposed to just wait and watch? Call out and hope it's a joke? Or slam the door before the sight behind it could be seen? The latter seemed the safest. Slam the door fast, then lock it and back away. Maybe call the police as well? But what would she say? The door opened?

Jessica took a step to the door and in the two steps, she was intending to kick the door shut. She took her next step and lifted her knee to her midsection to shoot her foot forward.

However, she froze with her foot in the air when door-opening culprit revealed themselves.

It was her son.

Sean was still dressed in his *Disney* Pjs she put him in while he was sleeping. She saw him but he didn't see her, his head was straight ahead while he crept to the hallway. The way he walked with wide steps and mute footing looked like he was sneaking in. But *why would a five-year-old sneak out?* she asked herself as she analyzed the scene.

"Sean?" she eventually choked, untrusting of her own eyes. The momentarily loss of words faded, it was like she had been watching a TV show or movie but then remembered she could interfere.

He stayed quiet and remained on path.

"Sean!"

No good, still walking. She caught up with him, then cut him off, and squatted to his height. And That's when Jessica Carver felt as if she could vomit her own heart out.

She hadn't noticed that his pajamas had been tugged and torn moments ago but if she would have, Jessica knew she would have reacted faster. He had a stunned, dumb look on his face that was colored with blood, bites, and burns. His cheeks looked like a hot fork had been pressed on him, maybe some lighters too. On his neck and right ear there had been teeth indentures. Dripping down his chin, his lips had been lathered in blood from a cut right down the middle.

"*Oh my god,*" she cried. Her eyes were shot with water in a second. "Sean! Baby! Tell me what happened? Are you okay? Who did this to you!"

He kept quiet and looked through her. It then hit Jessica that for the first time in her son's life, he had been sleepwalking.

But sleepwalking and attacked? She put her hands on his head and touched his hair while she hyperventilated. Examining him further, she pulled up his long sleeves and saw other burns that were destined to turn into blisters, scratches that looked like they could be from a mean house cat, and full-on bite marks that were no doubt from a person.

She wanted to scream, and nothing was going to stop her from doing so.

(11)

The police officer called to the scene arrived in under ten minutes, and in the meantime, Jessica tried and tried again to wake her son.

He had a doped look on his face that indicated laughing gas or some kind of pain medication. She was starting to think he might have been drugged, until the cop's knock at the door spooked him awake. He awoke with high energy and consciousness but with questions all around him and new lasting pain within. He wouldn't stop crying and spazzing for a while. Jessica tried to tell the policeman what had happened, but she knew little herself.

She spoke of the open door on more than one night, her roommate, Linn and the loud noise she heard the other night. Of course, not all the information given seemed useful or relevant to the officer but Jessica insisted on telling him. The door being wide open repeatedly seemed far too significant.

Officer Hawkins called an ambulance for the boy and he was evaluated all night. Once the doctors told her everything they knew, she felt a little better.

They assured her that there was no trace of molestation on Sean, and that the worst to come out of this was scarring, both physically and—the part they feared more—mentally. But since he didn't seem to remember anything, doc was willing to bet Sean may just forget about the entire thing with being so young, and especially, since he was *technically* sleeping when it happened.

By ten A.M, she was ready to take Sean home and it took an hour to convince some of the personnel at the hospital to let her.

Sean fell asleep (again) in the car on the way home. She carried him up when they got to stoneleigh. On the way up, she saw Linn's door closed over.

Jessica had already called whoever she needed to call to let know about Sean. She called her mom first, she cried hideously, and it made Jessica cry the exact same. Jessia's mother said she would be right over as soon as her plane landed. Next, she called Sean sr., and he didn't answer but she was certain he would call back later and blame her for everything. Meli answered on the third ring and her voice still echoed of anger regarding Jessi but went speechless when she heard and surprisingly sounded like she was about to cry.

Once Sean was back in his bed, Jessi had the urge to tell Linn what had happened. Although, she was uneasy with the idea of leaving her son alone now—and probably for the rest of his life, she thought, looking down at her son's burnt and bit face sleeping.

Going against her natural insticts just for a minute, she went out of the room and then quickly outside to the stairs and down to Linn's door. It was still falsely closed, so, she put her fingertips to it and shoved lightly.

She stuck her head in and called out. "Linn?"

She chose to step in, and Jessica instantly felt naïve, for this was the first time she had seen Linn's apartment. It was nice and very cozy. Filled with delicious and nostalgic smells and artwork. The crafts and paintings had mostly to do with night or nature. Above her wooden entertainment center with a bulky TV, Linn had a framed poster of Vincent van Gogh's *Starry Night*.

The symbol on top of that, she didn't recognize from anywhere. It was a piece the size of a kitchen plate and was assumingly made of black material. It was mysterious to say the least. She could see it being an animal or a plant, or maybe something to do with a different country. She had one more idea of what it could be, but she wasn't able to finalize her thought. There was a commotion in one of the bedrooms.

It sounded like the opening of a dresser. Jessi called out again, "Linn!"

Feeling like she had already been here for too long, she wandered speedily to Linn's Hall where the noise came from. She heard the roar of the drawer once more standing at the end of the hall. Two of Linn's doors were closed completely, but the third was merely closed over like the front door was.

She knocked on the door three times gently.

"*Linn?*"

The door opened a little more but not all the way from her soft knock. She could now see opened and empty drawers with a suitcase on the bed. Also, Jessica heard a pleasant and experienced humming of a woman inside. Jessica put her hand on the door and was just about to push it open. Though, beating her to it, the door ripped open, but the person looking back at her wasn't very familiar.

A woman opened up, about her height and size, dressed in dark Jeans and a flower shirt and she was, as a side note, agelessly gorgeous.

"Hello, there! That's funny, I thought I heard someone at the door, but I guess I'm just getting old ha-ha," she said and smiled wide after. Her teeth were the kind that could be accused of being fake, but Jessica could feel this woman's confidence radiating off her like a strong perfume. They had to be real, this woman was legitimate and someone could look at her for seconds and *know* that.

Her hair, black as coal and her eyes were as bright as spring grass. She was much more attractive than Jessi believed herself to be, but strangely, she had a hunch that she was younger than the woman before her. She projected this woman to be in her early forties but that guess wasn't from any age showing in her body or face. She just carried herself differently than any younger woman she had ever seen. This woman spoke and looked like she had been through it all and knew every single trick.

"You all right, doll?" the woman asked.

Jessica, collecting that she was just staring after she spoke to her, shook her hair and refocused. "I'm sorry, ma'am. I'm just looking for my neighbor, Linn. I ha—"

"Oh," the woman said quietly. She looked to the carpet, bit her bottom lip, and then her engaging eyes flooded. "She actually passed last night..."

Jessica's jaw, heart, and eyes seemed to fall. "What? How? What happened?"

"A heart attack I think, but I don't know. They just got her body out of here not too long ago," she said, rubbing her own arm and not looking at Jessi.

She then went back to the dresser and put more clothes in the suitcase.

"Oh my god… this morning… I just can't even..."

"Yeah."

"My son was attacked in the middle of the night."

The stranger in Linn's apartment cupped her mouth. "My god!" Her nails were painted black and sharp. Much like Linn's were. Actually, seeing the lady do that in that fashion, revealed an uncanny resemblance between the two. She figured she must have been related. Jessica felt like she wanted to cry for Linn. It upset her that she would never be able to tell Linn thank you for watching Sean all those times.

"I know, but I think he will be fine, I hope."

They nodded together and kept eye contact for the longest they had so far. Then, as if she were hearing a joke, she thought she knew before, Jessica caught on to the punchline before it was delivered.

This woman had the same exact eye color, eye shape, and eye everything as Linn. And even the mole next to her mouth. Everything was the same as Linn. The fucking clothes she's wore were Linn's.

"Who are you?"

The woman smiled at Jessi and it far from warmed her this time.

"My name is Veronica. Linda was my aunt." She stuck out her delicate and smooth hand for the introduction.

Jessica mindfully looked at it and stuck her own hand out to shake Veronica's. Her hand was firm and *steady* when she shook it, but she couldn't extinguish the feeling she had shook this same hand once before.

She felt so suspicious, it made her nauseous to keep digging into the idea. But suspicious of what? What exactly was she going to say or accuse her of?

Veronica saw the look of loss, or of being *lost* on Jessi, and spoke again. "I'm sorry if you and my mom were close. But I promise you, she is in a *far* better place now," she finished with her hands in praying style.

"I thought you said Linn was your aunt?"

Veronica stood motionless and looked to her right shortly. "She was. She just raised me the whole time. I'm sorry, I'm just a big ole mess right now."

Jessica only looked at her, questionably.

"Well, I better get all of her things packed up."

"Yeah. I guess I should leave."

"Yeah."

Veronica and Jessi looked at each other one last time. Jessica turned her back first and walked out the way she came. Before heading out under the sun, she looked behind her again. The beautiful and chilling woman was watching her walk out with the bedroom door in hand. She said, "I'm truly sorry to hear about your son. Take care." Then she closed the door and so did Jessica on her way out.

She put her back to the door and started to sob. Nothing had made any sense to her in the last seven hours, yet it happened so fast like it was planned. The young mother didn't know how to deal with the trauma that had been left for her son and her family. She prayed she wouldn't have to, and Sean would just forget. Then they would all forget. She never wanted any of this shitshow to resurface again. This was the first time and what she hoped to be the last time, that she was unable to keep her son safe.

Lifting her glasses to her forehead to wipe her wet eyes, Jessica then looked at how bad her own hands were shaking now.

Little Steps and Whispers

I was at home "sick" from school the day I started to feel uncomfortable being home alone. Well, I was mostly alone that day, just my black and white cat, Lucy and I. The night before, I stayed up hours after I told my mom I was going to bed and that I didn't feel well but really, I felt fine, and I stayed up working on my sick act for the next morning. My teacher that year—I believe it was my fourth-grade year—was giving out an end of the year spelling test of the year's hardest words. Considering I had already failed over half of the previous tests, I was very reluctant to take it. Though, when I think back to this now, I would have much rather failed the test that morning instead.

Unfortunately for me, my sick act was convincing and I was granted to stay home that sunny day. Just a little after seven was usually when my mother would take my little brother and I to school, but this morning she was running a little late to make sure I had all that I needed. Once my mom yelled from the top of the stairs, "Anthony! Alex and I are leaving! Get some rest!" then hearing the faint humming of my mother's car fade away from the house, I knew I was in the clear to start my 'sick' day, so I started up my PlayStation.

Before I go on about the last sick day I ever had, I want to describe my room at that time. In my childhood, my room was the house's unfinished basement. It was cool and remained dark for the most part and truthfully, it was too large for a child's bedroom. At first, when we moved in, it thrilled me that all of that space was mine but after this particular morning, I despised that room.

Once we moved in years before, we discovered the basement had little to no lighting available. It must have been something with the wiring and such, but we never really got to the bottom of it due to certain occurrences. There were no windows either, just a light at the very top of the stairs by the basement door; the switch was also there. Eventually and what was planned to be temporary, my father bought me a tall lamp that lit the room decently at best. He intended to actually install celling lights but not long after we moved in, he was killed in a fire at his work.

Anyway, I put the lamp about six feet away from my bed and it stayed there until after my "sick" day then I moved it closer to the stairs. The lamp provided a decent light like I mentioned but it was a pain in the ass because anytime I left the house, my mother insisted that I turn it off. So, every time I returned from anywhere, day or night, my room would appear near black from the top of the stairs. Whether I liked it or not, I had to always run down into the dark abysses of the basement, find the lamp and turn it on. An unsettling idea, right? Although before the room trade between my brother and I, I was pretty good at finding the lamp without hardly any visual at all.

Okay, back to where I was with that day. After my mom left, I turned on my PlayStation, like I said. I played for some time and Lucy was curled in a ball, vibrating with a constant purr on my lap the whole time. Those days, Lucy was an extremely clingy cat, some could even say strangely loyal. My mother always said we were best friends and at that time, I couldn't disagree. When I started kindergarten, I got her as a Christmas gift and ever since then, she always stayed close to me.

In time, Lucy got up from my lap, probably to use her litter box or eat but when she returned, she jumped on my bed then continued sleeping. It wasn't long after that when my own eyes got heavy with staring at the television for so long. In addition to that, I also did stay up much later working on the perfect cough and sick voice. I remember thinking there was some significance with Lucy getting in bed, like she was saying I needed to sleep. It's funny how much significance you give the little things in life when you're that young. I saved my game, turned off my console, then crawled in bed with Lucy on my pillow.

The happenings after I laid my head down to sleep, I reduced to a dream for a good fifteen years. Around my late twenties I became convinced it was all real and regretfully, not a nightmare. As soon as it was all over, I kept telling myself I had actually fallen asleep before I crawled into bed or that I fell asleep as soon as I closed my eyes, but I know that wasn't the case. It all happened exactly how I'm about to tell.

Everything around me was cool, dark and quiet but moments later, couldn't have been more than ten minutes, the silence was interrupted by what sounded like someone walking upstairs.

My eyes slowly spread open since I was so set on sleeping and I laid in the dark listening to whatever was going on above my room, the living room and kitchen area. I hadn't heard the front door open, so, from the start I was a little confused and a little frightened already. Although, as I reflect on this part now, once I heard the walking, I wasn't even entirely sure it was someone upstairs. It sounded more like tapping rather than an actual person walking. Similar to the sound of a dog's paw and nails clicking against a tile floor when it strolls around. I also knew exactly what walking upstairs sounded like, I heard it all the time, every day even. When you live beneath the rest of house, you hear everybody's movements frequently and usually you know who is in the house.

The more the tapping continued, the more intrigued and worried I grew with it. Lucy appeared to hear it as well since she got up from her curled position on my pillow, which made me both nervous and relieved at the same time. I was relieved I wasn't the only one hearing it but nervous we were hearing it in the first place. It wasn't long until I got myself out of bed, then hurried to turn the lamp on.

My first thought was that my mother came home to check up on me or maybe she had forgotten her lunch.

Though, I declined that idea once I got closer to the bottom of the stairs in seek of getting a better listen. Whoever was upstairs, wasn't my mother, and whoever it was, they had a friend because once I put a foot on the first step, I heard communication through whispers.

My gut rolled with fear. I couldn't quite make out what they were discussing but they were certainly planning something. I inferred that from how one of the voices whispered more than the other. Their voices were hard to identify from how quiet they spoke but a few times while they were communicating, both would burst into a high pitch cackle.

Tiny and speedy sounding, similar to what you would imagine a mouse's laugh sounding like if it could. The two or more whispered and walked all over above. Based off what I heard, they went through the kitchen, living room, my mother's room, my brother's room, and the bathrooms included. It seemed they were intent on looking through the entire house.

So why wouldn't they check the basement?

As soon as that idea hit me, that's when panic set in.

What could I do? At this day and age, cell phones were an upcoming thing and adults hardly had them, especially not children. I couldn't have even called the police if I wanted to. Which I would have but the home phone was upstairs, and so were they. It had crossed my mind to climb the stairs and try to catch a glimpse of one of them but the image of someone flinging the door open right as I made it to the top of the steps, made me feel physically ill.

I should just hide, I thought. Neither of them knew I was there, and I figured I could keep it that way if I just didn't make myself heard or seen. However, if the two upstairs thought they were all alone, *why whisper?*

None of what was happening made any sense to me and it still doesn't. I think about it quite often and when I do, I ask myself more questions each time.

Due to my growing fear and constant confusion, I couldn't think of a thing to do. I stayed at the bottom of the steps, listening and hoping they wouldn't open the door at the top. Lucy got up from my bed by this time and was now at my feet, looking up at the stairs as well. I'm sure she was just as curious as I was or maybe she was just curious to what I was doing. I wonder if cats can be as scared as humans. Sure, they run or jump when they get startled, and their fur gets big, but do they feel that lump in their throat? Do they quiver like their cold when they are exposed to such horror? Do they get that total transfixed feeling where they can't move a muscle because they are so terrified? I doubt it.

The tapping continued for a while, but the whispering ceased. They hadn't even been near the basement door, and I was beginning to think maybe they hadn't realized we had a basement at all or that it wasn't a priority to them. Either way, comfort was settling in rather than panic and I felt less afraid already. Despite the fact there were uninvited strangers in my house, they weren't bothering me. The whispering intruders may break things upstairs, more than likely steal too. But at least I was okay.

Then suddenly, the whispers sounded again, but this time, I could hear them better. They were closer to the basement door and for the first time since I've become aware of their presence, I actually could make out something they said. Just one word.

In a higher-toned voice much like their laugh, one of them whispered, *"Down."*

Instantly I backed off from the staircase and as if it was all part of somebody's plan, my lamp shut off and blackness surrounded once more. Panic was back and more gripping than before. The only thing I could think to do was hop in my bed and hide underneath the blankets. Although, before I could get underneath the covers, the basement door flung open.

Daylight poured from upstairs onto the staircase and I sat there watching on my bed, knowing I should be hiding but

I wanted to see them. Nevertheless, I didn't get the chance to. The basement door slammed shut and at first, I believed they had just ignored the basement but then I heard rapid tapping down the stairs. The whisperers were in the black room with me.

Fighting back tears and screaming, I heard little pitter patters tapping on the stone floor and around my bed as if a bunch of toddlers were searching through my basement. The lamp fell over and so did some crates of Christmas decorations my mother put away. They must have enjoyed that because with the crash of crates, that high pitch laugh came again but this time, it was no more than three feet away from me. As I was trying not to piss myself, and all over my bed—though, I may have—something else dawned on me. Lucy was still in the room. Soon she let out a growing growl and, in her way, a mighty hiss. She must have seen whatever was in the room with us.

Up until that precise moment of my life, as I hid underneath my comforter, I had never been so afraid. I also have never felt that sweat pouring and tear-jerking level of fear since then. While I shuddered with absolute fright, I kept listening to the ruckus they made and the diabolical giggles that followed. Our family wasn't the religious type, but I found myself mentally praying they wouldn't jump on my bed and find me. Although, it occurred to me even then that if Lucy could see them, *what if they could already see me*?

I had to get out of the basement and promptly.

Finding the stairs in pitch black was challenging, but not impossible. As I mentioned earlier, I had to find the lamp from the stairs in the dark quite frequently. Although, this scenario was the opposite, and I also had to run for my life instead of wandering in the dark pace.

Whenever I heard the steps a little farther from my bed, I bolted toward the direction of the stairs. I shoulder checked a wall that almost knocked me off my feet but I made it to the stairs. Actually, I *planted* on the stairs. The fall on the first step was painful on my hands and knees—still have a scar from it—but it didn't stall me for long. In the position I fell in, on all fours, I scaled up the stairs and opened the door and shut it behind me.

Everything upstairs looked normal, completely untouched and in order. Not a shred of forced entry evidence and no different from how it looked last night when I told my mother I wasn't feeling well. My knee hurt like hell and blood had seeped through my pajamas, but my attention was elsewhere, and I was still fearfully trembling from it. The door remained closed as I listened nearby to the fiends below. I felt I had them trapped. There was no possible way they could escape to my knowledge, but I almost opened the door when I heard Lucy's hiss.

Mistakenly, I had left her down there with them and as soon as I heard her defensive tactics, I began to sob.

After Lucy tried intimidating the intruders, she began to cry herself. Actually, no, she wasn't crying, she was *screaming* and trust me, cats can in fact scream. The only thing I could compare her wails to is when someone stepped on her paw or tail but that wouldn't do it justice. The pain she felt now sounded much worse. In the moments of her painful shrieks, she sounded more like a jungle cat than a domestic one. Lucy was in great agony and her wailing sounded violent and continued to get louder, like she was calling for help. To this day, I have never heard any living being cry or scream the way my cat did downstairs.

Then, the screaming came to a halt when a vivid crack that seemed to echo came from the basement. I stood there in front of the door, in the silence that now filled the once chaotic house, praying once again that it wasn't reality and that my cat was really alright. Tears soaked my cheeks, and I was still keeping them coming while I sobbed. After a minute or two, I couldn't help myself; I opened the door and yelled for her.

"Lucy!"

With my swollen eyes, I looked upon the downwards staircase that was only lit by the streams of window light and my thoughts ran madly through my head. I didn't know what to do, who to call, and especially, what I would tell them. And just when I thought things couldn't get any worse, they got intensely more mysterious.

Out of the basement's black surroundings and onto the poor lit steps, came Lucy.

Not a single scratch on her. She didn't look shaken up a bit, as if nothing ever happened and she wasn't just screaming to the heavens five minutes ago. Lucy walked right past me and looked both ways then pinned her sight on me. Before I returned a look, I glanced down at the basement and the lamp had come back on. No longer was I trembling but I was still as a stone with the same naked fear, only with more bewilderment, and that's saying something.

Her gaze on me was strange. It was a similar look to how one animal curiously looks at another animal of a different species. Not only was her stare different but her eyes were too. Not totally and obviously different, they were just *off*. At the time and for the next year or so, I didn't realize it, but her pupils looked lighter, nearly grey instead of jet black.

That night I didn't sleep in my room. Not even the next night or the night after that. I slept with my mom and told her I still wasn't feeling well but I would still go to school the next day. For the rest of my schooling, I had never had another sick day. In those days, I would have much rather suffered sick at school than be home alone with Lucy.

Ever since that morning, Lucy did just about everything differently. She quit lounging and sleeping where she could be found, hardly eats but still keeps her figure. I've never really seen her clean herself again either. When I would see her, she would always just sit in different spots of the house and stare with those dark grey centered eyes. On top of that, I haven't heard her make a sound since those cries. Not a hiss, growl, purr, or a meow. It seemed like she forgot how to, or she had never learned.

To no surprise, I quit letting her in my room and would normally walk away from her once she got close. Of course, I didn't tell my mother about this and never have I told anyone else. I suppose that's why I'm writing about it, just to express something that's kept me guessing for the majority of my life.

I'm writing this at the age of thirty-one and I was around ten years old when all this transpired. My black back but white bellied cat Lucy is still alive, which makes her twenty-four years old at the least. That's remarkable for a feline lifespan, almost unheard of but, sure, there are some instances where cats make it up to that age. Not like my cat though. Twenty-one years later, she looks the exact same and hasn't aged a day it seems. Okay, maybe not identically the same. The only thing that's different is the cataract in her left eye that she developed during the summer of that year. Other than that, she is the same. Still unsettling to be around with her gawking and silent roaming.

Of course, my mother and brother don't see it. She's just the old cat to them and they never paid much attention to her anyway.

I mean, she is my cat.

But they didn't experience what I did. Lucy still lives with my mother these days and because of that, I don't go over there much. I realize that sounds absolutely absurd but if you heard those little footsteps along with those whispers and cartoonish cackles upstairs, then the way my cat growled and screamed downstairs, you would know it wasn't the same cat as before. Perhaps, not even the same *thing*.

June

<u>After the Crash…</u>

Whenever I try to recall the weather of the night before my accident, I can remember it being nearly perfect outside. I had been knocked out in my boyfriend's bed all morning and the majority of the day, but once I got up then stepped outside, I instantly grew excited for the night… As if I was going to do something other than take an absurd amount of Xanax and completely *black out* for hours. But, of course, that's exactly what I had in mind.

The spring and summer of that year was nothing short of vague. I can only recall certain scenes and images of what really went on those days. In my head, it comes to me more like a movie I had seen but can't really remember the plot of. This was the peak of my addiction or 'binge' and my summer days were all melted together in the same pot. And as time goes by, the more solid it becomes, making those days harder to separate from each other.

Although, following the crash, my lack of memory halted that early morning in June. From that point on, I can remember everything. Especially the time I spent under the bridge and in the creek. And of course, the most memorable part, him.

Him, I could never forget. Despite how they justify it or what they suggest *really* happened, I know it happened like this.

***

Straight out of Dillton High I went to Butler University the next fall. Butler was a good fit for me, it wasn't too close to Dillton but it was still in Indiana. It gave me some nice breathing room from home and the freedom of that was a massive draw for me from the start. Though, besides the freedom, older boys, and the parties, I did enjoy college so far. Back then, I was a smaller, prettier, and unscarred girl and everyone seemed to want me there. Plus, school was never really that challenging to me as I did well at keeping my grades on point. Today, I still can't believe I sacrificed all of that for a boy when I took a year off school.

I had made that choice when I had fallen in "love" with Hunter. He was my age; I knew him the whole time growing up and I can say I always had a thing for him, but he didn't really develop feelings for me until I had come back the summer of my sophomore year. We spent that whole summer together and when it became time to return to school in the fall, I did not want to leave him. He didn't tell me to stay, nor did he tell me to go; he was just so indifferent about it; about everything really. For some stupid, naive reason, I loved that about him.

So, I spent the year with him, all the way to next summer that is. My parents were furious with me at the start, mostly about school but they also didn't trust Hunter much. That didn't stop me though, and they knew it wouldn't and, in the end, they let me make my own decisions. That whole year I stayed at his house almost every night. He didn't have his own place like I make it out to be though. Hunter lived with his dad, and Mr. Taylor just didn't care what his son did, no matter how irresponsible his actions were.

The particular night in which I'm writing about, we had a plan to hang out with two friends who were bringing Xanax gummies over. Justin and Marcus were actually his friends to be truthful. Marcus was really funny, and I did like him; Justin, on the other hand, was annoying and extremely flirty but really, he was border line rapey. He always got under my skin — or I mean, he would have liked to — by calling me *Riley* on purpose. I'm positive he knew my name was *Kylee* but that was just one of the small things he did that made me dislike him even more.

His friends came over around seven or so with the gummies. The gummies were these little green blocks no bigger than a fruit snack, but Marcus mentioned one cube was the equivalent to *three* bars of Xanax.

I took two. It's what I felt was necessary to get the high I desired. Around February is when I started taking Xanax and from that point to this point, they began to have less and less effect on me. The pills are all I had access to before then and the word was that gummies were "double dipped," so they were obviously stronger. They were more bitter going down, but Hunter told me to suck on them like he was. If I would have known that bitter and chewy cube was going to be my downfall, I would have never given myself the chance to taste it.

***

Fatigued or weak seems like a narrow way to put the effects of Xanax into words. Lethargy is absolutely one of the side effects, but I wouldn't say that it's from weakness or that it's the only result. Based off my experiences, I would say the lazy side of the high comes from feeling heavy. A weight is dropped onto the person and it stations them, yet, at the same time, a different weight is lifted mentally. All their concerns and anxieties flee, leaving them cool with anything and everything that's going on. That's what I would call, the first shade of the high.

Then, after a certain amount is taken, they look more like someone on their way out of this world. Pale in complexion and jaw loosely hanging open, sometimes even with their tongue out and their eyes practically closed. Looking from the outside, you would think that they're asleep and more than half the time, you'd be correct. Fighting a Xanax induced sleep is like staying dry at a waterpark. They might not get totally soaked, and the person on Xanax might stay awake for a little while, but inevitably, they will be splashed just like how the one on Xanax will find themselves with their eyes closed and unconscious.

Marcus was the first one I saw asleep, I think. Hunter could have been out before him though. If I had been focusing on him and not *Family Guy* on the TV, I might have been able to keep Hunter awake. Maybe Marcus too. Honestly, anybody but Justin would have been perfect.

I noticed Justin awake and looking at me after I had checked my phones time and messages. It was only 10:30ish and my mom had texted me to say goodnight and that she loved me—since every night I was never home for her to tell me in person, she usually did—and I saw I had three messages from an unknown number. They said, *"whatss upp"* with a drooling emoji.

It was Justin texting me from no more than three feet away.

I don't know how long I stayed inside once I realized, but I must have felt just as uneasy with him staring as I do now because I ended up outside sitting on some lawn chair in Hunter's back yard looking up at the stars. The night really was strangely gorgeous, that always stuck with me. Not before too long, Justin came out as well and with his own chair, the kind you place on the beach and tan in. He slugged over to me and placed his chair uncomfortably close, and nearly fell in it when he sat down.

What Justin said to me while we were outside, I don't have a clue. For as long as I've known him, I never really cared what he was saying whether I was sober or high. So, it doesn't really shock me that I can't make out anything he said that night. What I do remember from our exchange is precisely what made me get in my car and drive off.

Drunkenly, he called my name.

"Kyleeee" was just like how he said it, with an emphasis on the e in my name. Although surprised he didn't say Riley, I still ignored him and kept looking at anyway but his direction.

He laughed his stupid high pitch hyena laugh even with Xanax dragging him down. I wanted to get up as soon as he got out there, but I was so sluggish myself. Though, no substance could have kept me outside with Justin after his next move.

"Ky!" he shouted in the form of a whisper. I couldn't stand that he used *that* name so casually. That was a nickname reserved only by loved ones and I was frankly offended he even tried to use it. That's when I snapped back and saw it hanging out of his pants.

He had pulled his tiny dick out of his shorts and was playing with it right next to me. "Do ya wanna touch it?" the fucking creep asked me.

I bolted from my chair, flipping it on its back and went back inside. If I was out there a second longer, I was going to scream the neighborhood awake. Immediately, I wanted to tell Hunter what had happened but he was still in the same position I left him in. Harshly, I shook him and slapped his back while calling his name, but he was out for the night, most likely the day too from the amount he took.

Then I heard the back door open again; Justin was coming back inside.

I looked at Marcus and back at Hunter. They weren't waking up for anything, I was sure of that. Without much planning, I grabbed my car keys off the table and sloppily ran out the front door before Justin returned to the living room to see me.

***

When someone says they blacked out on Xanax, it's no exaggeration. It's as if an auto pilot mode is switched on and the cock pit becomes vacant. The pilot will return eventually, but sometimes when they do come back, they're somewhere else, maybe somewhere off track. The blackout may be merely minutes, or it could be hours with only brief moments of awareness in between.

Right when I got into my car, after frantically leaving Hunters, I went black.

Only for a few minutes though, and when I regained a better consciousness, I was on the outskirts of Dillton. To be specific, I was on Jones St. and just a little away from my parents. My auto pilot or subconscious must have known that.

I was all too familiar with Jones St, even as drugged up as I was. I drove on it every day during high school, avoiding the highway because Jones St. was more relaxed with only a forty-five-mph speed limit. The isolated road itself was a straight shot out or into town with farmlands, rich neighborhoods, and old trees on each side of it.

With my head dangerously close to the wheel of my Monte Carlo, I finally gathered that I was only eight miles from my parents. Regardless, those eight miles could have been eighty miles, I was a *Xaned* out mess. I shouldn't have been driving. My posture at the wheel was hunched and awful, I was pretty much leaning on it. Keeping my eyes open was as challenging as keeping them open in water and when they were open, the road wouldn't hold their attention like my phone was. Music was blaring loud, and my driver side window was down all in effort to keep me awake.

The summer night air rushing in through my driver side window felt excellent while I was flying down Jones. My speed was constant eagerly driving at sixty mph and I was edging closer to safety by the second.

Before I knew it, I was approaching Hiker Creek within a mile. Now turned ironic, every Easter with occasion in the summer, my cousins and I would make the three mile walk to Hiker to play in the creeks water. At the pinnacle of spring, it always held flowing water but, in the summer, it usually had little water or none at all. I looked forward to walking down to Hiker every year as a kid. However, as all of us grew older, they didn't come out this way as much, and when they did, the creek wasn't mentioned and like them, I quit going myself. And before my car tore through the steel guard rail on the bridge above the creek, I hadn't been there in seven years.

There was a song playing, and I didn't like it or just at that moment I didn't. I grabbed my phone in attempted to change the song. I can't remember if the wheel jerked out of my hand or if I had them on it in the first place. My Monte Carlo pulled to the right, and I heard a loud crash, then suddenly, I had the feeling as if I was on a roller coaster hurling down the track at top speed.

Seconds before my life changed not only painfully but spiritually, I looked toward the back of my car on the way down because something was telling me I wasn't alone. But I saw no one, and then nothing but black once I hit Hiker Creek.

***

As soon as I woke up, before my eyes even had the chance to see my surroundings, I believed I was safe. I thought I made it to my parents' house after all and I was curled up in the bed I left that summer. I wasn't that fortunate though.

The music I had been playing at an unreasonable volume was dead and gone, replaced only by a ticking and hissing from my now upside down and totaled engine. My hair had been in a loose bun all night but once I came to, my hair was down and dangling to the roof of my car. As my eyes looked toward my hair, I was hit with a massive light headed feeling and my face felt warm and numb. I looked to my rearview mirror and there were veins bulging in my forehead. They were thick and chock full of blood, feeling more like roots than veins.

Moving my arms from their hanging position gave me major discomfort. I tried to unstrap myself, but it was as if I was physically restrained from putting my hands near my lap. I ended up being able to put my hands at the top of the wheel, It's the farthest I could get them, and I hoped maybe that would make the blood even back out.

I was scared and confused, it took me quite some time to recall how I got there but once I was struck with the realization of my crash, I began to sob upside down. Despite that it was remarkable I had my seatbelt on and that I hadn't been smashed by my own car, I was still convinced death was waiting around the corner for me.

167

But other than the uncomfortable feeling my arms gave me from hanging above my head this whole time, I felt no other pain or agony. I wasn't bleeding from anywhere I could see. No scratches, gashes, or any place I could feel a potential bruise coming. I was fine, I was *alive,* but I didn't feel I should be. Especially with no damage like how it appeared. The car from the inside looked fine too. None of the interior had been smashed in and the rolled-up windows were still intact without a crack on any of them.

My driver side window was still down from when I was driving, and I could see all the healthy grass and weeds that my car was so close to smashing. From what the night allowed to be seen, the creek looked the same as it did every summer: dry with short weeds and grass covering the creek.

Outside seemed way later than when I was on the way over. Granted that it was already late when I crashed, but it seemed near black out now. I decided then I must have been unconscious for a few hours.

Although the time was irrelevant to me, I couldn't have known even if I wanted to. My car was dead and not able to display the time and my phone was missing. Way later, the police would bring me my iPhone in the hospital. They said it was yards away from where my car landed and my mother gasped, "Oh my god, no wonder you couldn't call for help!" I just nodded toward her in an agreeing fashion but truthfully, I doubt if I would have ever used my phone if I did have it.

***

During those isolated and uncomfortable hours, I strongly believed it was too late for me. No one ever used Jones at this time of night—except for drunk or drugged up drivers obviously—and by the time they would use the road, I figured I'd be dead by then. Plus, I was far too embarrassed and ashamed of being caught there in the first place and what got me there exactly.

Only three times did I cry out for help since I claimed myself be hopeless. When I cried out the first time, I thought hope was approaching.

A series of twigs snapped underneath what I assumed to be human feet. It sounded amazingly close to me, so I focused in.

Then I heard more.

Grass crunching with more twigs snapping but at a slow rate, like they were looking out for their steps or creeping up.

Right…left…right…left.

I took the opportunity just in case.

"Hello? Hey!" I yelped.

Praying it was a person and not just a nocturnal animal, I anticipated that their slow creep would speed up to the car. Discouragingly, no one made a reply and the steps I was hearing stopped for a moment.

"Help me?" I whined.

Suddenly the steps returned, but much different from before, now they weren't stepping, they were loudly stomping at the same slow pace.

RIGHT…LEFT…RIGHT…LEFT

Stomps that sounded like they were produced by a fictional giant filled the creek that morning. Closing in on my upside-down car with me trapped in, I held my breath on accident but felt the desire to scream. I recall thinking, *Is that you, Death? Coming up on me?*

I was struck with a case of odd luck because right when the steps were coming as close as they could before getting to me, blackness came upon me one more time.

***

Before my final black out, I assumed I was never going to see the light of day again. Thankfully, it was the first thing that stuck out to me when I woke up. The green in the grass was becoming more apparent, I could now see the cracks in the dry

dirt between patches of weeds and the uplifting sun had also
encouraged the birds to form their choir for the day.

Everything else was still in order though, and by in
order I mean I was still hanging upside down in my flipped car
under a bridge. Through the sun and birds, I felt relieved, even
if it was just a little tease of the day. It was hard for me to
fathom I had made it to dawn alive. The heavy steps I had
heard earlier had assured me I wasn't long for this life, but
seeing the world brighten before my eyes when it was once
appearing black, gave me hope.

My arms were back to dangling and were completely
numb by this point. There wasn't a possibility of me swinging
my arms to one side let alone put my hands back on the wheel.
Crying had crossed my mind again, but as noted, the rising sun
was giving me strength or at least that's what it felt like.

People would start driving on Jones soon, I figured. I
did have my doubts though; the bridge over Hiker was pretty
small, the creek only stretched like sixteen feet wide. My own
hope was someone seeing the rip in the bridges side guard or
maybe even see my car if they bothered to look out by the
bridge.

While practically praying for it to be over with, a soft
sound made me jolt and snatched my attention. Sticks were
being broken underneath what could be human feet. It
sounded just as nearby as earlier in the morning but normal
sounding and not *yet* menacing. I awaited to hear further steps
to be taken in my direction and when I did, I was hesitant and
afraid.

What was I going to do if it was the same thing I heard
before I blacked out? Just trying to get me to speak up so it
can reveal its true beastly self and devour me?

Right…left…right…

"Hello?" a man spoke.

My heart, while still upside down with the rest of my
body, jumped into my shoes when I heard his voice for the
first time.

"Yes! Hello!" I screamed. "I'm in here! I don't seem to be hurt but I've been in here all night! Can you please get me out or call somebody!"

Abnormally, there was no reply at first. Then he chimed back in like he had forgot he was even talking to someone.

"Oh, ha-ha, yeah. I can help you. What's your name, honey?"

"Kylee Richter."

Again, there was a long pause in our conversation.

"Hello?" I called back.

The silence dragged on and by the time he did speak back, I was close to thinking I was imagining his voice being there.

He actually returned with a laugh prior to talking.

"Yeah, I'm here, Ky. Don't worry."

It went right over my head then but I'm certain I'm quoting him accurately. The man outside the car saying *my* family\friend nickname gave me the feeling I knew him, or maybe he knew my family, which wasn't impossible if he was from the area. It was even kind of likely he did know me if that was the case.

His voice was friendly and had a touch of the country in it, he definitely sounded like anybody else from Dillton. The whole Midwest tone and slang was hard to detach yourself from if you grew up here and its easy as hell to hear it in somebody's voice. In the car, I couldn't decipher his age, but he wasn't too assertive like most grown men around Indiana like to be, he was more suggestive and supportive sounding.

"You say you're not banged up in there? You must be one lucky gal then, considering I've seen multiple bodies pulled out of wrecks in comfier positions than your car is in."

"I don't feel so lucky right now but I'm glad I'm alive. Have you called someone? Or could you get me out of here? I've been like this for so long I can't feel my arms!"

Another lull in conversation came from the man. Every time he did so I would get annoyed passed my limits. I didn't even bother calling out this time and I just waited for him to make his next move. I also thought he could be calling someone at any moment he wasn't speaking to me.

Waiting, I noticed the sun was starting to spread faster and brighter than before. From what I could see of the sky in my bent side mirrors, it was becoming blue and there were very few clouds. I predicted it to be a hot day with a small breeze. The day was assured to be absolutely beautiful from how I pictured it. I remember somewhat bargaining with God that if I got to live past that day, and continued on to have another chance at a different sunny day, I would never take drugs again. And as one could tell, I did get the day I asked for plus more, and I also kept my end of the bargain too.

During my admiring of the incoming day light, a foot dressed in a brown sandal stepped directly in my view. The shoe was Velcro strapped to an ordinary sized male foot but longer toenails than most.

"I'm comin' in there to unstrap you and getcha' out myself, all right? Try and get ready for me," he said while I tried to look up at his face, but was only able to see his foot.

On board with anything at this point, I agreed and anticipated my rescue.

***

Dillton, not unlike other small towns, has a tight community. Gas stations, grocery stores, and school events are constantly attended by mutual friends and even some family. It's truly difficult to not be recognized if a native goes into town. Everybody notices everybody, at least once. With that being said, when I got to see the man who pulled me out of my totaled car at five in the morning under a local bridge, I knew right off the bat I had never seen him a day in my life beforehand.

He looked to be the age of retirement, or he was just sneaking up on it. Not a large man by any means, though he was taller than me and stood with great posture that displayed some sort of confidence. His voice also sounded sure of himself but when looking at him while he spoke, it was the type of confidence that could be mistaken for charm.

"You sure you feel okay?" he said to me once I got to my feet, looking directly into my eyes.

His were a dusty green that assumingly were much brighter and clearer in his youth. Not to say he was brittle or a walking antique, because he didn't really come off that way. He seemed active in his everyday life and possibly even worked out to some degree. All in all, he gave off a look that he was in pretty good shape for his age.

To go with the sandals, he had khaki shorts on, and a vibrant red short sleeved shirt buttoned all the way to the top of his chest. The outfit was clean, lacking wrinkles, stains or tears in the clothing and it was complete by a grey John Deere hat that looked just as old as me.

I didn't say much when he first spoke to me once I got out of the car. Not only was I checking the man out, but I was still so downright astounded I was alive and even more amazed by the fact that like my car, there wasn't really any glaring damage on me. The feeling in my arms took a while to recover but it did before I started being more social toward him.

"Thank you so much for being here and getting me out. I honestly thought I was done for," I praised him as he circled my dead car.

Starting to become something like a signature around this time, he chuckled before replying to me. "Oh, no problem, dear. It was on my way."

That made me smile. "What's your name anyway?"

He replied swiftly but not with an answer to my question, but with his own. "Did you grow up here?"

"In Dillton?"

"In America."

It was as if I didn't comprehend his question.

In America? Clearly, I had. I didn't look like I could be from anywhere else as far as I knew, and I surely didn't have a foreign accent. The only thing I could think to do from his bizarre question was to stay silent while he looked for his answer.

"Never mind. We have to get you out of here, girl!"

I nodded back to him and assumed he meant by the ambulance or police that were on their way. Police potentially arriving did scare me though since they would probably have to investigate why I crashed, but after it was all said and done, I faced no sort of legal trouble for my actions.

Watching my surroundings brighten from the sun, I thought I would be hearing the sirens at any second. Although, they never blared, we sat there with only the frogs and crickets cussing while he evaluated my car and occasionally turned his head to smile at me.

"Alright, let's get goin'."

Entirely bewildered, I looked up at him with curious eyes. "What do you mean?"

"I'm going to get you out of here, just follow me."

"Wait, wait, where are you taking me?"

"Well don't make it sound like I'm kidnapping you now." He smiled. His voice was still so calm and strangely persuasive, he talked so matter-of-fact like. As if he did this kind of thing often.

"I don't know if I should. I don't understand wh-"

"Hey, kid, just trust me, and everything will be perfectly perfect again, okay? This is a hell of an accident you got yourself in and you're in shock, I get it. But just follow me and I'll work everything out."

I had no clue what he was talking about, or where he wanted me to go but I was beginning to trust him for unknown reasons. So, I followed him as he led the way down Hiker Creek.

***

Mr. Noname didn't speak while he led the way, but he did stroll with a soft whistle. When I first heard the tune, it didn't sound familiar to me, though now I can't get it out of my head.

The song gave off a tone that was dreamy and subtly melancholic like most old rock n roll songs from the 50s. Sometimes when I'm spacing out or just relaxing, I'll catch myself whistling it the way he did.

The sun was becoming more obvious than ever, shining beams of its light in between trees on the right side of Hiker, but not much of its shine got through. The creek was similar to how I remembered with its cool and generous shade. I could still feel the warmth coming in even with the shade, but it was just enough for it to be soothing. Despite the circumstances, it was sort of nice for a moment to take a hike down memory creek.

As the night transformed into the morning, the more I started thinking for myself, the shock was fading.

What the hell am I doing? I asked myself. *I have no idea who this is.*

He *did* save me though. I was out of the car *because* of him, and I was extremely appreciative about that. But *where was he taking me?*

I bit my tongue on that question, even though I was becoming more resistant the further we traveled down the creek.

On the walk, I hardly saw any water or puddles, but the weeds seemed to have no issue growing in its absence. All kinds of them covered the dirt in patches and some were tall enough to poke up my legs— or worse, what my legs lead up to. Small athletic shorts weren't the best choice of outfit for my journey but then again, it was an accident that started it all.

As much as the weeds were awful to walk through, they weren't everywhere and every once in a while, there would be nothing bothering or touching my legs at all.

I should have spoken up then.

Eventually, we came across a large part of the creek covered with these huge and leafless bushes. Instead of being puffy with bright green color, they were just branches coated with black thorns that looked like decaying teeth from a small shark. I have never seen any plant like it. Most plants symbolize life or love in one way or another but the plants that were ahead of me, looked to symbolize death or pain.

I couldn't believe my eyes when Noname started to walk right into it. And crazier than that, I couldn't help but follow.

Instantly they punctured my legs and arms, no matter how much I tried to maneuver around the thorns. Him on the other hand, his pace didn't stutter. He kept his head up and his whistling still blowing.

My patience faded and was long gone. "Hey, where are we going, dude? Is this really necessary?"

He didn't even stop whistling. That did it for me and I know that for others reading this, it'll be a no brainer, but I finally realized that none of this made *any* sense.

"Alright, fuck this." I stopped about a quarter of the way into the field. Noname kept going forward.

"Hello? Are you fucking with me? Where are you trying to take me?" I was beyond frustrated, confused, and scared while I spoke this, and I just wanted to be done with it and out of the creek for good.

It was like I wasn't there with him. He didn't give me the smallest signal to figure if he was listening or not. So, I took matters into my own hands, and turned around.

That got his attention, and he evidently didn't take my abandonment well.

"Where do ya think you're goin'?" he said, but in a tone beyond different from before. Now, he sounded angry, and his voice was starting to get raspy as if he suddenly developed a sore throat. "Ky, it would be best for you to come with me. So, keep walking. Right fucking now, girl!" he yelled.

"No," I confidently said to him once I turned to him again. "I'm not going with you anymore! We've been walking for at least a mile and you haven't said anything to me about where we are going, what the plan is, or even your name!" I turned back around. "Thanks for getting me out of the car. I'm going back to the road now so I can flag someone down. Goodbye."

A wild sharp pain came upon my entire right leg. I looked down and right before I saw them squeeze, I saw that the thorns were constricting up my right leg like pythons with an agenda.

In no time it spread to my other leg and wrist to stop me from swinging my arms. Thick amounts of blood leaked from where the thorns stabbed me and louder than I ever did in the car, I bellowed.

My screams were high pitched, powerful, and as genuine as could be. When I think about the worst pain I've ever experienced, I still think of those thorns and when I think about the most scared that I've ever been, I don't think about when I woke up trapped in a flipped car. No, every time that fear is brought into my head, I think of how Noname looked when I looked back up, and how he looked at me.

Looking like his skin was melting or sticking to his bones, his face began to resemble a skeleton with only a wax paper thin layer of skin on him. He looked at me and he smiled without showing his teeth, but I could still see them through his skin. His green eyes were swelling as well, and there were large dark bags under his eyes, the kind someone would get from lack of sleep or taking a downer drug like opium or *Xanax*.

"You can't go anywhere but with me," he said in a voice much raspier than before. His hat fell off when he stepped toward me in the sea of thorns and some dark hair that was underneath shed off with it. The top of his bald head was bumpy or spiky, and as if he still had a head of hair, he ran his hand over the top of it. His fingernails were now long like his toe nails.

He got face to face with me, put his index fingernail to my chin and pointed my head up to his.

"Listen to me and make no mistake, whore. *You* belong to me now. The life *you* lived and the world *you* inhabited have expired." His smile returned but this time he showed teeth, broken, dirty, and unhuman like.

"Your heart, your mind, your cunt, and your soul are all my possessions now, for I am your destination and fate, and *you* have arrived." He went in as if he were going to kiss me and I had no choice but to watch him get closer. So, I closed my eyes.

Suddenly, another voice spoke to me, but it sounded above, and it was a woman's voice. "*Hey*! Are you awake down there? Help is on the way!"

I opened my eyes to see I was in my car again. Upside down once more with my arms and hair dangling. Everything wasn't the same as before though, the sun was completely out and there was glass and blood everywhere. My car—even from the inside—looked demolished. Was I bleeding? Yes, and a lot. My nose, my eyebrows, and my lip all had gashes but there was still a lot more blood to be accounted for; it couldn't have all came from my face. Finally, I heard the sirens coming and I whined with them then passed out.

***

No question that I wasn't quite as unharmed as I once believed. It turns out I suffered four shattered thoracic vertebrae in my back that night and the surgery was just a little over six hours. I still consider myself lucky to be alive and the doctors, EMTs, and my family considered that as well.

My therapist, Dr. Langoria, told me it would be good for me to talk about my accident to others. '*To release myself from that creek*,' he says. Like a big slap in the face though, no one listens to my story. They don't buy it for one second. I can tell by their faces when I start talking about the footsteps growing huge or when I bring up Noname.

Although, they don't tell me I'm wrong, they just suggest the following, "The Xanax was making you have bizarre stressed induced dreams." Or "When you broke your back, you went into so much shock that you made up a dream or fantasy in your head to escape the pain while still being trapped."

Bullshit. He was there, I remember him vividly and when I go out into town, I'm afraid I'll run into him sometimes. The version I had first seen of him, not the second. I don't miss him or anything, but I guess I just want to be assured it wasn't just my imagination like the doctors or my parents say.

But it really doesn't matter what they say, because I know the truth. I don't know how I ended back in the car, but I know I got out before they got me out.

And when I look down to my wrist or my ankles and admire the scars the thorns left, it gives me closure.

Off the Trail

The night had been tedious, smoky, and strangely hot. It was cooler by the water, but humidity still hung around in the air, just like the smoke from all the fireworks did. Festivities of the fourth were simmering down now and the women of the Baker family were grateful for that. All the Baker men and boys, however, were wanting to ride out the night longer. Some drunk, others wanting to get in some trouble, but one Baker boy in particular, wanted nothing more than to just play.

They were a large, combined family rooting off a single mother and her two sons, Alan and Aaron Baker. As boys typically do, they grew up to be men and eventually found wives, and had their own children. Aaron was the first to make Carol Baker a grandmother when his wife, Anna, gave birth to a little girl. They named her Zoe.

A full year went by before Carol gained yet another grand baby, and after that, she was blessed with two more just like it within a four-year period. Alan, the eldest Baker brother and his wife had three boys. All about a year apart from each other. Their names were—from oldest to youngest—Tyler, Skylar, and Dakota.

Then, four years went by and one more baby was brought into the family, on Aarons side. When Zoe was eight years old her parents had Zane. The youngest Baker to date.

(2)

The woodland trail from their campsite to the docks was treacherously steep and narrow. Her walk down it with the rest of her cousins frazzled Zoe. The ongoing cramps she had been experiencing made matters that much more awful. The challenges weren't just defined with her cramps, though, she also had to carry her little brother down the trail. Zoe's mother had insisted she do this because she feared Zane would stumble into some poison ivy that potentially could be off the trail.

Whenever she was told that order from her mom, Zoe had been at the pinnacle of bratty. The young woman fussed and thought about cussing at her mom. *Why can't he just go down with you or dad? Or Aunt Leah or Uncle Alan? This is not fair!* Anna Baker was persistent, though. She told her Zane was fussing himself about going down with all of his cousins and his big sister. And after some slams and stomps with some grunts, Zoe ended up accepting the duty.

But that was hours ago from the current scene. The sun had expired, and hundreds of fireworks had been lit off since then. She also wound-up watching Zane the whole entire night. Which was understandable to her, and in addition, she didn't really care for fireworks anyway. She thought someone might consider it to be "unamerican" but her insight was that the fourth was just a money grab holiday. Items that are so cheaply produced and then sold at five times the value to the nearest redneck. Like her uncle, Alan, who had spent a startling $450.00 on fireworks this year.

Zoe also didn't complain about watching her little brother because it was obvious that she was the only one who could. Her father and uncle were drunk, lighting off the big fireworks at a safe distance away from where the girls and Zane were. Her mother was half drunk herself and Aunt Leah, after getting sick after some drinks, had been half asleep in a lawn chair for hours.

Grandma was also planted in a lawn chair, holding a low lidded stare at the lake. She looked like she was about to pass out right there, even with the fireworks being shot off not too far from her. Zoe knew she wanted to go back to the camper—the girl's camper—and end the night and she presumed her grandmother shared that same desire. Grandma Carol's camper would be so cold by now with its running A/C and there was plenty of room for all of them. And by all of them, she meant her mom, grandma, and aunt. The guys had one large tent just outside the camper. She wasn't sure who had the idea of letting the girls have the camper and the boys have a tent but if she had to guess, she thought it was probably Uncle Alans's idea, or maybe Grandma's.

Therefore, Zoe was the only one fit to watch Zane. Her cousins weren't even in question. There was no way her mother, or herself for that matter, could trust those dill-holes to watch her little brother, no matter how bad Zane actually wanted to be with his cousins. She understood of course, he just wanted to spend time with other boys, but it wasn't happening on her watch.

Uncle Alan's boys were a troublesome and annoying group of boys in Zoe's eyes. They made messes with even the simplest things, always said idiotic and gross boy things, and to top it off, they smelt almost constantly. Zoe was absolutely not going to let her brother transform into that type of boy when he got older. Keeping Zane by her side was ideal, really.

But, man, was she terribly exhausted and even more tired than she was directly after the walk down the trail. Her legs felt sore, her eyes weighed heavy, and yawning was occurring for her about every five minutes. *Can we get this over with?* she thought to herself. Her father and uncle were still lighting fireworks with her cousins watching. Zane was watching as well, but next to her and the other girls.

Then Zoe suddenly heard the back of her family's SUV open, and she felt happier than she had all day, maybe it was time to leave, she suspected. When Zoe looked over, she saw her grandmother and aunt were now standing and her mother was holding the lawn chairs they were just in. Anna Baker then threw the chairs in the back then slammed the back door down before walking over to her kids.

"Do you want a shower, hon?" her mother asked.

(3)

"I'm thinking about driving us to the shower house and leaving your father here," Anna added through a yawn after she stretched her arms toward the night sky. "My guess is that he'll want to stay here with Uncle Alan anyway, so."

"What, mom?" Zoe replied, stepping closer to her mother, and leaning her head forward so she could hear over the final firecrackers of the night being shot off. Her least favorite firework, especially at this precise moment.

"Do you want a shower, Zoe? Are you okay? Just tired?" She brushed a piece of loose blonde hair behind her daughter's ear.

"Yeah, I'm fine. I'm just really beat is all." Looking not at Anna but at Zane, who was apparently astonished by the last sparkler of this year's fourth.

"Thanks for watching him all night, Zoe. You're the best big sister anyone could ever ask for," Anna said as she shared her daughter's view. "How are you feeling with your cramps, though? Did the cranberry juice help at all?"

"I guess," she shrugged, but being her mother, Anna knew that meant *not really*.

"So, a shower then? Yeah?"

"Sure, Mom. That sounds kind of nice actually. Is there hot water at the shower house."

"There fuckin better be." Anna giggled. She was never really fond of cursing in front of her children, but she had been drinking a little tonight and she felt good and additionally, so what? Zoe would be thirteen this year and Zane would be six. *Damn,* she thought, *where did my babies go?*

"Let me go ask around and see if anybody else is interested in a shower."

Zoe nodded and stuck her attention back on her little brother.

Anna turned her back to her kids then flip flopped across the concrete parking lot of the docks to where her husband and his brother were putting on a drunken pyro show. Alan's sons moved closer to the water almost as soon as she started to approach their area. They looked like they were up to no good, but nothing was new there, except for the roman candle they were holding.

The father of the obnoxious little boys was polishing off another Budweiser by the time she got to conversation distance. Probably his seventh or eighth one, she assumed. He was always drinking, even when she had first met him when Aaron took her home to meet his family and he was only twenty at that time. Back then, Alan was handsome like Aaron and quite fit with a whole head of abundant black hair. Now a days, he had a bloated appearance and had lost most of his hair on top. She couldn't be sure if it was the drinking that had made him age so much faster or if it was his sons.

Her husband, drunk, but not as bad as Alan, was obviously looking for something in his brother's truck when she approached him.

"Aaron?" she called while his head was all the way down behind the passenger seat.

"Huh? What?" He popped his head up and saw Anna. "Oh, hey, babe!"

"What are you doing, Captain? Whatcha looking for?"

"Oh, um, it's called the Bonfire cracker," he slurred, trying to keep eye contact with her but couldn't help himself from searching still.

"The what?" she questioned.

"The bonfire cracker. It's a firework that Alan bought. We can't find it and I freakin know! I know! I know we didn't shoot it off!"

"Well, just keep on searching and I'm sure you'll find it." Though, she really didn't believe that. It was likely they did light it off already and they had just forgotten. They lit off so many tonight that it wasn't impossible to miss.

"Hey." Anna placed her hands on his defined chin and guided his head in her direction. She kissed him in a sort of aggressive but lustful way. The wine coolers she had indulged in the night had her feeling a bit frisky. "You taste like whiskey and Budweiser. And I kind of like it," she added, just an inch or two from Aaron's face.

"Oh yeah? What else do you like?" His hands slid down to her hips and then went up underneath her shirt, just on her nude sides. "It's a shame that only the girls get to use mom's camper because I would kill to have you to myself tonight."

Her grin was huge, and she couldn't help but let out a schoolgirl giggle due to her husband's smooth talking. "Well, too bad, Mr. Baker. You'll have to wait until we return to the windy city for that."

"What about the shower house?" he suggested.

"Oh, you mean the public shower house? Get real, Aaron." She pushed him off by his forehead using her fingers. "Speaking of that, though, I'm taking the car up to there for a shower run. Do you want a shower? Any of the guys you think?"

"Nah, babe. I'm fine but if I want one, I'll go up there myself. And as for the others, I wouldn't even bother with asking. You know how Alan and his boys love their Kansas funk on them.

"Noted," she finished, then walked away from him after giving him one more peck on the lips.

Returning to where she was before and within mind to leave as soon as she did, Anna was stopped by her brother-in-law when he heavily slurred her name. It sounded more like "Hanna."

"Yes, Alan?"

"You girls going back to site?" He burped on the last part.

"Eventually, but first we're going to the shower house to clean up. You ever considered that?"

"Not once," he laughed. "But do you think you could take my boys up with you guys? I'm pretty toasty and only going to get worse tonight so I don't think I can actually be held responsible for these shits."

"Your shits," she corrected.

"At least that's what she tells me." He smirked and pulled a cigarette from his quickly lessening pack.

Anna chose to ignore that. She liked Leah. Despite her boys being rather rowdy and not the cleanest group of boys, she was a good mother and humble at that. And considering what she had to deal with daily, Anna felt for her sister-in-law. Leah was also having a pretty rough night with getting sick earlier from the tequila shots they had taken. Although, Anna had only one shot and called quits, Leah, on the other hand, busted at six then puked in the lake. *Poor mama. Don't you know tequila isn't for us anymore?*

"Yeah, I'll take them up there, Al. Just don't light my husband on fire tonight, please."

He returned a wide and yellow smile. "Thank you. And I'll see what I can do."

(4)

Tyler Baker saw his aunt Anna walking toward where they were and quickly aborted his idea to steal a beer from his father's cooler. There was no real way she could have known what him and his brothers were up to, but he still felt like he was caught red handed.

The three brothers stood by the water after they had just shot off their last roman candle. The initial plan was to save it for after the beer but when their aunt went by the cooler and their dad's pick up, they immediately went to work on the candle to seem like they were just hanging out. And certainly not planning to steal a beer or two and maybe a cigarette if they could get their hands on the pack.

"Fuckin bitch," Tyler said to Skylar and Dakota when he saw her go up to their dad.

"How does she know?" Dakota asked. "Dad is going to fuckin kill us!"

"Shut up. We didn't do shit, and she doesn't know shit anyway," Tyler rapidly said. "She is just being nosey and bossy as usual."

Alan Baker's three sons didn't really care for their much more city accustomed Aunt Anna and the same feeling went for their future-bitch Cousin, Zoe who practically ignored them at all costs. Uncle Aaron was always cool but of course he was. He was a small-town kid too once. Just like their father and grandmother, Kansas born and raised. Although, his wife, was almost the complete opposite. A pretty city girl who latched on to their uncle and moved him to her world. She typically had something sour to say about their truck, their house, or even just the way Tyler and his brothers looked or smelt.

Tyler and his brothers have never been up to Chicago to visit, and he wasn't sure if it was because his dad just didn't want to or if it was Aunt anna not inviting them in the first place. Either way, the boys weren't hurt by it, they didn't want to go up there anyway. Why would they? A bunch of city snobs as far as he was concerned.

"Oh shit, she's walking over to us," Tyler muttered.

"Be cool."

"Hey boys." Aunt Anna asked, in a tone that sounded like she knew they were up to no good.

"Hey Aunt Anna," they said in unison.

"Your dad told me to take you guys to the campsite. Well, actually the shower house first to take a sh— "

"I don't want a shower," Tyler spoke up.

"Trust me, I could have predicted that, but I told your dad I would take you guys and it was his idea in the first place," Anna snapped back. They hated that a shower was being forced on them and that their night was coming to an end already but Tyler and the other two knew there were no point in arguing with what dad wanted. Especially when he's been drinking, which was pretty much all the time.

"Alright, so let's go, boys."

(5)

Where the hell did my lighter go? Alan frisked his own shorts. "Aaron!" he shouted.

The cab light was on in his truck, and he gave a drunk effort jog to get there. "Hey! Asshole, where's my lighter at?"

Aaron had just shut the door with both of his hands full right as his older brother approached. He had Alan's yellow lighter in his left hand and in the other hand, he was bearing a large green box with a black wick sticking out. Red and orange flame designs started from the bottom and were under huge font reading, "BONFIRE-CRACKER."

"You fuckin found it! Nice!" Alan laughed upwards.

"Yeah, it was near the back seat underneath a bunch of towels from earlier. Should be good still though, doesn't seem all that wet." He led back to the "Fire zone" as they referred to it earlier when the festivities began. "Is there any beer left?"

Alan followed his lead, plucking his cigarette in his mouth. "Most definitely, little brother. I stocked the fuck up before heading out." He went to his cooler nearby and pulled out two beers, one for himself and one for Aaron. "Now give me my lighter, dick."

His younger, more distinguished but drunk all the same brother tossed the lighter at Alan's chest. The BIC lighter thumped his chest, then fell to the floor right after. "Nice catch, Coach. Also, you shouldn't curse in front of your sons so much. They'll take that with them to school in the fall, you know."

"First of all," he said in an achy voice when he bent over to retrieve the lighter from the concrete and then stood straight with the lighter's flame already active. He sparked his slightly bent smoke before he continued his sentence. "Your pretty little city wife just took em' up to the shower house then they're all going back to the site and second of all, eat shit."

Aaron jolted his head toward where he last saw his three nephews and his brother was right. They were gone with only a burnt roman candle sitting where they were standing before. *Maybe the little slobs wanted to bathe for the first time,* he thought and let a smile out because of it.

"Oh, that's good, though. Now that the kids are all out of sight, there is nothing to keep us from getting shitfaced." He finally cracked his beer open, as did his older brother.

"Was never going to stop me, anyway."

"Really? I hadn't noticed," Aaron said in an undoubtedly sarcastic tone. "Let me see your lighter again, drunk." He bent down to where he sat the big green box with a wick.

'No, no, no, let's not light it right now. That'll be the main event. We'll do it a little later. When the rest of the family has left, and other people have cleared out too," Alan decided.

"Sure thing, boss. You bought the damn thing."

Alan smirked as smoke flowed out of his nose. He then took a heavy swig of his beer and put his lighter rightfully back in his pocket.

(6)

The SUVS metal exterior was still warm from baking in the sun all day. Carol Baker found it oddly soothing enough to close her eyes as she leaned her back on the passenger side door. Her daughter In-law, Anna, set off to tell her husband (Carol's son) they were going up to the shower house and when she ventured off, she forgot to give the keys to Carol or at least unlock the damn doors. Carol figured and hoped she would be back soon, the mother of two and grandmother of five was exhausted and ready to be done with a shower and enjoy the chill of her camper's A/C for the rest of the night.

While one daughter in-law conversed with Carol's drunk sons, the other was sitting right next to her in front of one of the SUV's front tires. Her head depending on her arms while they rested on her knees, remaining perfectly still with a puddle of drool under where her head was. Poor thing has been just about lifeless ever since the shots came back up. From a jealous standpoint, Carol did find humor that the girl who only had a few shots of tequila was already asleep and not the old woman or the new woman who had been taking care of her restless little brother all day and night.

Nevertheless, she did have empathy for Leah, and they were all on the same page anyway. *Finish the night up.*

"Grandma, grandma, are you asleep, grandma?" a voice said from below her.

Prying her relaxed eyes open, she saw him staring up at her. Zane, with his *SPACE JAM* T-shirt on and his tiny hands cupped by his belly. His hair was still blond but it was clearly getting darker as he got older and it just made his blue eyes seem even more bright. That was the Baker in him and just about the rest of the family had them too, but Zane's were different. They were seemingly more vibrant and sharper, full of life and they made you think that the child himself was fully and purely innocent.

"No, honey. I'm not asleep. Yet, anyway, if your momma doesn't hurry up."

"Oh, where are you guys goin?"

"We are all going to the shower house, stinky. Didn't your mom tell you or Zoe that?" She took her weight off the vehicle and stood straight up.

"Momma didn't tell me anything, Grandma. Zoe didn't too. She never ever tells me anything. She thinks I'm just a baby."

"Hm, are you a big kid then, Zaney?"

"Mhm! Yes, I am a big kid, and I don't want to shower tonight either. I just want to go back to the campsite."

You and I both, hon, Carol mentally agreed.

"But I think we are all going. Where is your sissy?"

"Sissy is on the other side of the car." He pointed straight ahead. "And not uh, Grandma. Kota, Tyler and Skylar won't go. I know it," Zane said, looking up at his beloved elder with a stern look on his face, displaying just how serious he was. "So, will you come back to the campsite with us, so we all don't *have* to go take a shower. Please, Grandma, *pweaseee.*" At the last of his proposal, he squinted his blue eyes shut and put on a massive smile while his cupped hands shifted in a praying form.

Carol couldn't resist laughing. He looked so much like Aaron when he was that age, just with lighter hair instead and his persuading was even the same. Almost as if they were making a birthday wish before blowing out the candles, they would close their eyes tight and shine their smile. Sometimes it worked for Aaron back then and she was sure Zane had gotten his way from it before too.

She ended her laughter with a sigh and once she opened her own eyes, Zane's smile had flipped, and he already looked disappointed. An answer hadn't been given yet, but she could gather that Zane took her laughing as a no. Which to him, it meant he would have to go to the shower house and not even with the boys, he would have to go with the girls so his mom could wash him properly. Part of Carol believed that may be for the best. To let Zane's mother have her way and end the night on her own terms, it was less complicated like that. *Everyone gets a shower then everyone goes to bed.* But another part of Carol understood her youngest grandchild's point of view all too well. A boy who is constantly smothered and supervised by the women in his life, practically chained to his older and strict sister all night, Zane very clearly just wanted some guy time. To be one of the boys finally, at least for a night and hang out or play with his cousins.

Then, as soon as she heard her other grandsons approach their area with the griping of their forced shower with Anna leading the pack, Carol decided to make Zane's night and perhaps his whole fourth of July.

"Hey, Anna," Carol said, exactly as Anna pulled the keys from her jean short's pockets.

Anna faced Carol almost instantly. "What's up?"

"I think I'm going to skip out on the shower run tonight," she said and nearby, Zane was listening and created a smile bigger than his persuading one. "I was thinking I would just take all the boys back to the campsite considering how bad they don't want to go."

"Yes!" Tyler and Zane both expressed their excitement at the same time. They traded a look before focusing back in on the grown-up's conversation.

Anna looked toward her exclaiming son and nephew then looked back at her mother in-law. "Really? Are you sure?"

"One hundred percent. You girls take the truck up to the showers and the boys and I will take the trail back to camp."

"If you say so, Mom," she said bending over and continued to shake Leah by her shoulders. "Get up, sister. Time to clean up before bed." Leah's head slowly came up with half open eyes. When Anna helped her to her feet by her arm, she slurred her words like her husband did earlier. Carol was pretty sure she said, "About fuckin time."

Zoe, who had been eavesdropping from the other side of the SUV, came around and tried to clear things up for herself. "Wait, so Grandma is going to watch Zane while we are at the showers?"

Visually warmed with her daughter's constant concern for her little brother, Anna smiled at her and laughed. "Yes, Zo. You can have some time off. I'm sure Grandma can handle it."

Carol swatted her hand at them both. "Of course, I can handle him and the other brats too. Hell, I changed all their diapers and their father's too." She placed her hands on her hips and she shot a gander at the boys then after, looked directly at her only granddaughter. "I got him, Zoe."

(7)

The moment the trash in their area was picked up, Anna, Leah, and Zoe all got in the SUV to head for the shower house. Right before Anna drove off with Zoe in the passenger side and the, again, unconscious Leah spread out across the back seats, she gave Carol a flashlight to hike up the trail with. The cautious mother also told her nephews to make sure to keep

Zane on the trail and keep him in the group. Basically, to watch him. Anna at first suggested Tyler carry him up the trail like how Zoe carried him down it but Zane spoke up and said he would be fine on his own feet. Though, to sooth his aunts' nerves, Dakota said he would keep Zane in front of him when they were on the trail.

At the entrance to the trail, Carol suggested to the boys that she should be behind the group as they walk and that meant that whoever was *brave* enough to lead them would hold the flashlight. About all the boys took that as a challenge when she emphasized about being brave enough, they bickered about it but not Zane. It then occurred to Carol that none of that mattered to him. It didn't matter where they were going, what they were doing or who was carrying the flashlight ahead of the group. The only thing that mattered to Zane was that he was there with them, finally able to be a part of the boys and their group, even if it was only for the forty minutes Anna said they would be gone.

Tyler was handed the flashlight and swung the beam of light toward the trees, then all five began their hike into the woods that held the trail to camp.

(8)

During the day, Carol had made her way down to the lakeside by vehicle. It took around ten minutes to get there in the SUV and by the time they arrived at the docks, the kids had already made it there through the trail. When Anna asked Zoe how the trail was, she vaguely said it was really steep but not too long. With that in mind, Carol expected the trail to be, well, a walk in the park. Halfway into the hike, she realized she had been way off.

Tyler evidently didn't consider the others while leading by how he was scaling up the steppingstones at a quick pace. That's what gave him the major lead on Carol who had been about a school buses length behind the flashlight. She could see Dakota had kept his word on keeping Zane in front of him, guiding him along the way and ahead of them by a few yards were Tyler and Skylar practically racing up the hill. At the height of their distance from her, Carol was guessing where she was stepping and sometimes, she would stumble into the plant life on the outside of the trail. The poison ivy or oak Anna had mentioned when Zoe carried Zane down didn't trouble her before, but now, she was really wanting Anna to be full of shit.

She was a spry elderly woman, no doubt, but the trail had still tested her limits. Sweat dampened her wrinkled forehead and her legs felt tighter than they had in what seemed to be eons and catching her breath at the moment was as difficult as starting a fire in forty-five mph winds.

Carol was just barely able to keep up with the boys enough to see them exit the trail and the woods. Dakota was the last to leave but even he had a considerable lead in front of her at his exit. Behind her was the last of the uphill stretch and now it was only level ground with a couple more yards to the end of the trail. She could see her campers outdoor light shining through the trees, just like a star peeking through the galaxy.

Fearing that her legs may give out from under her, a break, she felt, was necessary and deserved. She stood in one spot with her shaking legs and attempted to catch her rapid breath. To aid and regulate her breathing, she started to admire her surroundings around the trail, though, there was almost nothing to see. Besides her bright and yellow camper light peeking through branches, everything else around her was scarcely visible. The combination of being out of breath, exhausted, and the absence of moonlight had diminished any sort of night vision she may have had. The trees just seemed to blend in with each other, creating a black wall that gave nothing to see. What she assumed were bushes with thorns, leaves with potential poison ivy, and smaller trees all appeared to be nothing but darker splotches on a dark canvas.

She heard crickets but detected no movement in any sense. All stood still outside the trail. That made Carol relax, and the crickets constantly chirping, motivated her to find a constant and regular breathing pattern. Within a couple of minutes, her legs quit trembling as well and currently, she felt ready to continue to the exit.

Steely, she took her first step forward and followed up with another. Her thighs felt stiff as a new mattress and her hips were starting to ache awfully. She desperately needed to take a seat, though she urged herself to go on. The determined grandmother kept taking lethargic steps as she knew her camper was only a baseball throw away and she could finally sit there.

Only, she came to a sudden halt when the crickets went quiet. Now there was silence to go with the stillness of the night. Something made her look toward her right once more and when she did, Carol was stricken with a fear so instant, that a bolt of lightning could have delivered it.

One of the large darker splotches moved, completely disturbing the stillness on the outside of the trail.

It didn't move far or fast, more like it just swayed to the right like it was stepping aside. Curiously trying to fix her eyes on what was before her in the dark, Carol definitely saw something lurking behind some bushes and right in the apparent poison ivy. She couldn't see an exact shape, but a figure was certainly there.

What the hell is that? she nervously thought.

It had to be around seven or eight feet in height, but she knew massive beast of that stature didn't inhabit in Kansas. While calculating what her next move was, what was near her and if she was in danger, she stayed just as still as everything around her once was.

Listlessly, it swayed again. This time to the left and then back to the right, but not closer. Just subtly moving enough to where it looked like it was getting comfortable. It kept its distance and went back to remaining still but now her eyes were more fixed on it more than ever.

It was a man.

Or she assumed it was a man. No woman could ever be that tall, Carol wasn't even sure a man could be besides Andre the giant and she wasn't willing to bet he was in town. Little relief came upon her with the discovery of it being a human rather than a life threating animal.

Questions then arose in her head about the gangling man in the poison ivy like lanterns in the sky at a memorial service.

What in God's name is he even doing out there? Is he just drunk from celebrating the fourth and stumbled into the woods? Should I help him find his way? Maybe he's just using the restroom in a very hidden place.

At first thought, she wanted to just forget it and walk away, but on second thought, Carol wanted to get to the bottom of this enigma. She attempted to clear her throat as it was painfully dry from the trail and her fear.

"Hello? Do I see someone out there?" she inquired; despite that she was pretty sure someone was out there, maybe looking right back at her as intensely as she stared.

There was no swaying or movement of any kind. Not one signal that someone was actually out there, besides what she now thought she saw. Now she wasn't so confident in her eyes these days, but still, when she really did focus her gaze, it looked like someone could be standing right there.

"Sir?" she called once more out of complete impulse.

Maybe my old peepers are just playing tricks on me, she narrowed it down. Carol looked toward her light again and resisted looking back on the outside of the dirt trail. Eventually, she forced her weary body to leave the woodland area and the paradox with it.

(9)

The boys were all sitting around an inactive firepit by the time Carol came shambling out of the woods. The only one concerned with the way she moved, and her well-being was Zane. The other boys were all too busy talking about a game they wanted for their *Play-station.* As full of wonder as Zane was, he asked his grandmother what had taken her so long. Carol only for a second wanted to tell him she thought she saw someone in the middle of the woods, but in the end, she figured that would be too heavy for a child of his age. She didn't want to terrify him to the point where he didn't want to be outside or return to a lake ever again because of what his ancient grandmother might have seen. Her real answer was simply, "I'm an old fart."

Her comedic reply made all the boys laugh, but not Tyler. He smiled just a little, though, resisting the urge to laugh. He was in the adolescent stage and kiddie jokes like that weren't cool to crack up at anymore. At least, not to him. All he wanted these days was to be looked at as a teenager. In more ways than they realized—even though they were years apart in age—Zane and Tyler were in a more similar spot in life than they realized.

Tyler, who wanted recognition from his older peers in school and from the men in his life. And Zane, who wanted the older kids' recognition and to be accepted by the older boys around him, like Tyler for instance.

Carol didn't even consider sitting in the lawn chairs and continuing in the major humidity. The camper door was only two steps up the mini staircase that led to it and without a doubt, she knew the boys did not want to come in with her. Carol announced she would be going in and cooling down while she relaxed but also said the boys could stay outside the camper if they wanted—which they all did. The only thing she stressed was that they stay on the campsite and don't go too far. The boys loved this, and they swore to their grandma they wouldn't wonder off.

The instant she opened her camper door, a gust of refreshing and frigid air rushed toward her. It not only felt heavenly but also mitigating in a physical sense when she stepped in and that cool air comforted her whole body, seemingly aiding her sore joints and muscles. She had been waiting for this all night and now, it was finally time.

Taking a massive load off, Carol sat down in her camper's booth and fell in love with how the leather seats felt on her fatigued back. Her large camper was dimly lit and that made her even more tired. Already it felt like sleep was only a steppingstone away and the idea sounded more than appealing but with everyone gone at the shower house and the boys unsupervised, she was needed awake. Even though they'd be back in about twenty minutes, she guessed.

Twenty minutes, she dwindled on the time. Not long at all.

All of a sudden, she was now contemplating sleep like she once contemplated the figure she saw off the trail. *He wasn't really there,* Carol reflected but sleep was, and it pulled at her hard. Harder than it was staying up earlier when she sat by the water and surprisingly harder than the hike up the trail was. And that had been difficult. Probably the most challenging obstacle she had overcome since her fifties, but everything was a challenge in these later years of her life. Getting out of bed, driving, swimming, walking and likely the most difficult, staying awake.

Her eyes closed as her chin fell to her chest at the booth. *Twenty minutes,* the grandmother lastly thought before she fell into a fast and heavy sleep.

(10)

Just as their grandmother slipped into a near involuntary sleep, Tyler, Skylar, Dakota and their little cousin, Zane all sat quiet while mosquitos aggravated every one of them.

"I cannot fucking stand these bastards," Tyler mentioned, breaking the silence.

Zane tried not to display it, but he was absolutely dumbfounded and a little uncomfortable by Tyler's language. He had never heard anybody close to his age curse openly like that or at all for that matter. His own dad hardly ever cursed and when he did, mom would get on him about it instantly.

"I know I can't stop swatting these fuckers," Skylar added.

Baffled by what he was hearing, Zane just stared at his older and looked up to cousins. *Do Uncle Alan and Aunt Leah let them talk like that? Or is that just how boys talk when they're hanging out? Should I be cussing too?*

Suddenly, as if God were giving him the signal to do so, a mosquito flew onto his smooth skin and without much thought, Zane swatted the bug and released a frequently heard cuss word.

"Shit!" his tiny child voice spoke.

All heads shot to Zane and there was a silence found. Then, that silence was shattered by a bellow of laughter.

"Jesus, Zane!" Tyler laughed with his brothers.

"I didn't expect you to say that at all!" another one mentioned.

Never in Zane's few years of life had he felt the kind of acceptance and appreciation that was now present in him until he heard his cousin's laughter from something *he* said.

He smiled probably bigger than ever and even blushed. *Is this it?* He reflected. *Is this what it feels like to be one the of boys?*

His parents without a doubt would have scolded and spanked Zane if they would have heard him use that kind of language. Zane himself didn't care for the language either, but his cousins did. And his parents weren't here.

"What do you guys want to do now?" Skylar asked the group, looking at all their faces.

"Well, there's not a lot we *can* do honestly. Grandma seemed pretty serious on us not leaving the site," Dakota said in a matter-of-fact kind of tone.

"We don't have to leave the campsite to do something, dipshit," Skylar shot back at him.

"Fuck you, Skylar."

"Fuck you, little bitch."

"Alright, both of you shut up," the eldest brother and eldest of the group butted in. He then turned to Zane directly. "What do you want to do, little cus?"

Me? He second guessed. *He's asking me?*

Zane didn't know what to say at first. He wasn't even sure what older kids liked to do or what would be the cool thing to say. *A game?* he wondered.

"Hide n seek?" he said as if it was a question and as soon as the words left his mouth, he regretted saying it. *Hide n seek? They're going to think that is so kiddy and stupid.* Though, before he had the chance to cover up his tracks, his cousins jumped out of their chairs with great enthusiasm.

"In the dark? Hell yeah, Zane. Kickass idea," Tyler said.

With that massive grin on again and excitement incorporated with pride, Zane stood too.

"Who's seeking first then?" Dakota inquired.

Just like any other game of hide n seek that started, no one really wanted to be the seeker first. Everyone wanted the chance to hide first. No one spoke up for a moment then Skylar volunteered reluctantly.

"Okay, so sit in one of the chairs and close your eyes then count to forty-five." Tyler instructed.

Skylar took his seat and started the count in a hurry. Tyler, in a flash, took off to the other side of their grandmothers' trailer and crawled under it. Zane felt an instant pressure when Skylar began to count. He looked around to see a hiding spot and when the seeker got to the count of ten, Zane decided he was going to hide behind a tree that was on their site, but he was stopped when Dakota insisted he should hide with him in their tent. Dakota didn't express it vocally, but he did so because he still felt obligated to keep Zane with him, to watch over him. Or Maybe he figured Zane couldn't find a decent hiding spot by himself. Whether it be the obligation or that he thought Zane was too little to think for himself, it made him angry, but he went with Kota anyway.

They were found right after Tyler and since he was found first, Tyler was the seeker for the next round.

Not without some curse words and kicks, Tyler went to a lawn chair and told the others he would start his count now. At the count of six, Dakota went to the tree Zane was going to hide behind in the first round and climbed it. At the count of eleven, Dakota told Zane that they should hide on the other side of the camper and move when Tyler came around, but Zane was quick to reject the idea and his cousins help.

"I don't want to hide with you. Let me find my own place to hide!" Zane said quietly but still aggressively. The cousin closest to his age just looked at him with surprised eyes and his mouth slightly open from what he said. The count was at twenty-five now and Dakota ran off to fulfill his hiding spot idea. Zane, on the other hand, looked to the trail they had come off of earlier. He had the perfect hiding spot.

The little boy set off into the woods and on the trail but not too far. Only a few steps in, about the length of his father's SUV. It was especially dark once he got on the trail, but he looked around anyway. His grandmother's camper light was still visible but not really giving him any light to see with.

"Forty-five! Alright. Ready or not! Here I come, dickies!"

Tyler would no doubt see him if he just stayed right in front of the entrance of the trail, therefore, Zane thought it would be better if he stepped a little off the trail to elude any chance of being found easily. He brushed by some plants with thorns that stuck to his shirt, but he pulled away easily. Zane was going to stand by the tall trees just a little farther back. Yet, he found one that wasn't as tall as the others and it was oddly thin even for a small tree but there was a bush in front to block him from being seen if the night wasn't enough to hide him in the first place. He couldn't see much himself, anything really, but that was a plus since that meant Tyler wouldn't be able to see either.

Zane stood silent off the trail, in front of the slim and bizarrely proportioned tree. Eventually, Tyler would give up his search for him when he found Dakota and Skylar but not Zane. His hiding spot was better than theirs and he knew it was. Sure, he broke some rules by stepping off the site, but they also break the rules by cursing. Isn't that what all boys do? Just break the rules when no one was around to enforce them? Zane was beginning to think so. And he wasn't far from the campsite. He could still see all of them if he looked through the trees at the right angle. Grandma or his parents or Zoe would never know, just like how they would never know he swore earlier.

Within a couple of minutes, he heard that Tyler found Dakota on the other side of the camper. He actually had to chase after him and tackle him to clarify that he found him so he wouldn't just go hide somewhere else. Dakota started to cry right after the tackle and said he wouldn't help him find Zane or their brother—who was still up high in the site's tree—and that he didn't want to play anymore.

More minutes passed and Tyler still hadn't found Skylar or Zane. No matter how close he was to their campsite, the five-year-old was beginning to get frightened of his surroundings. He was imagining that a bush near him was actually a monster on all fours just starring at him with his thorny tail and that some of the sticks he felt on the ground were actually boy-eating snakes who were waiting for him to come out so they could suffocate him. However, the most chilling one was the tree that was closest to him. Zane was only about a quarter of the size of the tree he stood in front of and above his head was one of its branches hanging down. It looked like a skinny arm with a long-fingered hand with pointy nails but no thumbs.

"Where you at, little boy?" he heard Tyler say walking around the campsite. Hearing his voice got Zane's mind off the wicked shapes around him and he stayed quiet with a smile.

"How about you, little bro? Where are you at, As—?" Tyler started but was cut off by an unexpected series of explosions.

The gran explosion came from the docks and shot up the sky then red and orange filled and lit the night and the earth below for a brief moment. It was so loud and sudden it made not only all the boys jump but also made Skylar fall out of the tree, break his forearm on a branch on the way down and broke it again in another spot when he hit the ground.

Regrettably, it was also so bright that it revealed that the tree above Zane wasn't even a tree at all.

It was something Zane couldn't even begin to fathom. Something with a long face and blank eyes and gapping mouth with atrocious, lengthy teeth that crossed paths from top to bottom. Despite its monstrous appearance it was wearing a plaid shirt with holes in it with some lazy pants on. Zane screamed loud but not as loud as Skylar screamed over his snapped arm. The ghoul snatched Zane by his small head and ran in between the trees at a swift pace with its long legs.

(11)

The women of the Baker family returned no more than five minutes later and were instantly stricken with urgency when they saw Skylar's arm twisted. His now more sober and awake mother and aunt put him in the car and immediately drove off to Lawrence Memorial hospital with his mother calming him down in the back.

With all of this going on no one really thought about Zane's location until Zoe brought it up. The authorities were called from the ranger's office and brought to the lake. The only thing they found that night was his tore *SPACE JAM* T-shirt and, in the morning, they found one of the boy's arms tore off from the shoulder with poison ivy beginning to surface.

August

A Gut feeling

A Cambridge County sheriff car is cruising through the night and away from town on Iowa 16. Inside the car is sheriff Cole Fletcher. A locally grown man to these parts, and beloved by most in addition to being cherished by his family, friends, and peers. On this particular hot August night, just a half hour before midnight but only at the beginning of his twelve-hour shift, Cole was bearing a swelling and jittery anxiety he had developed before leaving early for work. He was in no sort of trouble nor was there any shred of dreading the near future. Sheriff Fletcher was just nervous. Nervous to become a father.

Earlier, just as he was buttoning up his tan uniform in front of their bathroom mirror, Cole had unexpectedly heard his wife enter through the front door. "Babe?" she had called to him from the living room. Her voice sounded achy, like she was hurt. Confused to why she was home but not yet alarmed, he answered Sydney, "Yeah, Syd?" Cole then met his sickly-looking wife in the living room. "What's wrong?" he asked with his shirt still unbuttoned at the top.

Sydney had told him that she left work early because she wasn't feeling well. Though, when he asked what exactly she was feeling, her face lit up as if it were four years ago and he was on his knee proposing all over again. "I think I might be pregnant," she smiled.

Cole loved Sydney, perhaps more than anything else on the planet and he suspected that he would love their baby even more than that. However, the potential news had shook him. There was a strong doubt within him that said he wasn't ready, and he also doubted that Cambridge would be the ideal place for their child. He was loved in the entire county but growing up as the only black kid in an entirely white school

207

did have its issues. Issues he wished he had never gone through and issues he would never wish upon his own child, or anybody else's child for that matter. But Cole had risen above that just fine here and Sydney truly believed times have changed and their own kid would be perfectly sound in Holden, or Greenfield or even in Cambridge City.

And to her credit, she was probably right. He thought that to himself as the first few cars he had seen on 16 zoomed past him. The town of Holden and all of Cambridge County had been pretty good to him when he boiled it down. It was just in his early days or his grade school years that he remembered some things being said. Some by his classmates with their parents and some of his friends even and worst of them all, some *teachers*. Though, as he grew older, the prejudice nature of the county seemed to go away, and everyone accepted Cole just as they should have in the beginning.

That maybe was the reason Cole stayed in the county in the first place. Eventually, the county had made him feel safe and a part of something, therefore, he became a sheriff to give back to his community in some sort of way.

Since Cole had become a part of the County's law five years ago, he earned the reputation and title of "the good cop." Letting speeders go, only writing warnings, helping anybody who seemed like they needed even a hint of it. Everyone came to trust him and to put him on some sort of mental pedestal. The community even suggested him to coach the local REC baseball team this previous season. "The Ultimate Warriors," and Cole had a fantastic season and they ended it undefeated.

A lot of the local fathers credited Cole to their team's awesome season. Now whenever Cole does decide to pop over to Angel's—the pub in Holden—there was always about three of the guys sitting at the bar who had sons on Cole's team and they would buy him a beer or two. Or five.

Though, his dismay was still present. And it wasn't that he felt he couldn't afford a baby, because he could and it wasn't because he felt his relationship with Sydney wasn't strong enough, because it was. No, when Cole really started to narrow it down in his nervous head, he came up with a different reason. Maybe he wouldn't be a good father, because his wasn't.

Cole swiftly decided he no longer wanted to cruise with this on his mind right now. He felt distracted and driving usually made him think more deeply about things. He knew Village Creek Rd was coming up soon on his left and there would be some late-night folks speeding away from the turnpike on this late but still fresh Friday night.

Never before had Cole deliberately looked to pull someone over, but tonight, he needed the distraction from what was distracting him just moments ago. When the street sign came, he took a wide left onto Village Creek.

(2)

Along Village Creek Rd, about five to six miles from the turnpike stood a red barred fence separating the abundant meadows from the road. The property in which the fence was a part of, was owned by the bank and was vacant as far as Cole was concerned. With that in mind, he decided no one was going to care if a sheriff stationed his cruiser at the entrance of the gate.

He turned off his lights to not disturb or confuse the people who did occupy the nearby houses but kept the engine running with the radio at a low volume. If someone or something needed his attention and dispatch couldn't get ahold of him, the repercussions could stunt his income and with what might be coming in a little less than a year, less income would make things nervously more troubling.

Cole sat there for more than twenty minutes before he saw his first car drive past him. Nothing special, just a blue jeep that might have been speeding at first but then gave a predictable break check when they must have saw his car's reflectors. Still with a lot on his mind, he watched the jeep drive from the way Cole came. No need to ruin their night, he thought.

Too nice, his superior had noted toward him when he saw the few numbers of traffic stops Cole had last month. Cole had shrugged and smirked then gave the humorous excuse "July was a slow month, sir. Literally for the drivers of the county." His boss looked stern and disapproving at first then returned a smirk of his own before dismissing Cole.

Just like everyone else in Cambridge County, the whole department was behind Cole in everything. They accepted him with open arms instantly and it wasn't long until he was the most recognized and respected enforcers in all the county. Friends within the department were impressed as well as happy for him from the beginning. While stationed in front of the red gate, he remembered what Dale, a fellow sheriff and friend under Cambridge had said to him about three years ago. "Damn, Cole, I gotta tell yah, you're probably the most white-loved black man since O.J… and we all know how that ended up." The laughter they shared after Dale said that was hard to keep quiet and was one of those jokes that forced your core to hurt from laughing.

Even at the moment, Cole had to resist laughing from the three-year-old joke. "Just like O.J.," he chuckled a little to himself.

The former words from a friend had done well to distract Cole from his thoughts of being a father, and for a few moments, he didn't feel nervous anymore. Just happy and sooner rather than later, the sheriff was thinking of other things that made him smile. Football Sundays, which were just around the corner, the spring that held his birthday and his favorite time to fish, and his mother, who was in great health and had a long life ahead of her. And of course, Sydney. The perfect partner in his eyes with her fair, soft skin and round perky breast and thick thighs but also her personality with her wide sense of humor, her ability to always keep things new and her sweet motherly nature.

Cole felt as if he had stepped on his own shoelace from contradicting himself totally. *Then why are you so damn worried? She's as close to perfect as anybody could ever get*, he silently lectured to himself. One can only be distracted from the inevitable for so long, Cole shrugged.

Within the next ten minutes or so, three more cars drove by. The officer presumed they were following each other by the amount of people in each car and by how close together the cars traveled behind each other. The first car must have seen Cole early on from how they gave an early break check to bring their selves and the followers back to the speed limit. Cole pondered on pulling them over, maybe the last car in line but why? For slowing down or having fun with a copious number of friends? Almost every damn car that will drive down Village Creek will do the same!

Cole was well aware of how the routine went. Going ten, perhaps fifteen over the fifty-five-speed limit, late at night just trying to get where they planned to spend it or end it. Fletcher guessed he just saw things more from a civilian's perspective rather than a sheriff. He was understanding, cooperative, and when he really tried to justify letting the speeders go, it was that there was nothing truly suspicious about it.

At 12:37, a silver Toyota flew past Cole and the cow pastors along the road. Even with the reoccurring break check, they were undeniably still going way over, yet, he let them fly by. He had pulled people over, without a doubt, many times in fact but those were cases where he felt those people were in a danger for themselves and/or others. Going a ridiculous speed or driving unwisely in certain weather conditions or maybe dim lights, or drunkenly driving. There really was nothing urging him to pull the Toyota over. Nothing forcing him to do so.

That urge didn't occur until exactly an hour after midnight when the most suspicious appearing vehicle slugged by the country scenery. It was a stained yellow beat-to-shit Ford Bronco with a flickering headlight that looked as if it was really a twitching eye. It strolled past going at least twenty-five *under*. There was no swerving and obviously no break check, the left back tire was on the flat side and when it drove past Cole, the individual driving didn't bat an eye to his direction. Which came off as unusual to the sheriff, or *suspicious*.

Without much thinking, or any truthfully, Cole whipped out onto the road before he even turned on his lights. It was as if something was pulling him from his gut to do so. Following his gut feeling, he turned on his head lights then his emergency lights right after. He got up right behind the Bronco and when he saw his red and blue lights reflecting off its rusted but still silver bumper, he giggled at a coincidence.

"Just like O.J.," he said to himself.

(3)

The infamous Ford didn't surrender from its unusual speed for another mile down Village Creek. Cole drove just about fender to bumper with them until they ceased driving and pulled to the side. While they were pulling over together, it was evident that the Bronco wasn't using their brakes to stop. Either that or the brake lights were out but by the way the vehicle came to a halt, he inferred that they just let off the gas and let the Ford stop naturally. Now even further from the turnpike, the only thing surrounding them was vacant fields. Acers away from any houses or anybody.

Finally, break lights brightened on the Ford. The engine whined and the vehicle's body rattled in the cruisers red and blue emergency lights. Cole wasn't able to run their tags as their license plate was caked in dirt, though he could tell the tags were from Texas and they were expired. The minute the Ford came near Cole early on, he had smelt gas and it only got more potent when he got behind them. Currently with the gas fumes, it was nearly hard to take a full breath once Cole stepped out of his vehicle to approach the conspicuous truck.

During the day, whenever Cole was fast asleep resting for his shift, he thought he had heard it storming for the majority of his time in bed. After he closed the door on his cruiser, the feel of the night had really soaked in. There was little wind, and it was a tad humid but still cool, like it did in fact storm earlier or that it was about to.

The driver side window was still up by the time Cole approached. He could only see the silhouette of the individual. As far as Cole could see, it was a heavier set man with a trucker hat loosely placed on top of his head. The window still being up when Cole was on the other side of the door did come off as concerning but instead of losing his cool or assuming anything, he knocked three times with two knuckles on the glass.

The sheriff waited a generous amount of time for the driver to comply. There was no change, the window remained up and the driver stayed staring ahead.

Cole wasn't one to shine his always handy flashlight into the cars he pulled over. Especially not directly into the face of the driver or the driver's side for that matter. However, this time, he retrieved it from his belt, clicked its button and began to raise it but he stopped as soon as the window started to roll down with a constant creak.

Flashlight still active in hand, Cole was taken by surprised by an unsettling fume that rushed at him once the window opened. It was so unpleasant and powerful that it over came the smell of gas that was once so hard to escape.

Then he saw the driver. A very tan man, mid-forties to fifties with a thick jet-black mustache looking forward at the hood of his truck, entirely soaked with sweat. *That's the smell,* Cole believed.

Generally, whenever there is a traffic stop, the officers first words to the driver would be something classic along the lines of, "Licenses and registration" or "Do you know why I pulled you over?" Although, in this scenario, Cole opened with something different when he saw the aggressively perspiring man staring blankly.

"Are you okay, sir?" he asked with sincere concern.

No acknowledgement of Coles question nor presence came from the man. He merely kept gazing without a blink but with slouched eye lids.

Feeling certain that this was a reasonable cause to point his flashlight, he raised it to the mute man. "Sir," Cole called.

The bright light didn't have any effect on him. He kept his gawk straight and Cole could now see even more of the man in the light. His pupils were massive for starters but also there was a fat glob of snot that stretched across his mustache and almost into his mouth. Below that, he was wearing a grey stained T-shirt with a string of drool forming a puddle on his chest from the right side of his mouth. The drool had a constant stream as if he were about to vomit right on his steering wheel and soon enough, the man actually gave up his first dose of movement and sound right there.

He hiccupped. His chest jolted with it and then he went back to being totally frozen. The moment Cole heard the potential hiccup, he became more troubled from just how it came out. Something more like a croak or a deep gag. The kind someone makes when something is lodged in the throat, getting little air but not enough.

Drunk. He's gotta be, Cole thought to himself. Maybe a little high on something too. That seemed more likely than anything, and honestly, that was the easiest to deal with. He needed to get him out of the car and perhaps get some answers before he called the medics down and reported this whole thing.

"Sir, I'm going to need you to shut off the vehicle and step out. Are you able to do that for me?"

He wasn't shocked whenever the driver didn't answer and Cole followed by taking it upon himself to reach over considerately then turning the key, shutting off the noisy Bronco.

(4)

Getting the presumed drunk man out of the truck and into Cole's car only took a minute. Though, not without some stumbles on the way. He was able to stand on his own, but he would only walk when Cole had a hand on the man's back guiding him ahead. Currently, the sweaty civilian was confined in the officer's still lit up cruiser, staring through the glass that separated the front and back seats.

Whenever Cole got him out of the driver seat, he frisked him first thing and came up with nothing but a pack of Pall Malls blues. No sort of identification was found in the Bronco besides the trucks title. It was registered in the name of Gilbert White and while Cole couldn't be entirely sure, the dark man in the back of his Cruiser, trance-like staring straight sure didn't look like a Gilbert White.

Post putting him in the back and briefly searching his truck, Cole joined him in the car and proceeded to call everything in. Procedure says if a driver in a traffic stop is incoherent or clearly under the influence of an unknown substance, an ambulance will be called to the scene to evaluate the individual, or perhaps take them to the hospital. The ETA of the paramedics coming from Cambridge central was approximately eight minutes at best. Even with it being so late, there had to be a traffic in the city on a Friday night creeping into Saturday morning.

(5)

Uncomfortably, they sat together divided by the glass. In the rear-view mirror, officer Fletcher could see the sloppy gaze staring back at him, although, he wasn't quite sure the gaze was on him. The man's face gave off the impression he wasn't on earth with the rest of us—day dreaming, to put into simpler words—but Cole still could not stand to look back at him in the mirror.

He made the officer feel uneasy and well, just downright creeped him out. He hadn't let out one of those strange hiccups in some time now and Cambridge's most beloved sheriff was grateful for that. A few times, Cole thought about checking the mirror when he got too quiet but eventually, he would hear him breathe and that ended up reassuring him enough not to look.

Once, he checked the mirror but not due to the silence. He believed he heard a voice but when he checked, the man's mouth wasn't moving. Additionally, the voice didn't sound too clear, it was very muffled, as if he were carrying a radio or phone with him. *Impossible,* Cole knew he had searched him well. Yet, he swore he could hear something making a noise that sounded eerily like speaking. That also had made him feel on edge. To be truthful, this whole damn exchange had put him on edge already. His hands were clammy, and he kept frantically checking the time to see how much longer they had until the EMT arrived. They were only on their second minute together, but it felt as if it had been half of an hour.

Cole Fletcher had such an ominous feeling swimming within him about the entire day, night, this traffic stop, and especially, the mysterious unidentified man in the back.

Despite how this traffic stop went and how unsettled Cole grew from it, he was strangely kind of glad it happened. It was exactly what he had been asking for in retrospect. The perfect distraction from thinking about his future with the love of his life and their surely amazing child to be.

Then, as if a cool breeze blew away his stress, Cole had felt like a complete fool. How could he be so worried from something that was always thought about? He had wanted Syd to have his children for years and now that they're on track to have their first panic seeps in?

In fine detail, Cole had imagined their family before. Their child would be mixed and hopefully with Syd's eyes and her contagious smile paired with her little dimples. And if somehow, they could have her rational thinking and her outgoing personality, that would be good with him as well.

Cole wasn't positive of what he would want the kid to get from him but with how much he adored Sydney and everything about her, merely his last name would be enough. The sheriff felt a slight grin move on his face from his own wit and from the thought of his wife, who might as well be credited as his life and more importantly, the mother of their child.

More than ever, he wanted to embrace her and spill how excited he is to be the father he always wanted to be. He just had to get through this shift to d—.

"*Ayúdame…*" A faint and scratchy voice called from behind.

Whenever Cole had first heard the voice from the back, he believed it to be just another guttural sound or hiccup but within seconds of reflecting on what he heard, it dawned on him that it was Spanish. Quickly he put his eyes to the rear-view mirror only to see the man finally doing something other than staring ahead. His head was now looking up to the roof of the car like a baby with no support on its neck, and additionally there was a white syrupy substance oozing from his mouth and nose while he quivered violently.

Help me, my god he said help me!

Without a minute to lose, Cole hopped out of his Cruiser and tended to the perhaps seizing Mexican. The instant the back door was opened by Cole, the man flung himself out onto the road. He landed straight on his knees and hands then vomited what seemed like a bucket full below him. Cole watched with disturbed amazement, and he continued to watch the man flop into his white puke with tears streaming from his bloodshot eyes.

Cole then snapped out of it and got on his own knee to speak to the man. "Sir! Stay with me, okay? The EMTs are on their way! They are on their way!" The panic-struck officer grabbed one of the man's shoulders, "Sir, I'm going to put you on your back, okay?" Carefully, he was flipped onto his back and the foam shot up into the sky like coke erupting from a bottle after a Mentos was dropped inside.

Then, again, he went silent but a different type of silence. The man ceased shivering and kept an even blanker stare than before. Covered in his own bizarre vomit, he was dead. Cole hadn't checked for a pulse yet, but he knew as soon as he looked down at him entirely. There wasn't any sort of movement going on. No stomach and chest rising for breathing, no nostrils flaring or mouth moving from letting out air and the choking had completely quit as well. The EMT would arrive to a dead man on Village Creek rd. tonight and Cole would have one hell of a report to wr—.

"… …" A muffle of life came from below Cole before he got back on his feet. He looked down to the thought to be dead man. He looked the same. Though, the officer heard it again. "W… …" as if someone was underneath the heavy corpse, the muffled speaking was back.

Cole stayed on his knees completely over filling with perturbation and irrational thoughts while staring down at him. Slowly, he frisked the dead body to see if he had missed anything on him from before. Nothing in any of his pockets and nothing stashed in his underwear or pants but there was a bump on the back of his shoulder Cole had not felt before.

It was the size of a pineapple and seemed to have some intricate detail pressed into his skin from the inside. He put his hand under his shirt and felt it thoroughly. Then, swiftly, it scattered under the fat man's skin and away from Cole's hand.

He ripped the man's grey shirt down the middle and looked for what he had just felt. Utterly sickened and confused, he felt the body for the bump, but it was nowhere to be found.

The corpse's gut was round, slightly hairy, and still. Cole stared into it wondering just what the hell has happened here tonight. These had been the longest fifteen minutes of his life and easily the most traumatizing since he had become a sheriff. He wanted to go home even more than the last time he thought of it. Home to his bed and to his wife who he could not wait to share this with.

"w… u…" There it went again but a little more understandable. Cole leaned in to get a better listen. Maybe it'll do it again. His face was inches away from the belly of the man, anticipating a muffle but then he got a scream.

A narrow face appeared in the gut, etched into the skin like it was pushing its face against the outside of his stomach but from the inside.

"*Wake up!*" it screamed.

The once dead Mexican came to life with a gasp then at the same time, Cole froze still on his knees, closer to the man than he ever wanted to be.

"*KILL HIM!*"

All in fluent movement, he unhooked Cole's harness, took the gun, and shot Cole point blank in the forehead.

He stood up just fine on his feet, shirt tore open, face still coated in thick puke and retreated to his Bronco. He started the truck and took one last look in his rear-view mirror of the dead cop on the rain drenched road and returned his emotionless stare to the road before driving off.

The Ford was quiet for almost ten minutes before the face in his gut spoke again. It said, "*To the heartland.*"

Only in flashes

By 10:50 PM the windows had become foggy, and the storm grew belligerent. It was nearly impossible to see anything out of it, yet Matthew Ferguson kept his tipsy gaze on the window as if he could see the harsh storm on the other side. After hours of teasing mist-like rain and bolts of lightning striking and lighting the night sky, the storm had finally made its way to the town of Vincent. Now the showers were heavy and constant, and the lightning flashed more than ever but there was still no sound of thunder.

Matt sat on the sofa with crown royal on his breath, and eyes tired but staring, frustrated and feeling stuck. Any other night, storms came with great nostalgia for him. Memories of being in bed with a warm fleshed woman of his past always came to mind. Listening to the thunder and the rain pour at home, with feeling each other's slow breathing as they fell asleep totally content. The thought always put a smile on his face and rightfully so. However, that was in his early twenties and separate ways followed. These days he didn't have a woman.

He also wasn't even home at the moment.

(2)

It was a Friday and during Matt's shift at the warehouse, a gregarious work acquaintance extended an invitation toward him.

"Hey man, why don't you stop by after we get out of here tonight? I got some cold beer and some crown in my freezer that's been calling my name for the last couple of days, I think it knows your name too." That is what Devin, the co-worker offered.

A thoughtful invite from a nice enough guy but Matt was still hesitant on accepting. He came straight home after his shift and gave some thought on the invitation. Matt didn't have a lot of friends in Vincent, practically any friends really. In just the last year, he had moved to Colorado from Missouri and didn't exactly make a lasting impression or hit it off with the people he had met so far. Besides Devin, apparently. It sounds unfortunate but Matt ended up liking his solitude and lack of friends.

Devin was a great co-worker. Someone Matt would joke around with on the floor or talk about football with occasionally, though that was the jest of it. It wasn't surprising that Devin reached out. He was polite, funny, and they both had common interest but Matt was a little more than a decade older than him. On the other hand, the idea of some cold beer and maybe some whisky appealed to Matt.

Also, Devin only lived about six duplexes down the street from Matt. So, if he did go, it wouldn't be very challenging to leave. Or that's at least what he thought at first. Within the hour of being home after work, he pushed himself to accept the invite.

Getting ready to head out, Matthew closed all his doors, any windows that were slightly open and made sure everything was off, then grabbed his house key. Standing at the front door from the inside, he observed his grey lit duplex. Tidy, simple, and all on one level, he admired it as he thought of anything he might want to bring to Devin's. Matt drew a blank and turned around to walk out the front door and locked it from the outside.

Later on, when Matt reflected back to his walk down Wisconsin Ave while he stared at the dreaded foggy window, he felt foolish for not seeing this chaotic storm coming.

Around 6:16 PM, post leaving his house but before the moon took over the cloudy sky, Matt could smell the rain lingering in the breeze. In addition to that, there was a chill present and that made it colder than a usual September evening. The world appeared Smokey on the walk over, it was a grey, wet, and cold night that eventually would seem endless to Matt.

Every duplex on Wisconsin Ave looked almost identical to each other. All one level and most likely had two bedrooms with a decent size living room that connected with the smaller kitchen. He assumed Devin's was like that and once Matt made it there, he noticed he was right. Though, more importantly, when he arrived at Devin's doorstep, the sky had started to sprinkle.

That was the first warning Matthew didn't take.

(3)

Alcohol, or any other kind of mind-altering substance, can make one looser or potentially sharper, but it could also make someone completely vulnerable. While they were indulging in their drinks, Matt and Devin had become oblivious to the brewing storm. But really, it wasn't that they didn't know it was sprinkling or that the clouds looked dark, it was just that they didn't care.

They shared many laughs and stories over their drinks as lightning started to illuminate the sky brighter than day. While they poured their shots of whiskey, rain poured harder. Neither of them mentioned the rain nor lightning all night and by the time the weather was undeniable, they were considered drunk.

A little after 10:00 PM, Devin announced he would be going to bed. He offered Matt the couch if he didn't want to make the trip home, he even jokingly offered his own bed, but the catch was that he would be in it too. That sent both men into a moment of hard laughter, a great way to end their night he thought. Unbeknownst to Matthew Ferguson, his night wasn't even close to being over.

Now caught up to Matt's stare down with the foggy window, he sat on the sofa in the quiet and dark living room of his work acquaintance's abode. Or perhaps, they were friends now. Matt did enjoy the night with Devin's company. The more he thought of it, the more accepting Matt was of Devin being his friend. Earlier in the night, they had even discussed going to a Denver *Broncos* football game in October. Isn't that what friends do? Matt thought so.

Despite the fact he now considered Devin a friend, Matt still wasn't on board with sleeping over. The sofa wasn't that comfortable, Devin didn't give him a blanket, and knowing his own home and bed were only about a block away, staying seemed silly in a way. The only reason he didn't leave right when Devin said goodnight was the flooding rain outside. It sounded strong and had a constant rhythm with the way it fell on the roof then onto the window. The lightening was just as intimidating. The window flashed as if there was a red-carpet event smothered with paparazzi right outside.

Therefore, Matt waited for the rage of the storm to pause for a moment and in that hopeful moment, he would make his way home.

(4)

It was now a quarter past 11:00 PM, and Matt had become so aggravated with the rain that presently, he was at the open front door. Watching the rain fall, waiting for it the cease.

The streets looked flooded and as the rain showered, it looked thick as snow. As far as he could see, there wasn't a single living thing out. No vermin in sight, no rebellious teen and surprisingly not one running car. This was the kind of rain that would force people to stay off the roads and avoid going outside at all. From the open door, Matt could feel the cold air rushing in. It was some of the coldest rain that could ever fall and when it did fall, it would make the roads or sidewalks hazardous to be on.

The lack of activity began to make more sense to him as he watched what the weather was doing. No one would want to be caught in this storm and no one should be.

And suddenly, as Matthew tried to remember if he had heard any thunder tonight, the rain took a break.

This was his chance and maybe the only one he was going to get until the morning. Without thinking or even locking Devin's front door, Matt took off with a fast-paced walk into the streets. It was still raining but the rain falling now was nothing compared to how it was before. For the moment anyway.

Both sides of Wisconsin Ave had large streams of water flowing toward the storm drains. Matt splashed in the inch of water on the road and kept his pace in the opposite direction of where the water was flowing. He was getting closer with his swift walking, but the cold urged him to go faster, to run the rest.

At first, he decided against running, he could easily slip on the concrete, and once he had heard that someone is more likely to get drenched in the rain if they run rather than walk.

Throwing that true or false statistic along with the caution of slipping on the road, he started to run home.

Shoes drenched and socks soaked, he made it to his unlit doorstep. Beforehand, Matt knew his front light wouldn't be on but what came off as unusual to him, was how dripping wet the doorknob was. Though, he didn't spend more than a minute lingering on the thought. It was immediately justified. *It's just the rain.*

Out of his damp jeans, he pulled out his house key and seconds later, he busted in the house. He closed the door, nearly slamming it shut from complete relief of being home and done with the storm. The first task he tended to, before he even turned on any sort of light was taking off his drenched shoes and socks since he didn't want to make footprints in the carpet.

Then, a strange and vile aroma that filled the house stopped him right after his first shoe was off. The smell was sour and could potentially make someone gag. The more Matt smelt it, the more he could identify what it smelt like. A smell that we've all had to smell sometime, it was the stench of urine. He quickly flipped on his celling light and his heart seemed to jump to his tonsils at what he saw underneath the light.

There were wet foot tracks all over his living room floor.

(5)

Within the first few minutes after Matt's discovery of his home invasion, he was seemingly snapped right back into sobriety. His body went hot as he evaluated the wet steps all over his carpet and his stomach churned painfully while inhaling the ghastly funk the house reeked of. Before he could think of any action to take or a peep to make, a frightening but realistic thought came to him.

What if the intruder is still here?

Matt's jaw might as well have been wired shut like a corpse. It took all his courage and maybe stupidity to muster a word.

"He-Hello?" he called. "Anybody there?"

Of course, there was no response.

Still stationed by the door, he looked at his living room and beyond with the same feeling of absolute surprise he started with. Every door he had closed before leaving was now wide open with the prints leading everywhere. They were wild and directionless; impossible to identify where they had gone first or last. The tracks were so random it looked like the intruder was coming in and going out of the same room more than once.

With caution, he stuck out his neck to check around the corner and into the kitchen. The tile had been soaked with tracks like the carpet and all of his cabinets had been open, but nothing seemed to be missing. Matthew didn't know who had been at his home or what they had been up to, but he did know they had covered all the house. The kitchen, the living room, the restroom, then the spare room, and worst of them all, his bedroom.

While in his state of complete shock, Matthew felt as if he hasn't taken a single breath. Although, certainly, he had but the discomfort and fear that ran through his mind and body was enough to make him forget to keep breathing.

"I-I'm going to call the police!" he shouted still from the front door, acting like the person who invaded his house was still there.

Or maybe she or he was, Matt didn't know for sure.

(6)

Currently, outside's chill forced shivering upon anyone who stepped out, yet Matt still stood by his doorstep light, awaiting the police. The rain had picked up again, but it still wasn't back to its original greatness. While he quivered outside with his wet hair and clothes, Matt tried to pinpoint when exactly the intruder broke in.

Was it right after I left? He didn't think so. The tracks looked fresh, and that sour stench was potent by the time he got home. More than likely, he assumed they broke in a little before he decided to leave Devin's, around ten.

Then that thought hatched another. *When did they leave? Right before I walked in? If they did leave that is.*

Headlights from down the street stole his attention, hoping it was the police since the cold was becoming unbearable after twenty minutes of waiting. When the car drove farther down Wisconsin Ave, he saw the Vincent police sticker on the side. Matt was curious to why they didn't have their lights on at first, but he quickly decided they didn't want to disturb the peace. He was just grateful they had finally arrived.

The police car parked on the street right in front of the duplex and two officers stepped out. The driver was a tall and thin woman and from the passenger side was a stocky man who was shorter than his partner. Not wasting anytime, they rushed to Matt and out of the rain and away from their white squad car.

"Mr. Ferguson?" the female officer called, approaching him.

"Y-Yes that's me." He shivered, either from the cold or from the reason the police were at his house in the first place.

"This is Officer Rhodes and I'm Officer Jen," she introduced. Rhodes extended his hand and a smile; officer Jen did neither. Matt ignored her and took Rhode's hand, then shook it. "You believe someone broke into your place?" Rhodes asked as he released Matt's hand.

Before he answered, Matt noticed Officer Jen was seemingly examining him. She had this certain cramp on her face that could only be described as a judging expression.

"I know someone broke in." Matt wiped his nose. The cold was really starting to get to him at this point. "Here, come inside, it'd be easier to explain if I just show you." He led the officers into his home that still smelt like it was just a giant porta potty. Instantly, the two officers reacted to the smell by the look on their faces and then they saw the foot tracks.

"I don't know what the smell is, it wasn't there before I left which was around six," Matt noted. "Same with the footsteps, obviously."

Rhodes stood with his hands on his hips while he looked all around the living room floor. "It could be a gas leak; we'll call the fire department to send someone down here so they can check the levels."

"Where did you go tonight, Mr. Ferguson?" Jen chimed in, almost interrupting Rhodes.

Thrown off by her question, Matt gave her a confused look before he answered. "I went to a friend's house just down the street here." He pointed toward Devin's.

"Hm, did you have some Friday night drinks?"

The confusion thickened then he became slightly angry. "As a matter of fact, I did, but what does that have to do with anything?"

"Just seeing what the night was like, sir," Rhodes quickly said in a much sweeter tone than his partners questioning. "Did they take anything?"

"No" Matt shook his head. "I don't believe so, but I haven't really checked."

While the two men in the house conversed about the break in, the dominant officer bent down to get a more defined look at the tracks. Rhodes had his notepad handy and was taking notes from what Matt was stating about the break in. "How much of the house did they cover?" Rhodes asked with pen in hand. In an aggravated fashion, Matt brushed his hair back and let out a deep breath. "I think all of it, but again, I'm not sure, I haven't checked the whole house." Rhodes nodded and continued with his questioning. "Do you know anybody who could have do-"

"These tracks are barefoot," Jen interrupted from the floor.

"Huh?" Both men replied.

"These tracks, all of them, they look barefoot." She stood back up to her tall height. "You mentioned you hadn't searched the whole place. Why is that? Do you think they are still here?"

Hearing that question out loud made Matt go pale. Now that exact idea that floated in his head seemed more real than he ever wanted it to be. "I mean, I don't know."

In that precise moment, Officer Jen got even more serious. She took off down Matt's hallway and cautiously checked the open doors. First, Jen approached the open bathroom and wasn't shocked to find water all over the tile. It splashed mildly when she stepped in, but besides the water, everything seemed to be fine.

Without much dialogue, she left the bathroom and continued on to the spare bedroom with Matt and Rhodes trailing behind her. The spare room probably had the least number of tracks. Jen and Rhodes didn't vocalize it, but they assumed the intruder spent less time there because the room didn't have much in it.

"When exactly did you move to Vincent?" Rhodes asked.

"Just about a year ago. I'm from Missouri."

"Any family up here?" Jen interrupted like usual.

"No. You could say I moved up here just to get away from everyone."

"Hm, okay." She turned to her partner. "Well, while I'm checking Mr. Ferguson's room, you should go get ahold of the fire department so they can check for a leak.

"10-4, boss," he replied then went back out the door.

Like the spare room's door and the bathroom door before it, Matt's bedroom door was wide open. Though, unlike the spare room, this room had triple the amount of footprints. The sight made Matt's body run hot once more, he could feel a cool drop of nervous sweat trickle down one of his arm pits. Also, to make things more nerve racking, his room was by far the worst smelling. It was as if his bedroom was where the foul urine stench was coming from. In attempt to escape the smell, Matt turned to leave the hall but he was stopped when officer Jen inquired something.

"Mr. Ferguson, how much have you had to drink tonight?"

Immediately after hearing her question, he felt incredibly frustrated with the officer. Rather than ignoring her again and just heading out the door, he turned around and answered. "Officer, what does that have to do with anything?"

"With all due respect, it may have to do with everything."

"I had a couple of beers, that's all," he answered, leaving out his shots of whisky.

"Uh-huh, we-"

"Why do you keep asking about the drinks I had earlier tonight?"

Jen could easily see Matt had become angry and for the first time since her arrival, she went for a sweeter tone. "Mr. Ferguson, I'm not accusing you of anything, okay?" She got closer to him, nearly face to face. "But you have been drinking all night, I'm not sure if you were just drinking beer or not but I could tell as soon as we approached you tonight."

"What the hell are you saying?"

Officer Jen stood eye to eye with Matt, which was unusual to him since she was a woman, and he was a little over six foot. She hadn't said a word yet but the way her eyes looked at him and looked at the wet steps all over the floor then back at him said it all.

"You think I did all of this?"

"Mr. Fergu-"

"Are you kidding me?" Matt turned his back to the female officer and brushed his hair back again in that aggravated way. Whenever he turned back around to face her, Matt had a grin on his face, like he was humored by her accusation. "So, what you're saying is that during my drinking at my friend's house, I ran out into the storm, drunk, and walked into my house soaking wet and made this mess? Oh, yeah, I must have taken my shoes off before entering, huh?"

"Sir, calm down. I'm just saying people have done stranger things while under the influence and at this point, if it was you that did this, then that's the best-case scenario," Jen snapped back at him.

His face was red from how flustered he was with her accusing, but he kept giggling like it were some sort of joke. He couldn't believe what his night had transformed into and now he found himself wishing he would have stayed home instead of going out after work.

"If it was me, then why would I call the police?"

Jen shrugged "Maybe you forgot, people tend to do that while drinking. Like I said, stranger things have happened."

"I didn't have tha-"

Just then officer Rhodes barged in from the cold storm and came between Jen and Matt's dispute. "The fire department is on the way," he announced as he wiped the rain drops off his bald head. "Did you check the place good?"

Before answering Officer Rhodes, Jen was still staring at Matt with her accusing eyes. Instead of staring back at her or giving her a piece of his mind, he went outside in a pissed off fashion. "Not yet, I'll keep searching and see if I can find anything. But I doubt it..."

(7)

Two men from the fire department arrived at the Ferguson residence around midnight and then left within twenty-five minutes. There was no sign of a gas leak, and the strange aroma remained a mystery, just like the foot tracks discovered with it.

Matthew sat on his sofa with his head resting in his hands, frustrated and demented as well as tired and perhaps still a little drunk. Rhodes and Jen were still present at the house. Both appeared almost as tired as Matt. Rhodes sat on a recliner across from the resting victim and the once accusing Officer Jen stood with her back against a wall near the front door.

"Mr. Ferguson," she called as she pushed her back off the wall. Her call jolted Matt awake.

"Yes?"

"I believe we have done all that we can tonight," she said walking toward him. Rhodes quickly got to his feet, seeming very eager to leave. "We are going to head out now. There is no sign of gas, and the intruder is long gone but we're still sorry for your troubles."

"Wait, so that's it?" Matt questioned while putting his hands up. "Are you guys going to find this person? Will I hear from you again about this? Or are you gu-"

"Sir, we've done all we can. They're gone." Rhodes surprisingly interrupted. It appeared to Matt that Rhodes had left his side due to the stress and length of the night.

"He's right. We've checked the house thoroughly and there's nothing but these damp footsteps and that awful smell. And both will fade in time." They both stood above Matt in their matching navy-blue uniforms and looked down on him as Jen continued. "Maybe light some candles for the smell and I'm sure it'll go away. You'll be just fine. Like we said, we've checked this place in fine detail. Outside, all the rooms, the closets, under the bed, everywhere. There's no monsters here, Mr. Ferguson."

That monster line slowly made Matt's head rise, and a grin formed on his face. "No monsters, huh?" he scoffed. "That's great."

Both officers headed for the door, but Rhodes stopped before exiting and mentioned something else in attempt to comfort Matt. "We'll keep a squad car by if it makes you feel any better. Sleep tight, sir."

Then they went out and into the cold and to their car. Matt found the energy to get up once they left and shut the door behind them, locking the top and bottom lock after. He thought back to the last thing Rhodes said about putting a squad car close by and realized he didn't believe what the officer had said. But the police were convinced the rest of the night would be safe, and Matt began to believe it would be best if he convinced himself of that too.

(8)

By 1:20 AM a red berry candle had been burning in Matthew's room for about an hour and not only did the storm return to its original wrath, but much greater than before. The lightening, pouring rain, and all. However, there was still no thunder.

The foul smell still lingered in the house but as far as the bedroom with the candle went, it was back to normal. Fortunately, some of the less soaked foot tracks had dried in the spare room and most of the ones in the living room had as well. Unfortunately, the ones in the now red berry smelling room still had more than a dozen tracks.

To speed up the process, he laid just about all his towels on the wet spots of his bathroom, kitchen, and bedroom. Once he finished laying towels, Matt felt that sleep was well deserved, since this was the first opportunity he's had gotten since Devin went to bed hours ago. Matt wondered if he was going to mention the nights strange events when he saw Devin. Without a lot of thinking on the idea, he concluded that of course he was. He'll probably tell anybody with a working set of ears.

As soon as he finished brushing his teeth and got rid of the taste of the liquor he once drank when the night was still youthful and not yet dreadful, he went straight to his bedroom with the hope of falling fast asleep. Notwithstanding that his mind was on edge from the night's curious findings and that he couldn't help but let his thoughts wonder.

A fan at full blast while sleeping is an essential to many and that included Matt. He turned its round knob and the constant roar of the fan started. His bedroom on this night was only lit by a lamp and the candle, both on a nightstand on the right of his bed and he intended to keep a light on for the rest of the night. Also on the nightstand, was the candle lighter he used to light the wick. Finding a lighter around his house wasn't easy since he quit smoking in his late twenties. Though, with what the night had put on his shoulders, a cigarette sounded perfect now. Despite the police's belief and no matter how hard he tried to convince himself, the house still didn't feel safe, especially not safe enough to be in the dark alone.

The bed was warm, but Matt's body shivered as if he were outside in the cold storm. Just knowing someone came into his home uninvited and unwanted, particularly when he wasn't home chilled his bones more than Colorado weather ever could. Having said that, it was the unusual findings that troubled him the most.

Why did they take off their shoes? Or were they shoeless from the start?
What exactly was that smell?
Why didn't they steal anything?
Why did they pick this house?

But even with those paranoid thoughts running a marathon in his head, laying in his bed was easily the most relaxed Matt had felt tonight. To soothe him, he focused on the continuous pouring rain and the humming of the fan. He could feel himself drifting away, and slowly but surely the nerve-racking ideas blew away like loose gravel during high winds.

Moments before falling asleep, he remembered the active candle by his bed and thought it would be best if he put it out. The last thing he wanted was the fire department and the police returning over a lit candle accident.

When the flame was out, he sank back into his bed and continued to fade. And then, unexpectedly, with his eyes closed and sleep within his grasp, the fan slowed down and eventually stopped.

Matt opened his eyes and saw the lamp had been shut off as well. It was obvious the power was out due to the storm. Without the pouring rain and the rapid lightening, the room would have been entirely dark and silent. The power out didn't surprise him in the slightest, given the storms aggression. There was nothing he could really do about it either and he was already so close to sleep he might as well just continue. The power would come back on by itself anyhow, fan and lamp included. So, he shut his eyes once more, but it wasn't long until he opened them again when he heard an off-putting sound that made him instantly sweat.

It wasn't a certainty, but to Matt it sounded like something was breathing and wheezing in the room with him.

His eye lids burst open and the second they did, a sudden flash of lightning struck and what he saw during that brief flash forced him to sit straight up and clench his comforter.

Someone was standing in the corner.

All he wanted to do was doubt himself and what he was experiencing. Mentally praying what he witnessed and what he was hearing was strictly his imagination. He didn't want to entertain the idea or possibility that the intruder really was still in the house Matt denied and denied, until yet another flash of lightening came through the window and convinced him otherwise. The intruder was there. But closer than before.

It was all too real. He could really hear the breathing mixed with wheezing. He could really see someone else in the room with him, but not who. The lightening's flash was too quick.

Already covered in sweat produced by raw fear, he rolled out of bed and mistakenly bumped something off the nightstand. His heart beat felt faster than the pace the rain fell outside, and on the verge of tears, he screamed. "Who's there!"

Similar to when he called out earlier, there was no response. More lightening illuminated the room for milliseconds each time it struck and every time it did, the intruder was closer, cornering him. As the intruder approached closer, it appeared to be a man, a bald man the height of Matt. He was confined in his pitch-black bedroom with the man who broke into his home and absolute panic was starting to settle in.

He took a step back, then put his hands up, waiting for contact or a clear visual but when another flash came, he saw nothing. Befuddled, he stepped forward and felt something cold, hard, and slim underneath his bare feet. It was the lighter.

As fast as his quivering body would allow, he retrieved the long lighter from the floor and sparked its flame, on his last hope he got worked up for nothing and there really wasn't anybody there.

The bald man was there though.

He was so pale it was uncanny, and he also wasn't just in the room but right on the other side of the flame, no more than a foot way. Face to face, the stench had come back and worse than ever, it easily would make someone sick, but Matt was too mesmerized to vomit or scream.

Nude, visibly drenched, and dripping, and as if he were frightened of Matt, he screamed violently. He had no eyebrows or eye lashes and no eye color. Just a black dot in the center. They looked like eyes that belonged to a rat. His face was round and had little to no neck. There was nothing specific to his body, no gentiles, nipples, wrinkles, or anything else personal, like he was made out of clay then smoothed out completely. While he screamed, Matt saw he had no teeth, only the blackest gums.

Exactly as Matt began to scream back, the pale man-like thing's scream formed into a wild laughter while he stood on the other side of the lighter's flame, staring at him with those beady eyes.

Then just as fast as the power went out, it came back on, and the laughter and the "man" was gone. Vanished with the dark when the light returned. Gone with only a pair of wet foot marks and the horrible stench left behind. Matthew Ferguson stayed standing in the same spot across the foot tracks, trying to process what he had just seen when finally, the thunder *crashed*.

Murphy Family Nightmare

The sun is sinking down under the immense tree line which surrounds the eastern Kansas town of Pleasant. John Murphy is on his nightly drive to his country home. Not only to his home, but to his beloved wife, Julie, and his occasionally ungrateful child, Jacob.

God damn it, who was he kidding? No one but himself, that was for certain. Jacob was always bitching about something. Whether it be John's parenting or Julie's cooking, Jake always had a mouthful of bratty remarks. John gripped the wheel and eased on the gas, so he didn't slide on the country road's loose gravel. He could feel anxiety sprouting in his stomach and knew it was about coming home from a long day at work only to open his front door to his disrespectful and unpleasant son. It was a similar feeling a teenager would get coming home to a mentally or physically abusive parent, but it wasn't a parent John was dreading coming home to. It was his child; his only one.

The car engine shuts off, then John removes his hand from the ignition, pulling out the key. He takes a deep breath. Julie comes marching through the front door and turns the corner of the garage.

"Do you know where Jake is?" Julie asked in a nervous tone.

"No." John steps out of the SUV. "He hasn't been ho-"

"Not since he left at eleven this morning," Julie interrupted.

Afterwards they went into the house to try and get ahold of their missing son.

Jacob was a spoiled, annoying, and troublesome boy, and he showed that at home. Of course, it was normal for teenagers to rebel and be disrespectful to their parents, but

Jacob had only just turned twelve. Showing up hours late for dinner, stealing money out of Julie's purse, or sneaking out of the house after midnight. The list seemed endless. At times, it seemed Jacob was doing whatever he could do to lash out at his parents. But even if Jacob Murphy really did hate his mother and especially his father for any reason, they still loved him and were his parents. Instead of John's fire red hair and light green eyes, he had Julie's smooth brown hair and her soul staring brown eyes, but he did, however, have John's face.

(2)

With no sign of Jacob by 10:30 that night, they texted the cell phone Julie insisted upon him carrying. No response came from Jacob.

The chore of staying up for Jake fell on John's shoulders since it was a Tuesday night and Julie had to be up and out by 5:45 AM. It's never an easy thing for Julie to just check out for the night when her son was out past ten; not knowing exactly where he was didn't sit well with her. She always assumed the worst when he was out of her sight. Almost as if he were still a baby, but that was exactly the thing; he would always be her baby. His birth was a blessing she thought she'd never accomplish. This night, like many, John comforted her and promised her he would wait up for their son.

Avoiding sleep was easier for John with television; just some old reruns of The Twilight Zone and himself. He tried to relax as he nursed his Budweiser. John had opened the window to the right of his recliner prior to making himself comfortable, not only for the cool breeze of a fall night to keep him awake but also so he could hear his son's footsteps walk up the driveway.

But, three Twilight Zone episodes, four bottles of Budweiser, and three shots of Captain Morgan later, Jake still had not come home.

It was now midnight. John kept getting more and more frustrated with Jake's absence from home. He could even admit he was furious. Although the alcohol he had been consuming may have contributed to his rage, he felt drinking was necessary tonight. Both Julie and Jake hated when John was drinking. Alcohol made John more aggressive and a little more outspoken about his awful son. From Julie's perspective, John was too hard on their son after a few buds.

His beer was nearing empty. John patted his arm rest and stood on his feet to retrieve another Budweiser. Right before John turned to walk into the kitchen, his eyes were stolen by a picture of a newborn baby on the T.V. The television was showing a Catholic anti-abortion ad during the commercial break. *"There is never a reason to murder a child,"* the screen displayed in bold, white letters but the word *"murder"* was in red.

Tears began to fill John's grass-colored eyes at the thought of a baby taken for granted and only to be cut off by its parents. As a biologist, the conception of life, to John, was a miracle. Why? Why would someone kill what some are unable to have? John wondered as he dried his wet eyes.

Killing something that's a part of you. To John, abortion was the equivalent of tearing a piece of your heart off voluntarily. He would never hurt Jake. How could he?

That was his only child; the one that survived.

John began to think of Julie's miscarriages, and this was not the subject he wanted to think on while he was indulging in alcohol. Their unborn children's names were going to be Josie and Jack. Twins at the beginning of the pregnancy, but it followed that two babies turned into one then one turned into none for the Murphy family.

In the medical field, they call it Vanishing Twin Syndrome. This occurred when the other twin was absorbed by the stronger fetus. In the Murphy's case, the stronger fetus was Josie. Despite that fact, Josie went on not to achieve birth either. Julie was blessed with her baby boy, Jake, after the death of the twins about a year later, but John never got the daughter he had always dreamed of.

John threw another shot of rum to the back of his throat to shake off his drunken thoughts of his unborn daughter.

(4)

Cracking open his fifth Budweiser, he decided to retire back to his recliner by the open window. Then the sound of gravel shuffling under walking feet came from outside. No jacket, just his old Kansas University T-shirt and his cargo shorts but the liquor kept him warm as the crisp October air surrounded his body. John quickly turned the corner of the garage to meet his son walking up the driveway.

Jake's eyes held a look of surprise when they settled on his father.

"Where have you been, Jake? Your mother has been scared out of her wits!" John said in a loud but not-quite-angry voice.

"Dad, I just went to a friend's house. Is that a crime?" Jake stepped right of John to escape to the front door. He was stopped by his father's hand.

"Where do you think you're going? I'm talking to you!" John nearly shouted.

"I don't want to talk. I'm going to my room to call a friend," Jake snapped back at him, removing his father's hand.

"The hell you are!" John reached out his hand, "Give me your phone. Now, Jacob."

"No," Jake said, rolling his eyes and that simple "no" sent John over the edge.

He quickly and aggressively grabbed his son by his scrawny wrist.

"Let me go, asshole!" Jake screamed in agony.

"Give it here, then!" Jake pulled his phone out of his hoodie and surrendered it to his father.

John let go of his son's now red wrist. Out of his drunken rage and with all his might, he spiked he cell phone on the hard stone ground destroying it into several pieces. But even right after shattering Jake's phone, it seemed to John that still didn't feel drastic enough for his son's actions.

"This is my fucking house, Jacob, and you are my son! You live by my rules because you wouldn't even be living without me in the first place." John, at this point, was nose-to-nose with his son, gazing into his brown eyes; the same brown eyes his wife has. He saw fear in those soul-staring brown eyes. Fear wasn't far from respect to John Murphy.

Without a single word, Jake turned to walk to the front door only to stop right at the doorknob.

"I hate you!" Jake sobbed, sounding like an infant with lack of sleep. John looked up at him while he was picking up the pieces of the destroyed phone. "You're a drunk and you were never meant to be a father. The kids who didn't survive are better off dead and I-I would be too!" Jake then stormed off inside followed by the slamming of the front door, leaving his father speechless in the crisp October night air.

(5)

Moments after the intense confrontation between John and his son, John quietly crept into bed with his wife. He was too drunk to stay awake, but his shaking fury kept him staring at the rotating ceiling fan. Due to that same loud rusty fan, he wasn't surprised Julie didn't wake up when Jake slammed the front door, or even when he was screaming in pain while John held his wrist tight.

"You were never meant to be a father."

Could his pesky son be correct? Was that what God was trying to get across when the twins didn't survive the pregnancy?

All these thoughts made John grind his teeth. "I hate you," his son had shouted at him and with tears welling up in his own eyes, John took a deep breath with that last thought of what his son had said earlier and quietly said, "I hate you too, son."

He then rolled to his right to embrace Julie then blinked, keeping his eyes shut for about three seconds. His eyelids were getting heavier, he noticed.

On Julie's side of the bed was an alarm clock poised on a nightstand with a picture of the Murphy family right next to it. The clock read 1:06 AM and the picture depicted Jake with a mediocre smile in-between John and Julie. Another long blink came upon John. This time, his eyes kept shut for about ten seconds and a tear escaped the corner of his eye. The cool teardrop slid down across John's resting head. His heavy wet eyes blinked, and they stayed shut until he saw light appearing through his eyelids. It was the sun flaring through the window.

(6)

John's eyelids burst open with confusion. Julie was nowhere to be seen but how could it be morning already?

He observed the room, hearing the roar of the noisy fan. "I don't remember falling asleep," John said aloud but quietly to himself. Rubbing his tired eyes, he looked at the alarm clock on Julie's side. The clock read 8:06 AM. "That's about two hours early, my friend," he smiled. John began to roll over to close his eyes again but instead, he whipped his body to the nightstand to observe the family photo.

The photo that included the Murphy trio now included a fourth person; a little red-headed girl.

Right next to Jake's mediocre smile was a girl that held a bright smile and even brighter green eyes. His jaw dropped along with his eyes, which opened as wide as a window in the spring, and John sat baffled.

Who is that little girl? What is going on? This has to be a dre-

Then John's heart dropped in his chest when he met eyes with that exact red-head girl just standing right in the doorway.

She was about Jacob's age but a little shorter. The girl shared the same green eyes and red hair as John but looked remarkably like Julie in the face.

"Can I turn this off now?" she asked with her hand on the switch for the fan.

John sat with a knot in his stomach and without a word.

There's no way this could be real, but he could hear the birds whistling outside; he could feel the heat shining through the glass of the window, and his stomach moving from his heavy breathing. The eye contact between the two was locked. For John, it was like looking into a reflection of his own eyes.

The fan started to power down after the girl flipped the switch. "Dad, I'm about to eat breakfast. Do you want to join me?" She was still looking into his eyes.

John moved his feet off the bed and onto the floor, breaking the stare. He took a huge breath and noticed his cargo shorts where he left them before bed.

"I'll take that as a yes, weirdo." She then giggled, walking down the hall.

This had to be a dream ran through his head, though the booze from last night was still strong on his breath. Despite his preference of just going back to bed and hopefully waking up normal and not in an episode of The Twilight Zone, he put on his shorts and left the bedroom.

(7)

Walking past Jake's and the guest room, he noticed the hallway, which had always contained family pictures, seemed to double in content. New photos lined the walls and he scanned them on his way to the kitchen.

John's eye was caught by a picture of the red head holding a certificate. In bold, black letters, the certificate said: **First place Science Olympiad awarded to Josie Murphy**.

The tight knot in his stomach constricted even further.

"*Josie*," he gasped.

"Yes, Dad?" she answered, standing to his right as if she were standing there the whole time.

He swallowed hard with the intention to speak but had no idea what he was going to say.

"Hi, Josie," came from his mouth in a bewildered voice.

She smiled big.

"Hi."

Josie had a wonderful smile with straight teeth and the most beautiful dimples, much like Julie's.

"What's the matter, Dad?"

Her smile swept his confusion away and the knot in his stomach was gone. John couldn't help himself from smiling.

"Oh nothing, honey. Just a little tired, I guess."

"Okay, whatever you say, Daddio" Her smile turned into a laugh, and she hugged him tight, then she walked away into the kitchen.

John didn't know what to think but he felt happy. *This had to be a dream,* but maybe it was just a dream come true.

(8)

He made it to the kitchen and Josie was sitting on a barstool at the kitchen counter. Resting her head in her hand, she found John's eyes with her own.

"How's it going, *Joes*?"

Where the hell did that nickname come from? He thought. It just came so naturally.

"Good! But I've been up ever since Mom left for work this morning and I'm starving now."

Right before John had the chance to reply, he felt a chilling breeze roll in from the window he left open last night. Swiftly, he went and closed the window.

"Hey, Dad? I'm going to go and see if I can get Jake up." She hopped off the stool and skipped down the hall.

Jacob.

John Murphy had almost forgotten about his son. He began to think of the tight grip he had on his son's wrist and then smashing his cell phone.

Oh man, he'd been drunk and now he felt the guilt.

Like a dog with his tail between his legs, he walked to the trashcan to see if the pieces of the phone were still there.

But at that exact moment, coming from down the hall, he heard a crunch and the sound of an open mouth eating. Abandoning the shameful path to the trashcan, he started to walk toward the hall that held the sound.

(9)

Approaching Jake's closed door, the sound of feeding got louder and more ferocious.

"Maybe we also got a tiger," John joked to himself right before he pushed open the door to see the unimaginable.

His son's body was lying still on the bed with his stomach ripped wide open. Standing above him was Josie, smothered in Jake's entrails looking like a baby with tomato sauce after a spaghetti incident. Her soaked hair was matted with the blood of her brother. Pieces of Jake's torn flesh stuck around her mouth and, ignoring John's entry, she kept ransacking inside Jake's corpse.

Meanwhile, John stood, petrified with fear, gazing at his son's head staring up at the ceiling through his soulless brown eyes. In that moment, Josie's head shot up and locked eyes with her father. In her right hand, she held Jake's blood-dripping and still-beating heart. When her beautiful smile turned sinister, she brought the throbbing organ to her teeth and ripped off a piece of Jake's heart.

Blood flooded out of Josie's mouth as she began to speak, but her voice was deep and monstrous.

"You were never meant to be—"

All of a sudden, John was awake in his dark bedroom. But it wasn't the horrifying, cannibalistic dream with his unborn daughter that shot him back into reality.

No, John Murphy woke up to liquid, impossible breaths, realizing only after he began to choke on his own blood that someone had slit his throat. After struggling, he felt his arms and legs tied to the top and bottom of the bed frame and duct tape slapped over his mouth. He looked around the dim room to identify the slasher, but it was no use since the sun had not fully risen yet. All he could see was a silhouette of the killer standing, watching his blood drain from his paling body. While his blood poured profusely out of his open neck, soaking the sheets and his own body, all he could think about was his son.

Was he alright?

Did the killer spare his child…?

Or was he already dead?

At John's weakest point, when he was bleeding to death with no hope of survival, he thought only of Jacob and his regret of how he'd treated him. The sun rose over the strong tree line and shone through the bedroom window. Rays of sunlight glinted off a straight razor while the light cascaded over John's only child's face.

Jacob remained until the end, staring down at his father's demise.

AT THE DEAD OF NIGHT

The first nightmarish novel written by Wayne
Hopkins, and a sequel to the short story, "Shut
and lock the door".

<u>Suppose</u>

You're a young man who has just moved
away from your smothering mother and into
your apartment. Suppose that when you do,
you're driven insane by the same unnerving
nightmares that plagued your childhood.
Suppose that just when you think you have it
figured out, it's already too late and the
deranged woman in your dreams has you
within grasp…

Well, that's what happened to Sean
Carver Jr…. or did it?

Chapter 1

July 19th

Sean could have sworn he was safe in bed just a minute ago.

He vaguely considered the idea he had sleepwalked, but he wasn't willing to bet on it. He hadn't caught himself sleepwalking in years. Given how weightless and foggy he felt, Sean believed he could have fallen here from another dream he couldn't recall.

No, that couldn't be it either, he knew how he dreamt. Sean was confident that if he had felt a falling sensation, he would have sat up in bed immediately. And, despite how rare dreams had become for him in the last ten years, he was certain what he was seeing was just that. A bizarre but vivid dream.

The ground he stood on was a gravel road that led up to a high point and steeped down the other side. He stood barefoot at the highest point, only his briefs saving him from complete nudity.

The first trait of the dream he took in was his position. The second was the crowd of stars above, and the third was the fact the moon was hiding from the night sky. Only starlight made the dreamscape somewhat visible. From the peak of the hill, he could oversee the eerily dull scenery before him. There was nothing but trees along the road and acres of fields or farmland on the other side of them.

A sudden flare of light appeared.

He didn't see it fall nor shoot, but a star was burning a hole in the earth in the distance. One of the fields at the bottom of the hill looked to have a tiny mouth of fire. Tiny from *this* distance.

Sean decided it was a star from the glow it gave off. It was an astronomical red with scratches of a sunlike blinding gold. And the heat it radiated was a hybrid of warmth he had never been exposed to before. From this far, dream or not, it was like experiencing magic.

In Sean's actively dreaming mind, he supposed he must be closer to the light than he appeared.

Closer than he believed, or *realized*.

Sean Carver had already known there wasn't a chance of an easy-going Saturday morning when he went to bed the night before. He lived under his mother's roof, and knew how damn particular she was going to be about the party later. He looked forward to having his own roof someday, but the day where his mom wouldn't be so particular about everything might never come.

She stormed into his room early, just as the summer sun was beginning to stretch across his face and extinguished the vague, but at the same time, life-like dream he was having.

"*Sean.*" she called gently.

He purposely failed to respond, hoping she would just leave.

"Sean!" She sharpened her voice.

"Mom!" he mocked with his eyes still shut.

"You need to get up, boy. I have things we need to put in your car for your party."

Yet another attempt to ignore her away.

"Sean! Wake the hell up."

"I'm awake. Jesus, Mom, just leave." He sat up, eyes closed still and his hair looking like an abused paint brush.

"Well, all right then, Jr!" She scoffed. "Sarah is also on her way, just so you know."

His mother took the silent bait and left this time. Sean removed his covers and instantly felt the house's cool A.C. grace his naked legs. After swinging his feet off the bed, he retrieved his *iPhone* from the floor. He had two unread messages and opened them immediately.

The newest message was from Sarah and it read,

Good morning, Baby! I'm getting ready

and then I'll be headed over to help set up

The text was sent around seven that morning.

Sean scoffed at the thought of the women in his life getting up before seven on a weekend and how he despised it. He just wanted to be able to sleep in.

The oldest message, received shortly after two a.m., was from his dad.

I'll be in town around one or two-ish. I have something to talk to you about.

That took Sean by surprise.

Not that the message was sent so late, his dad always ran around at night, being a regular drinker and so called 'womanizer.' Knowing that, he was sure his old man wasn't alone or feeling lonely when he sent the text, whether it had been a new woman or a familiar whisky.

Regardless of whatever company he may have had, Sean was simply shocked his dad had something to talk about.

The father and son had a thin bond and not much of a relationship. Sean couldn't recall a time where his parents even liked each other, or a time where they all lived in the same house. Early on, Sean's father went onto a financial child support system and only saw his son bi-monthly, or whenever else it was forced upon him.

Sean anticipated another shout or visit from his mom, and if he were still sitting in bed when that happened, she would herd him into one of his 'dickish' moods. Whenever his mom saw this side of him, she made things more troubling by calling him Jr. It was a cruel blow every time she said it because it was actually part of his real name, and because she knew precisely *when* to use it. Around the time he was growing into a teenager, he heard her talking to his Aunt Meli on the phone about it.

"Oh, Mel, guess what? Whenever Sean starts getting that whole man-of-the-house tone with me, I've just started calling him Jr." She chuckled. "Because that's when he reminds me of the *asshole* the most."

He put on a clean shirt and pair of tan shorts while thinking of the hot weather and his full name. He was named after his dad, but outside of some looks and the name, that's all they shared. Sean Jr. didn't hate his dad, but he didn't he feel that any part of their father and son relationship was genuine. Besides the obvious DNA.

Sean heard his suspicions come true when his mom yelled his name again.

"Mom! Okay! I just got dressed! Get off my back."

"I wasn't hollering for that. But good, you better be, Jr!" she yelled back with a giggle at the nickname. "Your little girlfriend just pulled up."

Sarah decided to leave her car at Ms. Carver's house—or Jessica, on a good day—and rode shotgun in Sean's half packed blazer. He had expected more of a load than what his mom had actually had for him, which he was no doubt pleased with. Nothing too overboard, guess the surprises didn't cease with just one parent today. She had sent him over with some set up plastic white tables, generic graduation party decorations and a poster board decorated with photos of Sean from kindergarten all the way up to his senior year of high school.

The VFW Park was a mile and a half from the Carver's home. It wasn't a unique party venue, everyone knew that, half the kids in town had had their own grad parties there. Matter of fact, that was the sole reason Jessica Carver had picked July to have Sean's party there; to avoid getting his stepped on by another party. And there was no way Jessica or Sean were settling with having a party at any of the other venues Pleasant offered. One was another park a block away from the VFW, but it was loaded with children. The only other, and the worst, was an indoor building that was typically used by the 4-H community. Sean told his mom he refused to do it there because it smelt of moth balls and bad hygiene, and she couldn't disagree with him.

Sean pulled into the park's unorganized lot, which looked more like a unkept road caged up with steel rope. He put his truck in park and kept it running while he checked to see if his Aunt Meli was already there. He didn't see her and when he checked his right side, he was tackled into a trance by the sight of Sarah's thighs barely hiding beneath her dress. They looked freshly shaved and shined in the sun, falsely wet from moisturizing them with coconut lotion earlier.

Above her youthful thighs, in which he was constantly wanting to be in between, was her smart phone. As she skimmed her feed, her auburn hair dangled to the screen but only the wavy strips of hair that were purposely kept out of her bun.

Sarah soon looked up from her phone as if she had a feeling she was being admired. She shot a look to the near empty lot and not at Sean. "Anybody here yet? Wasn't your aunt supposed to meet us here soon?" She turned to him, and the couple locked eyes, as Sean intended, but he came up speechless from her gaze. Their eyes were both a shade of brown, as was their hair, but her eyes were lighter and more on the hazel side. Her eyes also seemed to have more of an effect on people. Sean often thought that a lot of Sarah had an effect on him.

"Yeah, but I don't see her. I'll call if I don't see her pull in soon." He found his words, luckily.

She titled her head. "Is this the same gay aunt I met at graduation?"

Sean knew it was. Not only because he just had one aunt he actually counted, but more for the reason that a certain impression had been set when the two first met. Aunt Meli didn't care for Sarah at all.

"Yeah, babe." He left it at that. He hoped his family would eventually warm up to Sarah, but he would have to stop her from referring to his aunt as the 'gay' one first.

Sean took another look at the lot, at the gazebo with the gardens surrounding it and at the restraints that made up the parking lot. There was still no one in sight.

He decided to say what was on his mind in order to keep a potentially awkward silence away. "I'm not really sure when Goose and Al are going to show up. I know Goose had family over at his house yesterday to say goodbye, but Al shouldn't be doing shit. I'm sure they'll both make it before my dad though."

"Who needs 'em, baby? All of them, honestly." She laughed, but in a petty tone that came naturally. "I wonder if your dad is even going to show up this time?"

He laughed lightly with her and shrugged off her implication. He didn't care about her dissing his dad, but Al and Goose never did anything to deserve the bashing Sarah regularly dished out. At least if he laughed, she wouldn't drag it into a fight. If he defended them, she would've gone to war, and if he stayed silent, she would've gone to war just the same.

Alberto and Gage, aka Goose, were, without a reasonable doubt, Sean's best friends for the last four years. Neither of them played sports, nor did they concern themselves with getting fucked up on whatever pills or booze they could get their hands on like a good chunk of teens in town tended to do.

The trio couldn't be boiled down to a single adjective like typical high school schoolers. They hid in a gray area of Pleasant High's social genres and weren't given a second look. And that was fine with them, they enjoyed each other's company the best anyway.

Sarah, whom Sean had only been dating since October, usually looked for any reason to hate Al and Goose. She even went so far as to tell Sean's mom her feelings over dinner one night. Saying that Al and Goose were "*so* dumb" and Al was greasy and gross while Goose was a straight-up freak.

Maybe that was why his mom didn't care much for Sarah either, he thought while he kept looking out for Aunt Meli. The comment Sarah made at dinner was not only rude and pompous sounding, it came off as somewhat racist when talking about Al. Sean knew it, and he knew his mom has certainly picked up on it, too. And that shit never played out well with his mother.

Jessica never actually told her son she didn't like his girlfriend but he knew something there rubbed her the wrong way. He dwelled over this for a minute or two, and came to the conclusion that, truthfully, there could have been numerous things she didn't like

"You wanna take a picture with me, baby? I did my make-up super-hot today." Sarah broke the silence.

She did look, well, hot. Her make up skills did wonders for her looks. Never an ugly girl, but with the eye liner, contouring and foundation, years were added and she was a beautiful, more mature, lustful woman in an hour.

"You fuckin' bet I do. It'll do massive things for my street cred," he exclaimed, even though he really didn't care for a picture, but the attitude she would carry afterwards, he did care for.

He got in real close with her as she laughed at his answer. The coconut lotion was more potent than ever now, and the smell of strawberry was now apparent too. He really felt he was a terribly lucky guy to have her as his girlfriend, even if she was a little younger. That didn't matter much to him though, she would be out of school soon and he could trust her. Who cared if his mom didn't?

Sarah held her phone up, and took time to gain steady hands for a good shot.

"Make sure there isn't a glare in my glasses, babe," Sean noted but didn't bother to look at the photo when it was taken. His Aunt had pulled up.

Sean could count on one hand the family members he was close with, and all of them were women. His mother had not remarried after her divorce, and neither had *her* mother. The similarities in the family tree didn't end there. Jessica, like her son, had also been an only child. Luckily for him though, she had found a lifelong friend in Pleasant's slim diversity while growing up. Melissa had